BY

ALEXA

ESCAPE FROM FURNACE

LOCKDOWN
SOLITARY
DEATH SENTENCE
FUGITIVES
EXECUTION

ALEXANDER GORDON SMITH

SOLITARY

ESCAPE FROM FURNACE 2

SQUARE
FISH

FARRAR STRAUS GIROUX
NEW YORK

SQUARE
FISH

An Imprint of Macmillan

Library of Congress Cataloging-in-Publication Data
Smith, Alexander Gordon, 1979–
    Solitary / Alexander Gordon Smith.
        p.   cm. — (Escape from Furnace 2)
    Summary: Imprisoned for a murder he did not commit,
fourteen-year-old Alex Sawyer thinks that he has escaped the
hellish Furnace Penitentiary, but instead he winds up in solitary
confinement, where new horrors await him.
    ISBN 978-0-312-67476-2
    [1. Prisons—Fiction.   2. Horror stories.   3. Science fiction.]
    I. Title.

PZ7.S6423So 2010
[Fic]—dc22

2009030843

First published in Great Britain by Faber and Faber Limited, 2009
Originally published in the United States by Farrar Straus Giroux
First Square Fish Edition: July 2011
Square Fish logo designed by Filomena Tuosto
Book designed by Jay Colvin and Christian Fuenfhausen
macteenbooks.com

10   9   8   7   6

AR: 6.5 / LEXILE: 960L

TO DAD,

*the architect of, and the inspiration for,
so much of what is good in my life.
I told you this was a proper job!*

SOLITARY

BENEATH HEAVEN IS HELL.
BENEATH HELL IS FURNACE.

ESCAPE FROM FURNACE 2

CONFESSION

I HAVE A CONFESSION.

I'm not a good person.

I always said that I only stole from strangers, that I only took stuff they'd never really miss: money and electronics and the sort of things you can't cry over.

But that was a lie. I didn't stop there; I couldn't. I stole from the people I loved, and took the things that meant the most to them. I didn't just break into their cupboards and drawers, I broke into their hearts and ripped out whatever I wanted, anything that would get me some easy money down at the market.

So don't go fooling yourself that I'm a good person, that I'm an innocent victim, someone who didn't deserve to be locked up inside the hell on earth known as Furnace Penitentiary. I'm not. Don't get me wrong: I didn't kill my best friend Toby when we broke into that house. No, the blacksuits did it, they shot him then they framed me for his murder. But I've done things that are just as bad. I've killed little parts of people; I've cut them up inside, hurt them so much they wished they were dead.

There isn't time to confess everything, but I have to get this off my chest. If I don't do it now then I might never get the chance. Death's coming up fast. I can feel its cold fingers around my throat.

Two years ago, when I was twelve, my gran died—had a fit in the middle of the night and swallowed her tongue. Mom was devastated, like any daughter would be. She cried for weeks, she didn't eat, she hardly spoke to me or Dad. She'd just sit and hold the little silver locket that Gran had left her, gently stroking the scarred and crumpled photos inside.

I guess I don't really need to tell you what I did. But I'm going to anyway. *I need to.*

I waited till she was asleep one night, ten days or so after Gran had been buried. Then I sneaked into her room and pried that locket from her hand. Ten quid. Ten lousy quid is what I got for it. A handful of dirty coins for the only thing my mom had left of her mom. I watched the man I'd sold it to rip the photos out from inside and chuck them in the bin, and I didn't feel a shred of remorse.

Mom knew I was the one who'd taken it. She never said anything but I could see it in her eyes. There was no warmth there anymore, no love. It was like she looked right through me, at a phantom over my shoulder, at the son she wished she could have, the son she'd lost forever.

See what I mean? I'm not a good person. Don't forget that. It'll make my story easier to stomach if you know that I deserved to be punished for Toby's death, even though it wasn't me who pulled the trigger—that I deserved to be sent away for life in Furnace, deep in the rancid guts of the planet.

And that I deserved everything that happened to me there.

Because Furnace is no ordinary prison, it's a living nightmare perfectly designed for people like me. A place where freaks in gas masks—wheezers, as we called them—stalk the corridors at night and carry boys screaming from their cells. Where those stolen kids are brought back as monsters, all rippling muscles beneath stitched skin. And where the same poor wretches are eventually turned into blacksuits, the warden's soulless guards.

I saw it happen with my own eyes. I saw it happen to Monty. I saw what he'd become, right before he died.

So, never let yourself forget that I'm a bad person, that all us cons are, even the "good guys" I met inside like Donovan and Zee and Toby (no, not my old friend I'm supposed to have killed—a new friend with the same name). The four of us thought we'd found a way to escape, blowing a hole in the chipping room floor with gas smuggled out of the kitchen. But nobody can run from their own demons. Donovan was taken by the wheezers the night before we broke, and as for the rest of us—me and Zee and my new friend Toby—well, maybe even Furnace was too good for us. It was certainly too good for Gary Owens, the hardcase headcase who discovered our plan and followed along like a bad smell.

No, maybe our fate was to find out what horrors lay in the tunnels *beneath* the prison.

Because that was our way out: the river that runs deep underground below the bowels of Furnace. We didn't know where it led to. We didn't care. Anywhere that wasn't Furnace was good enough for us.

Or so we thought.

Oh yes, beneath heaven is hell, and beneath hell is Furnace. But the horrors that crawl and feast beneath *that*—now that's a truly fitting punishment for someone like me.

So there you have it, my confession. It may not seem like the best time to share it, but it's funny what races through your head when you're plummeting into the darkness with only razor-sharp rocks and rapids to break your fall.

THE RIVER

FALLING INTO THAT RIVER was like falling into death.

The first thing it stole was my breath, knocked from me as I plunged into liquid ice. I felt my lungs shrivel, every last scrap of oxygen forced out. I tried to snatch in another breath but all I got was cold water, dead fingers forced down my windpipe and filling me with darkness.

The current was too strong, grabbing my body and tossing it from rock to rock like a rag doll. I felt pain tear up my left leg, then my head exploded into light and white noise as I was hurled against the jagged stone. I tried to swim, tried to grab the walls of the tunnel, tried to do anything other than be pounded into a bloody mess of flesh by the sheer force of the water.

And at first I thought I was succeeding, the pain leaving me and making me feel like I was drifting down a river of silk. Only I knew I was still being torn to shreds, the agony replaced by numbness and the kind of sickening warmth you know is just a trick of the mind to keep you calm while the last few drops of life ebb away.

I stopped fighting it, giving myself up to my watery grave. It wasn't fair. Donovan, Zee, Toby, and I, we'd done everything right—we'd found the crack in the floor in Room Two, smuggled in the gas-filled gloves from the kitchen, and blown the place to splinters. We should have been free. The river was supposed to have been our own private expressway out of Furnace, carrying us laughing to the surface where we could bathe in starlight and howl at the moon and feel the gentle breath of night on our skin.

But instead it was like another of the warden's vicious beasts, a nightmare dog that held us in its foaming jaws and shook us until we were broken.

I was going to die down here, I knew it. And suddenly that didn't seem preferable to life in Furnace. Suddenly I wanted to be back in my cell, in the light and the heat. Because even the most sadistic guard and the cruelest Skull gang member could be bargained with. The river was a force of unrelenting fury that made even the warden seem human.

I felt my body lurch, felt something in the blackness deep inside me snap. I tried again to breathe, my lungs bursting. The roar of the water began to fade as the river took my hearing. I wasn't scared, I wasn't sad. I wasn't anything.

Because that was the last little piece of me that the river stole, bleeding my emotions out and leaving me an empty husk buried in a casket of ice at the bottom of the world.

I WANTED TO OPEN MY EYES but I couldn't. *You're dead*, said a voice, maybe someone else's, maybe my own. *Dead people don't open their eyes.*

That made sense, but I still wanted to open them. Only I couldn't quite remember how. I stared at the darkness, willing something to happen, praying for my vision to work. Very slowly the black screen in front of me parted, a crack of weak golden light sliding into my brain. It carried no heat, but all the same it began to chase away the chills inside my body.

I could feel the numbness recede, and in its place came a deep, pounding agony so profound that I threw up. It was mainly river water, but I could feel something else vomited from me too, something barbed and heavy that had been wrapped around my guts ever since I'd jumped.

I tipped back my head, my entire body gripped by freezing fire, and tried to focus on the light. I knew what it was, of course. It was the end, it was the afterlife calling me, the thing people see right on the edge of death. I didn't care anymore. It could take me wherever I deserved to go, just so long as it made the pain stop.

I tried to hold out my hands, tried to welcome it. And for a moment the light grew brighter, so intense that I felt like I was bathed in gold. Then it snapped off, dropping me back into darkness, into pain.

You're bad, said the voice, my delirious mind. *And bad people don't go to heaven.*

I tried to scream, but it was too much. The world slipped, shuddered, and fell away.

The trembling ground brought me back, pulling me up from the abyss. I didn't even try to open my eyes this time, just clung to the sensation of movement from beneath me, the slightest tremor which let me know I still existed. Although my body throbbed with pain I could tell that I wasn't lying on the cold stone of the tunnel. Whatever it was it was soft and gave out a slight warmth which I gripped with the last of my strength.

I felt a weight on my shoulders, something pulling me toward it. For a moment my mind snapped and I was lying on my bed at home, just a kid snared by fever, my mom hugging me close and refusing to let go even when I tried to squirm away.

Then I heard the roar of the river and it all rushed back like a splash of acid—the explosion, the fight with the blacksuits, the sound of the mutant dogs as they tried to burrow through the rockfall behind us, then the leap into the unknown. I fought to bring back the memory of my mom, but it was gone, sucked into the shadows like every other part of me. I put my head against the soft ground, trying to burrow into the heat, trying to hide from the fear and the pain.

But they found me, and once again I was pulled into oblivion.

VOICES THIS TIME. Hammered through my subconscious so hard that I could feel them as much as hear them.

". . . got to move . . ."

". . . not leaving him . . ."

". . . slit the little man, we're all gonna die 'cause of him . . ."

". . . can't go, you've got the only light, you can't . . ."

". . . gut him good, better move or you'll get it too . . ."

Drifting out, a black cloud settling over my mind again. I panicked. Something was happening, I needed to be awake. I fought against the agony, against the part of me that just wanted to fade away into nothing. The ground was moving, something holding me tight. Thin arms around my shoulders.

"Gary, back off, he can still get us out of here. Just give him another minute." With each word the shape beneath me vibrated. More memories came flooding back—two friends, jumping by my side, and a third. Gary Owens. The psychopath who'd taken over the Skulls, who'd already stolen God knows how many lives in cold blood.

The thought of him pumped more adrenaline into me than the river had done, and this time I managed to open my eyes. The light was still there, timid and more silver than gold. It beamed out from a shadow beneath it, a black form against the gray walls that was moving my way. I blinked, seeing the red veins of my own retinas splashed across the darkness. The shadow focused, took shape—a muscular body with a dead face that sneered at me.

"Just in time, little man," said Gary, spitting a wad of bloody phlegm onto the rock. I noticed that his face was cut up pretty badly, and a steady stream of crimson droplets fell from his left sleeve. "You messed up, got us all killed."

"Alex?" said a voice from right behind me, making the ground tremble again. I looked up, feeling as though someone was pulling the tendons from my neck with a pair of red-hot tongs. Zee was sitting next to me, cradling me, his body still shivering. I tried to get up but for a second he wouldn't let me, his arms locked tight. I placed a hand on his, squeezing as hard as my sprained fingers would allow, and he finally surrendered.

"Jesus, I thought you were a goner back there," he said as I struggled upright. "I saw you go headfirst into a rock."

"Did one of you . . . ?" I stuttered, trying to keep as still as possible so that the pain wouldn't flare up again. It wasn't working. I put my hands to my temples and they both came away red.

"I did," said Zee. "I managed to get a hand on you, drag you out."

"What about Toby?" I asked. There was silence for a moment, until Zee's shuddering sigh broke it.

"There was no way he was going to make it," he said finally. "He was messed up from that explosion. I'm sorry, Alex."

"We should have left him up there," I said, the sadness clawing up from my stomach, causing as much agony as the wounds on my skin. My world spun again, visions of Toby—the younger kid I'd met in Furnace—bruised and broken on the rock merged with visions of my old friend with the same name, shot in the head by the blacksuits and resting on his bloody bed. It was too much, the darkness of the tunnel creeping into my vision once again, the sound of the river muted.

"Alex, Alex! Stay with us; fight it!"

The words brought me back again, each one a life raft that buoyed me up over the shadows.

"Did we make it?" I repeated, staring back down the river. It might have been a product of my feverish mind, but I thought I could see a shaft of light punching down from the roof of the tunnel behind us. It was the hole we'd jumped through, and from it came the unmistakable sound of a siren.

"Yeah, we made it," Gary hissed. "Made it pissing distance. Great plan, little man."

Gary turned, and from the light on his helmet I could make out that we were in a narrow stretch of tunnel, the foaming ribbon of water tearing by like it was trying to suck us back in. It curled off to the left, away from the strip of red rock we were on: not quite large enough for a bank but low enough to scramble onto.

"We're still too close," Zee said.

"What we do now?" said Gary, limping across the narrow ledge until he was towering over me. "You better tell me or I swear I'm gonna bust your skull open."

"Why do I have to—" I attempted, but Gary spat his answer at me before I could finish.

"You dragged us down here, you get us out."

"But there's no way they'll come after us," I said, trying not to scream as I shifted my leg, needles in every nerve. "It's suicide. Not even the blacksuits would make that jump."

I knew as soon as I'd said it that I should have kept my mouth closed. I mean, if I'd learned anything in Furnace it was not to tempt fate. Because fate wants nothing more to do with people like me, except to see us suffer.

Something tumbled from the hole in the ceiling, a writhing form that spun through the flickering light and struck the raging torrent with a splash that was far too big for a man.

"Oh Jesus, they're not sending the guards," said Zee, his voice breaking.

Another form dropped like a dead weight, this one howling as it hit the water.

"They're sending the dogs."

HUNTED

I TRIED TO GET UP but my body wouldn't let me. Fortunately Gary was more than happy to lend a helping hand. Two, actually. He ran forward and grabbed the collar of my tattered prison overalls, hoisting me to my feet and shaking me hard enough to make my teeth chatter. He pulled me close, glaring at me with the soulless eyes of a spider.

"Where now?" he screamed, flecks of blood and spittle hitting my face. "You better have a plan or I'm gonna feed you to them myself."

A plan. I could think of one. *Lie down and die.* It's all my legs wanted to do, just fold beneath me and leave me there for the dogs. It would be quick, I thought. Those immense canine jaws, the skinless muscles bulging, and those teeth—one bite, maybe two, and it would all be over. I must have still been delirious, because the thought of being free of this bruised flesh almost made me giggle.

"Why don't you think of one?" I spat. "I got us this far; it's your turn."

Gary looked at me like he was going to rip off my head, then with a grunt of disgust he shoved me backward. I stumbled, but

Zee caught me before I could fall. A wet howl bubbled from the water, too close.

"Come on, Alex," whispered Zee in my ear. "We've got to think of something. I don't want to die down here, not like this."

His words cleared the madness from my mind, snapping me to attention. Gary's helmet lamp was veering wildly from left to right as he searched for a way out, but there were no exits, no passageways. The only thing I could see in every direction was rock.

Every direction but one.

"We have to go back in," I shouted over the roar of the river.

"No way, man," Gary replied, his voice shaky. "Almost died the last time. No way I get back in there."

"We don't have a choice," I went on, stumbling over the uneven ledge to the raging water. It pummeled the rock beneath my feet, desperate to get hold of us again so it could finish the job it had started. But there really was no alternative—in seconds the warden's monstrosities would be on us. "You wanna wait here and get torn to pieces? We get back in, it will be easier this time."

Gary stomped toward me again, fists raised, but whatever he was planning he never got the chance. A throbbing snarl rose up to our side and he swung around, the lamp picking out two silver eyes and countless needled teeth emerging from the foam. The dog was straining to free itself from the current, its claws firing off sparks as they ripped across the rock. It howled, lurching its body onto solid ground, its back legs scrabbling for purchase.

"Go!" I yelled, taking a deep breath and throwing myself back into the flood. This time I knew what to expect, bracing myself for the cold and managing to keep the air in my lungs. I felt the river grip me and pull me forward but I spread my arms and curled up my legs, keeping one hand against the wall to my left to steady my passage.

Behind me I heard two more splashes. Somebody screamed, a choked cry drowned out by the rush of water in my ears. I turned, my shoulder grazing against the cheese-grater rock. What little light there was from Gary's helmet lamp was half submerged, the glow like some deep-sea jellyfish. He was still beneath it, writhing in the water and trying to break back up to the surface.

Zee had disappeared. I couldn't see the dogs either, but that didn't mean they weren't there in the darkness of the tunnel.

I fought the panic, trying to swim against the current toward Gary. I couldn't have cared less if he drowned, but we needed that light. I reached beneath the surface, grabbing a handful of cloth and skin and pulling as hard as I could. He bobbed up, gasping for breath and clinging to me with iron fists.

"Keep your head forward," I shouted, coughing as the river dipped and filled my lungs with water. "Look for a ledge, a slope, anything!"

I don't know if he heard me or not, his panicked breathing and muttered curses not even stopping when he slammed into a rock. He spun around, the lamp illuminating the way we'd come for the briefest of seconds but leaving an image in my mind that lasted a lot longer—Zee's panicked face, and behind him four glinting devil's eyes gaining fast. Too fast.

I swerved to avoid another jagged black blade looming from the water, then clutched Gary's overalls as the river dropped again. The water closed in over my head as we plunged down a near vertical shaft, but it wasn't a long drop and I managed to snatch another breath as it leveled out again. It was just as well, as dead ahead the ceiling of the tunnel dropped right to the surface, the river disappearing through a hole in the floor.

Great. Death by mauling behind us, death by drowning ahead.

And that was all I had time to think before I was sucked down into the whirling abyss. It felt like I was in a washing machine, my body spun so fast that I thought my limbs were going to fly off and my eyeballs pop out as it forced us deeper and deeper into the earth.

We burst out in another stretch of tunnel, the water still flowing fast but the river wider now, less furious. I saw Gary and clutched him, feeling his arms around me as though we'd been best friends for years. There was a choked shout as Zee flew free, then a set of whimpered barks as the dogs drew breath.

"There!" I said, taking hold of Gary's head and twisting it so that his helmet lamp was pointing at a section of broken wall to our left. A series of shadowed grooves led up to a narrow ledge high above the water—steep, but we could climb them. "Get up there," I said breathlessly. "Least till dogs have gone."

We let go of each other and swam for it, my limbs feeling as if they'd been hollowed out and filled with lead, my head chiming like I was standing right next to a church bell. The river almost dragged us past, but I managed to grab an exposed hook of rock and pull myself free of its icy grip. Gary was already ahead, scaling the wall with a speed born from terror.

There was a cry from behind me and I saw Zee struggling against the current. I tightened my grip on the rock and reached out for him, taking hold of his hand as he blasted past. The flow was almost too powerful, threatening to suck us both back in, but with a scream of defiance I reeled him close.

It was just as well. Almost as soon as he'd lifted himself up out of the water a muzzle broke free, splintered teeth snapping shut inches from his heel. The dog threw itself at us, its raw flesh reflecting the dying light from Gary's lamp. But there was no bank, no shore for it to gain purchase. It clung onto the rock for what seemed like forever, its jaws thrashing wildly. Then the other dog sped past, snared fast in the current and whining. It smacked straight into the first, knocking it from the rock and sending them both careening into the darkness.

"Gary, wait up," wheezed Zee as we listened to the whimpered snarling fade. "We can't see a thing down here."

God only knows how I had the strength to climb. Yet somehow I did, dredging something up from deep inside me, some primal strength. Each time I reached for the next handhold or foothold I felt like I was back in the prison gym, fighting the Skulls, kicks and blows raining down on me. But that's the funny thing about pain: the more familiar it becomes, the easier it is to tune it out.

I noticed that the light up ahead was no longer moving. Gary had reached the ledge, and although he didn't offer either of us a hand as we pulled ourselves over the lip of rock, he did move his leg out of the way so we could clamber up. From Gary, that was the equivalent of him saying he loved us. Zee collapsed and I sat next to him, peering back down at the river. It was lost in shadow, its undying roar the only thing letting me know it was still there.

"Where we gonna go now?" spat Gary eventually. "We've lost the dogs but where's the way out, little man? You messed this up big."

I ignored him, trying to get a sense of our surroundings. The ledge we were on was narrow but stretched out along the length of the cavern. Bathed in weak light, the rough walls were made up of pockets of darkness that looked like those in the chipping halls. Most were probably nothing more than grooves in the rock, but there had to be a passageway or something up ahead.

Had to be? my mind echoed. There didn't have to be anything. This wasn't part of the prison, it hadn't been designed by an architect and carved out of the rock by logical minds. It was a river more than a mile beneath the surface sculpted by the cruel and chaotic forces of nature. Nobody had ever set foot down here before. We were the first, and it wasn't going to let us go.

"No way out," Gary mumbled to himself, rocking back and forth and making shadows sweep across the cavern. "Got us killed. Got us killed bad."

"No, we'll find a way," said Zee, sitting up and putting a hand on my shoulder. "You got us out of Furnace, right, and nobody has ever done that before. We'll find a way, I know it."

I wanted to agree, wanted to get up and charge down the ledge and find that escape route. But I knew in my gut that Gary was right.

"We buried alive down here," he said. "Buried alive."

And we were. The warden may have locked us up in Furnace, but I was the one who had arranged our execution. Because this wasn't a way out at all. It was a tomb.

BURIED ALIVE

WHEN YOU'RE SCARED—and I mean *really* scared, not just hearing a noise in the night, or standing toe to toe with someone twice your size who wants to pound you into the earth—it feels as if you're being injected with darkness. It's like black water as cold as ice settling in your body where your blood and marrow used to be, pushing every other feeling out as it fills you from your feet to your scalp. It leaves you with nothing.

That's how I felt sitting on the ledge. It wasn't the dogs that terrified me, and it wasn't Gary. Or the thought of being caught again. It wasn't even the idea that I might die shivering helplessly on the rock like some strange fungus. No, it was the thought of what might happen *after* death.

I could accept my life ending, because there would be no more fear and no more pain. But what if death wasn't the end? What if some part of me, my soul perhaps, lived on? And what if it was trapped here in the guts of Furnace for the rest of time, never again to see the sun or hear the sound of laughter? It was that which made it seem like my body was a pit devoid of life and light. It was that which was driving me toward madness.

"We move that way," I said, more to chase away the voices in my head than because I had a plan. Light burned my retinas as Gary turned to look at me. I stuck my hand out, pointing down the slope in the same direction the river ran below. "Gary, you've got the light, you take the lead. Make sure you don't miss any passageways, one of them might be our way out."

"Might?" snapped Gary, as menacing as a pistol shot. But he obviously didn't have any better ideas as he scrambled to his feet and turned his head in the direction I was still pointing. His helmet lamp illuminated the narrow ledge ahead, which seemed to disappear into darkness far too quickly.

"Just take it slowly," I stammered as a shiver passed through my body, making every nerve end burn. "Watch your feet; if you fall over the edge then we're all screwed."

Gary didn't answer, keeping his head forward as he shuffled carefully along the rock. His feet kicked scraps of stone over into the void and I tried to ignore the sound of them hitting the foaming spray below. The river had let us live twice now, but I was willing to bet it wouldn't show the same mercy if we tumbled in again.

"Come on," I whispered, offering Zee a hand and hauling him up. "Before that idiot leaves us behind."

We eased our way after Gary, treading carefully in his shadow and doing our best to peer past his enormous shoulders. Each step he took made the gloom along the wall twitch, and it was impossible not to think of the wheezers—the warden's gas-mask-wearing freaks—lurching and staggering like injured birds in front of us. Every time I saw movement my heart hammered, which wasn't a bad thing since fear seemed to be the only thing keeping it going.

"This isn't getting us nowhere," came Gary's uneven voice. "It's all the same up here, no doors or nothing."

"You were expecting a door?" I asked, unable to stop the

haggard laugh breaking from my throat. He didn't reply, and he didn't turn around, but even so I swore I could feel the air thicken like he was about to explode. And he was right. No matter how many paces we took, the wall to our left and the pitch-black abyss to our right stayed exactly the same. Each stumbled movement forward brought a fraction more light to the ledge up ahead, but it also pinched it off right behind us. We could have been walking on a treadmill.

The image brought back my terror of becoming a ghost trapped here for all eternity. Weakened to the point of insanity by everything that had happened, my mind started telling me that I was already dead, and that this was my personal hell.

And it could have been. I mean, more than anything our progress through the darkness reminded me of the times I had broken into houses and crept through the shadows while the owners were asleep, desperately trying not to make a noise and always panicking that I wouldn't be able to escape in an emergency. What could be a better punishment for a criminal like me than to be doomed to an eternity walking along a ledge in a pocket of light and air that constantly felt like it was shrinking?

"Watch it!" came Gary's voice as I smacked into his back. "You trying to push me over? I'll gut you if you try it. You hear me?"

I'd been so wrapped up in my own mortality that I hadn't noticed him come to a halt. I mumbled an apology, bracing a hand on the wall before stepping up on my tiptoes to see what had stopped him. The view was identical to the one that had greeted us for the last few minutes, except for a jagged scar running vertically down the wall. It cut straight through the ledge, splitting it in two and resembling a crude crucifix, like this was a massive cathedral and we were trespassing on the altar.

"Go on then," I said, no longer caring about antagonizing him. "That might be it."

"You go," he replied, his voice shaky. "Don't feel right."

I wondered what had spooked him. The ledge ahead didn't look any more treacherous than it had all along, except further up where it had been sheared in half. The gaping wound in the wall was dark, but shadows couldn't hurt us.

Then I heard it, a noise rising up above the numbing roar of the river below. It was so loud that I didn't know how none of us had noticed it before—a whistle that rose in pitch like an old kettle before sputtering out and vanishing into its own echo.

"It's the wind," I said, but I was so unsure that it came out like a question.

"That means we're near the surface, right?" came Zee's voice from behind me. I shook my head.

"There's wind in these caves just like there's water. Doesn't mean anything."

The whistle came again, closer and louder and longer. Another rose up on the back of it, a shrill call that sounded more like a scream before being sucked back down below the thunder of the water. *It's wind*, I thought to myself, trying to hammer the words into my head so hard that I wouldn't question them. *The wind in the tunnels, caused by pressure changes in the water.*

But I knew that whatever it was we were hearing, it wasn't made by anything as innocent as air. More whistles, three or four this time, fighting each other for supremacy. Gary swore and turned to me, his pupils so large and the whites of his eyes glowing so fiercely around them that he looked like an animal. He whispered something that I couldn't make out, but I knew what his lips had spelled.

Wheezers.

"Is it them?" asked Zee, almost crying. "Please God, not them."

I shook my head until all thoughts of the freaks in gas masks had disappeared, then took a step forward. Easing myself past Gary, I made my way toward the crack in the rock, my heart so far up my throat that I could feel its beat on my tonsils.

"It might not be them," I said over my shoulder as I reached the edge of the precipice. "It could be anything. We're just afraid, paranoid. Forget about the noise, okay? We've just got to find a way out. We'll worry about the wheezers when we have to."

A clutter of remarks met the end of my sentence but nobody argued with it. I took that as a good sign, grabbing the edge of the cracked rock and peering around it. The scar was maybe two meters wide, the ledge continuing on the other side but too far away for us to jump to it. Without the light I couldn't make out where, if anywhere, the crack in the rock led.

"Gary, I need the lamp."

Instead of handing it to me he walked to my side, his rough hands on my arm a promise that if he tripped and fell he'd take me with him. Tentatively he leaned out and aimed the fluttering beam into the shadows. They parted reluctantly, as if this was the first time they had ever seen light. The crevice thinned to a point— there was no passageway.

"Look up," I commanded. If I'd spoken to Gary like this in Furnace, then he'd have shanked me without thinking twice. But down here things were different. He tilted his head back, rocking unsteadily on the edge of the precipice and digging his fingers into my bruises. The pain was worth it, though, as the weak glow picked out another peak of rock that led off into shadows. I had my mouth open to point this out when the noise came again, and the way it dropped screeching from the very darkness I was looking at made it clear where it was coming from.

"Find another way," said Gary, his voice dead.

"There is no—" I started, but before I could finish, his hands had left my overalls and were around my neck. He swiveled, twisting his body and mine until I was scrabbling for purchase on the lip of the ledge. I could feel the cold air of the river below me, like an icy tongue trying to pull me in, and for a moment I thought I was falling.

"I said find another way," screamed Gary. "Or you go swimming."

"Gary!" yelled Zee, but I didn't fight. Part of me wanted him to let go, drop me to my death. Part of me wanted to become a ghost just so I could see him struggle to find a way out without me, just so I could laugh as he slowly starved to death at the bottom of the world. I almost said as much, but thankfully I managed to keep my mouth shut. You don't call the bluff of people like Gary.

"There is no other way," I repeated, never taking my eyes off his. "We can't go back. We can't make that jump to the other side of the ledge. We don't have a choice."

"What's that down there?" said Zee. I dropped my gaze and Gary saw that as a sign of submission. Hauling me back onto the ledge he pushed Zee aside and looked down into the crack. I joined them, peering past their tangled limbs to see a ragged circle of darkness a few meters below us. "That's a tunnel, right?"

"It might not be," I answered. The hole in the rock didn't look much wider than any of us, and the thought of climbing into it not knowing where it led or how much more it shrank made my stomach churn. "We're better off heading up, anyway. Even if that is a tunnel it looks like it goes deeper."

"Doesn't matter," said Gary. "Not going anywhere near the wheezers."

There was no arguing with him. With another eerie dance of light and shadow he started climbing down the vertical scar, grunting as he eased himself toward the hole.

"This is wrong," I said to Zee. "I've got a really bad feeling about this. We should be heading up."

But even as I said it another guttural scream skidded down the wall like fingernails on a blackboard, and before it had ended Zee was following Gary. I would happily have left them to it, so great was my terror of crawling even deeper into our stone sarcophagus. But if I let them go I'd be alone in the darkness, and that would truly have driven me to insanity.

"This is wrong," I said again to deaf ears. Then I grabbed hold of the rock, swung my body around, and descended into the abyss.

THE THROAT

IT SEEMED TO TAKE FOREVER to climb down that fractured wall. It was so dark that I had to run my fingers over the slick, cold rock to find a grip, and pretty much every step I took one of my feet would slip, threatening to plunge me into the void. I felt like a piece of bait—a maggot pinned on a hook and squirming in pain as I was lowered toward the throat of some nightmare predator.

By the time I'd reached the hole three more haunting calls had dropped from the ledge above, each louder and more frenzied than the last. My damned imagination projected the image of the wheezers onto the stone in front of me—hundreds of them swarming over each other like flies over a corpse. It was crazy, of course: there couldn't have been that many of them. But the growing volume of the shrieks made it clear that the crowd up there was swelling.

"Move it!" came a voice from below. I assumed it was Gary's, but when I angled my head down I saw Zee directly beneath me, clinging to the lip of the darkness and gesturing me on with his head. Gary was next to him, on the other side of the opening. I wasn't sure why neither of them had climbed in, but I should have guessed.

"Ladies first," hissed Gary when I scrabbled down the last stretch and braced my foot in the hole.

"You've got the light," I protested. I should have saved my breath.

"Won't tell you again," the bigger boy growled. "Get in there."

I looked at Zee but he didn't meet my eyes. Not that I blamed him. The tunnel was barely wide enough for any of us to clamber into, the same width and height as a coffin.

Cursing with every foul word I knew, I dropped past Zee and thrust my head into the shadows. The air inside had none of the freshness of the river. It was hot and heavy, like the breath of some ancient creature. Like it had been back in the prison.

"This is wrong," I said again, the darkness swallowing my words so quickly that neither Gary nor Zee seemed to hear them. Biting my lip to stop myself from screaming, I eased my shoulders into the throat and shuffled until my entire body was inside.

The panic set in immediately, the feeling that there was no oxygen, and that the rock pressed against my stomach and my back was closing in, crushing my lungs. I tried to reverse—better to fall to my death in the river, or be caught by the wheezers, than to die cowering in some hole clawing for the last scrap of air—but Gary was already halfway in. The light from his helmet barely had enough room to squeeze past me, and by its strained yellow fingers I could see the red ragged walls of the tunnel shrinking in on each other ahead.

I thought back to the things that had happened in general population, the main prison. I remembered the time Zee and I had been chased by the dogs, rescued by Donovan; the day I'd nearly been caught by Moleface as I crawled free of Room Two; the fight between me and the Skulls in the arena; the moment we'd made our break, Toby and I held up by giant hands as the fuse burned down toward the explosive gloves.

At the time each one of those events had been terrifying, and I'd been convinced that death had finally caught up with me. As I looked back now, however, everything that had happened up top seemed like a game, like a school trip. I wished I was back in my cell, Donovan by my side, laughing about Zee having to clean the toilets or something. Because compared to the guts of Furnace, to the merciless river and this gullet of ancient rock, gen pop was a country club.

"Go," Gary said, his voice muffled. I took as big a breath as I was able, then eased my way deeper, my elbows grating against the stone as they pushed me along. With every movement the claustrophobia threatened to consume me, and several times I had to stop as the fear rang bells in my brain, making my entire body convulse.

I don't know how long we were in that tunnel. It could have been a lifetime. Each agonizing inch seemed to take hours, and every time I managed to wrench my body forward I thought it would be my eternal resting place. Somewhere in my mind I pictured what would happen if I did just die. Gary and Zee would have to retreat backward down the pipe. Then I imagined Gary's fate if both Zee and I were to perish right here—trapped between two corpses as the darkness came to collect him.

Despite the horror of the thought, or maybe because of it, I started to laugh again—shallow gasps that sounded more like sobs.

"You see anything?" came Gary's voice after what might have been an hour, or a day, or a minute. "Air's getting thin in here, better be a way out ahead."

"Nothing," I replied after another age. "Tunnel's dropping." It was, the angle getting steeper, sloping downward. It was narrow-ing too. I could feel its cold embrace on both my shoulders, its knuckles on my scalp. "We have to go back, there's no room."

"Can't go back," came Zee's voice, faint and echoey like it was coming from a mile away. "No way, we can't turn around."

"Right, we go on. Just go on," Gary said, although his voice was a whisper broken up by the breaths he snatched in after every word. This was hell for me, but for him with his tree-trunk chest it must have been infinitely worse.

I wiped the sweat from my brow and obeyed, feeling the blood rush to my head as I wormed down the slope. The tunnel was be-coming less smooth, blades of ragged stone jutting out at every angle and threatening to slice my arms to shreds. It only got worse up ahead, the broken walls forming a knot of stone that was so tight I couldn't see what lay beyond it.

"Dead end," I said, shuddering to a halt. "There's no way we'll get past that."

"Don't stop," Gary barked, as if by shouting the words he could somehow weaken the blockage ahead. I felt his hands on my legs, pinching and pushing, and I could picture his fat lips sucking down all the air. It was all I could do not to lash out, kick him until he wasn't breathing anymore, but instead I opened my mouth and flooded my lungs with oxygen until the panic had gone. Then I shuffled onward, praying we'd be able to find a way through.

I don't know if anything heard me. I can't see how. I mean, we were crawling through a stone coffin with more than a mile of solid rock and a hell of a lot more worthy prayers above our heads. But when we reached the knot I saw that it wasn't as tight as I'd first thought. The tunnel was blocked by a shard of stone hanging from the ceiling like a guillotine blade, and a short distance past that was a solid mound that rose from the floor. If they'd been any closer together, then we would have rotted right there, but it looked like there was just enough room to weasel past.

I pushed my head beneath the blade, its unforgiving edge scraping the hair from my skull and gouging its mark along my neck. I pushed hard with my feet, yelling in pain as I wrapped my arms around the mound and pulled myself up. For a moment I thought the angle was too much, that my spine would just snap, but then I squeezed my bony backside through the gap and was free.

To my utter relief the tunnel seemed to have widened out on this side of the knot, and as Gary's head emerged from the twisted rock I saw why. The throat had opened up into a cavern, so big that the writhing helmet lamp failed to illuminate a floor, a ceiling, or even the walls. It was like we'd emerged in deepest, darkest space, with only a crumbling ledge between us and infinity.

"Give me a hand," wheezed Gary, his words close to cries of distress. "I'm stuck."

It would have been so easy to leave him there, caught fast in a bear trap of solid stone, to steal the helmet and just run. Only I could hear Zee's frantic cries squeezed from the tunnel, begging us to hurry up. I knelt and grabbed Gary's trembling arms, feeling the hot, sticky sheen of blood on his skin. He burst free with such comical speed that I swore I could hear a pop. His momentum caught me off guard and together we tumbled down a slope and crunched to a halt on the cavern floor.

I was the lucky one, landing on Gary's chest so hard that a fountain of blood arced up from his lips, silhouetted against the flickering light. He coughed wetly then shoved me off, groaning as he sat up.

"Did that . . . on purpose," he said, but the words carried none of their usual force. Gary was a tank, but something bad had happened inside him. You couldn't bleed like that and still have all your guts intact.

"You okay?" I asked. He looked up at me, his face barely visible beneath the lamp on his helmet, and his expression seemed like one of surprise.

"Gonna be," he said eventually. "Gonna be fine, soon as we get out of here."

"Guys," came a voice from above our heads, further up than I thought. "How'd you get down there? I can't see anything."

"We rolled," I suggested.

"Rolled?" echoed Zee. I could hear him muttering as he tried to scramble down the slope. There was a clatter of stones on the floor, followed by a squawk as he fell. He staggered, then found his feet, chuckling with relief. "Thank Christ we made it out of there. I thought I was gonna die with Gary's butt in my face. Hey, man, you all right?"

Gary snorted, and I wondered if it had been a laugh. He wiped his hand across his mouth, giving himself a bandanna of blood, then tried to stand. It took him a couple of attempts, and by the time he was upright he was swaying and panting equally hard.

"Just took a few hits, that's all. Not the first time I've had the crap beaten out of me. That river was a pansy compared to my old man."

Zee and I exchanged a look that neither of us could really interpret, then turned our eyes in the direction of Gary's beam. The darkness in the cavern was so profound that it seemed to devour the sickly light before it could travel more than a couple of meters. But every now and again as it swept across the floor the golden edge of a stalagmite would rise up from the shadows before fading as the search continued.

"You reckon there's a way out from here?" said Zee, helping me to my feet. I didn't dignify his stupid question with an answer, just followed Gary as he set off across the cavern. Each step we took echoed from the ceiling—God only knew how far above our heads—the muffled sound like the patter of giant raindrops. It was enough to make me smile, until I realized there was something wrong with the sound.

"Stop a minute," I whispered, halting and grabbing Gary's shirt to make sure he did the same. I felt Zee's hand on my shoulder, but despite the fact we were all as silent and still as the stone pillars around us the sound of footsteps didn't recede. There was the distinct slap of bare feet on wet rock, followed by its echo. Two steps, three, four, and then silence.

"What was that?" I asked, realizing that my question was as pointless as Zee's.

"Probably just water dripping," Zee suggested. "That's how these things form, stalagmites and stalactites. I saw it on a documentary once with my mom and dad. Know how to remember the difference between the two?"

There was no answer except for the patter of light steps, faster this time, like someone running.

"That's not water," said Gary, turning and pointing the lamp behind us. The whole cave seemed to move as the beam swept around, shadows coming to life like beetles. More steps, off to the left, the clack of insect legs.

"There," said Zee, pointing in the direction of the sound. "No, further over."

The lamp lurched, picking out another needle of stone that rose from the floor nearby. Only this one had two silver eyes which reflected the light back at us like distant planets.

The shadow screamed, a vast wet maw opening in the misshapen lump where its head should be, then it lunged forward. In the split second before Gary ripped the light away I made out a body of glistening sinew, packed with muscles too large for its skin and stitched together like a rag doll. I assumed it was a dog, only it was pounding toward us on two feet and reaching its skeletal fingers out for our throats.

Then the darkness of the cavern washed over it, leaving only the relentless slap of its feet and the gargle of blood in its throat to let us know death was approaching.

DAYLIGHT

I MIGHT HAVE HAD A CHANCE, might have outrun the beast, if Gary hadn't decided to use me as bait. For an instant the light blazed, brighter than ever, and I felt rough hands on my chest shoving me backward. Then the boundless night reasserted itself and I floundered on the uneven ground, bouncing off a shape that loomed up before me and caused us both to trip hard.

I thought it was the creature, and expected to feel teeth in my neck, filthy claws in my skin. Lashing out, I caught it on the jaw with my palm, heard a choked cry.

"Alex, it's me!"

Zee, his hands held up to his face to guard against my blows. I put my fists to better use, pushing myself off the wet stone and helping him get to his feet. The footsteps were so close I could feel them, the tremor traveling up my shins, and I was almost grateful that Gary was now so distant that only the merest flicker of yellow light remained—it meant I couldn't see the nightmare at our heels.

"Run!" I yelled, although it was hardly necessary. Zee was already ahead of me, nothing but smoke against shadow, his guttural breathing the only thing giving him away.

I managed to run too, sprinting across the cavern even though my legs felt like they'd been broken in a million places. It's funny how much strength the human body can find when it's really pushed, and there's nothing like the fear of a grotesque monster breathing down your neck to help you reach your full potential.

I'd only taken a dozen strides when I struck something on the floor beneath me. I cried out, more in shock than in pain, feeling the cavern spin as I cartwheeled over the broken rock.

It was on me before I could pick myself up—a skid of feet, then fingers like iron on my chest. It screamed, a shriek of triumph that pierced my ears and my heart, a fog of sickening breath smothering me like a net. I tried to think, tried to pull my arms free, tried to fight it, tried to do anything other than wait for it to take my life. But the truth is I was too scared to move, too scared to breathe, too scared to think. I lay there as motionless and silent as if it had already killed me.

I'm not sure what happened next. I could hear more feet pounding toward me, surely too quickly to be human. I heard a crack right above my head and the dead weight lifted. There was a shout, another scream, the scuffling of cloth on rock and the dull thump of fist on flesh, snarling, spitting, then incredibly a voice seeming to rise from the confusion.

"Go," it said, the sound of sandpaper on wood. "There isn't much time, get up and run."

I didn't need to be told again. I heaved my aching body off the ground and staggered blindly away, not caring where I was going so long as the madness was behind me. There was another crunch, this time followed by a pitiful groan, then I felt hands on my arms again, wrenching my body around, the grip so hot I could feel the sting even through my overalls. They twisted me to my left then pushed me forward.

"This way," said the voice, a whisper that nevertheless seemed to make the air tremble. "Watch your feet."

I lifted my leg high, feeling a rock graze the bottom of my foot. There was a chilling shriek from behind me, followed by another, and the arms pushed with more urgency, guiding me around a stalagmite that I could never have seen.

"Who are you?" I asked between gasped breaths.

"It doesn't matter. You need to go."

"But why are—" I stopped as we rounded a corner and a light came into view, so insubstantial that it looked like the last scraps of a morning mist. The pressure on my arms vanished, leaving only the memory of its touch, and I turned to see my guide. But he was already retreating, his body blurring into what looked like a starry sky.

Except the glinting sparks I saw before me weren't stars. They were the demonic eyes of a dozen creatures tearing this way.

I turned and fled, the light now bright enough to make out any obstacles that stood in my way. I raced around a pillar of stone expecting to see Gary, but the glow wasn't emanating from there. It was flowing down a passageway ahead, too bright to be coming from a helmet lamp. Surely too bright, too pure, to be coming from any artificial source.

Something in my gut twisted so hard that it felt like I was being tickled by an invisible hand, and it took me a moment to realize what it was. Hope. It had been so long since I'd felt it that the sensation was like something living inside me, something wonderful waiting to break free, just like I was.

The sound of screams, and the clatter of rocks being thrown, snapped me to attention. I cast a sightless look back into the cavern, which sounded like it was home to a full-blown riot, then focused on the light, letting its warm touch pull me forward. It seemed to gain in strength as I rounded a corner, the corridor growing wider and taller as if the stone itself was being pushed back by the glow. It ended in a gnarled trunk of rock, but there was a gap large enough for me to squeeze into. When I clawed my way through to the other side I saw Zee there, pacing the identical passageway beyond and chewing what little was left of his nails. He looked up when he saw me, his expression morphing from fear to surprise to relief in a fraction of a second.

"You okay?" he said, running over. "I thought you were done for."

I nodded up ahead to where the light seemed to stream in with even more strength, picking out every last detail on the splintered walls.

"That looks like . . ." I said, but I couldn't bring myself to finish the sentence for fear of jinxing it. Zee managed a tired smile as he slung my arm over his shoulder and helped me stagger forward.

"What happened back there?" he asked after a couple of steps.

I shook my head. "It doesn't matter," I replied eventually, echoing the thing that had saved me. "I'll tell you about it when we're out in the open, when we're home free, okay?"

"That's a deal," he said. "Can't be much farther, light's pretty bright. Bet Gary's already there."

We reeled around the bend and were almost blinded. The corridor ended maybe thirty yards away, the opening blazing with so much light that the sun could have been hanging right outside. We were drenched in it, its touch like honey on our bruised skin.

And it flooded inside us too, chasing away every last scrap of darkness, every last breath of cold. I'm pretty sure we could have floated down the rest of that passageway if we'd wanted to, buoyed up and brought home by a river of golden light.

We were so busy dreaming that neither of us took the time to wonder how daylight could ever penetrate so deep underground; so busy laughing that we didn't notice the walls around us weren't natural, that they'd been chiseled from the stone by picks and hammers. For a blissful instant we'd made it, we were free.

Then we stepped into that portal of light together, our laughter one step ahead of us, and we saw what we both knew deep down we would. There was no sky, only rock. No sun, just remorseless spotlights scouring away all but the most persistent shadow from the tombstone walls. No trees, no life, other than the cluster of grinning forms standing before us, so close that we could make out the silver eyes and black suits, the rusting masks and filthy trench coats, the glistening lips peeled back past canine teeth.

And there was no freedom, just the warden and his leather face welcoming us back with the devil's grin.

WELCOMING PARTY

FOR WHAT SEEMED LIKE AN ETERNITY nobody moved. It was as if the entire cavern was frozen, a nightmare tableau stripped of motion. Or maybe it was just that time slowed down, my horror so profound that one single second of gut-wrenching realization would haunt me for a lifetime.

Eventually the world seemed to catch up, time snapping back into place and bringing the scene to life. The first thing I noticed was Gary, sprawled on the floor beneath a blacksuit. His face was a mess, but bubbles of air were bursting on his bloody lips so I knew he was alive. Despite everything he'd done to me I felt anger flood my veins at the sight of his injuries. Somewhere between jumping into the river and bursting into this cavern he'd become one of us.

Zee was muttering something to my side, and when I heard the scuff of feet on rock I thought he was trying to make a break for it, back the way we'd come. But when I turned to follow I saw that he'd collapsed, his face so pale that it looked like parchment, almost transparent.

Maybe if I'd seen him run I might have had the strength to follow, but I couldn't go alone. I had nothing left. I had a sudden flash of how I looked right then: just as ghost-like as Zee, the only sign of color the spreading crimson stains where my life force was still draining out of me. My entire body was rice-paper frail, ready to fold and crumple. I'd only felt this weak once before, that night so long ago when Toby had been shot, when I'd been framed—running toward my mom, toward safety, but unable to reach home. I hadn't made it then, and I wasn't going to make it now. Both times I failed, and both times I was captured. Only this time my punishment had to be death.

I tried to take a step back but my legs refused to obey, turning so numb and insubstantial that I didn't even feel pain when I crashed to my knees.

The sound of a pistol shot filled the cavern. A second followed, then a third, and by the fifth crack I realized it wasn't a gun at all but the warden's hands. He was clapping slowly, each slap of his palms echoing from the walls and making me flinch. He strolled toward us, his applause relentless, before coming to a halt almost close enough to touch.

Clap. I twisted my head, studying his pristine black shoes. *Clap.* A gray suit without the slightest trace of a crease or a stain. *Clap.* His lean body, his leathery neck so strung with tendons that it looked as if there was wire coiled beneath the ancient skin. *Clap.* And his face, so ordinary yet so wrong, like he was wearing someone else's over his own.

Clap. I tried to meet his eyes, knowing that I wouldn't be able to. I was right: just when I thought I was looking at them I realized my gaze had slipped to his clothes or to the cavern walls. Caught in the corner of my vision I couldn't have even told you if he had eyes, just black sockets, which seemed to suck the light from around him, which seemed to drain away what little warmth was left in my bones.

Clap. I tried again, and this time I almost caught them. It was like being plunged into freezing water, my body cramping, my lungs growing so heavy I couldn't take a breath. In that instant I witnessed things in my head that I couldn't even begin to describe— blood, decay, screams—forced from his mind into mine, threatening to drive me insane.

Clap. And just like that they were gone, leaving only a pulsing headache where they had been probing with their filthy fingers. I shuddered, gagged, and wrenched my eyes away, the cavern swimming back into focus. The blacksuits and their dogs hadn't moved, and the wheezers in their shadows were motionless too, save for the occasional spasm. I guess they knew we weren't going to mess with the warden.

He clapped once more, keeping his hands poised prayer-like in front of his chest for a moment before lowering them into his trouser pockets. I just stared at the ground as if the pebbles before me could offer a way out.

"Bravo," he said, his voice like a rasp being dragged across the inside of my skull. "I have to confess that I am very impressed."

"Please don't kill us," came a hoarse cry from Zee. "We didn't mean any harm, we . . ." He trailed off, his words lost in his sobs.

"Very impressed," the warden went on as if he hadn't been interrupted. "To find a way out of my prison, to escape from Furnace itself, it's quite remarkable really."

"Do we get a reward?" I whispered, but it was so quiet I didn't think anyone could have heard it. To my surprise, however, the warden began to laugh—a ragged breath that was as dry and lifeless as his face.

"Oh yes, you'll have your reward, Sawyer. And a fitting one it is." He took his hands from his pockets and clasped them behind his back. "Where's the fourth?"

I shuddered, wondering where Toby was now. There was no way he could have survived, caught in the jaws of the river with no bones left to break. But maybe his body had made it out, spat from the rock and laid to rest beneath the endless blue sky. I'm not lying when I say at that moment I would have traded my fate for his without a second thought. Better to be a spirit with the earth beneath you than a corpse pinned tight by the weight of the world.

"He didn't make it," I replied eventually. "He was injured in the explosion, but he jumped anyway. He's dead."

The warden clucked his tongue as if deep in thought. He was probably trying to work out whether I was telling the truth or whether to keep looking for Toby in the sprawling guts beneath the prison. I frowned, shaking some of the confusion from my brain.

"How did you find us?" I asked. "How did you know we'd be here?"

Even though I wasn't looking at his face I could feel his lips part like those of a cadaver, a dead smile all teeth and white-gummed. But when his voice came again, growled like distant thunder, there was anger there rather than humor. It seemed to radiate from him like a cold current in the ocean.

"We didn't. *They* did. Those infected little bastards appear to have served a purpose after all." He was muttering, apparently talking to himself rather than me. "They followed the stench of your fear and we simply followed them. Always hungry, the rats. Did you see them?"

Rats? I thought about the creature that had attacked me in the cave, its twisted mouth surely too wide to be human, and filled with rows of dripping shark teeth that seemed to stretch all the way back to its red-raw gullet. Then I thought of the other figure, the one who had saved me and guided my blind body to safety. It was too strange to make any sense of, so I simply shook my head.

"Just as well, just as well. You were lucky." He laughed again, that soulless snatch of air. "Or maybe not."

"Why? What are you going to do with us?" Zee asked through snot and saliva.

The warden raised his arms and the flock of dark forms behind him seemed to come to life. The dogs began to growl, the black-suits struggling to hold them back with steel leashes. Lurking behind them, the wheezers seemed to take a single asthmatic breath, their limbs jerking like they were puppets.

"As you know all too well, obedience is the difference between life, death, and the other forms of existence on offer in Furnace," said the warden, his voice quieter yet seeming to pulse around the cavern with even more force. "Your actions have cost me a great deal of time, money, and respect from the other prisoners—who have all been told that you died in the explosion, I should add. I would have you strung up and slaughtered like the vermin you are, only you are far more useful to me as *specimens*." He said the last word with a relish that made my skin crawl, bending down so that his face was inches from mine. "Your punishment for trying to escape will be death—of a kind, anyway. But long before it comes you will be begging to be put out of your misery."

Until that moment, none of it seemed real. Maybe I was so tired I couldn't process it, it was all too absurd. But right then, with the warden's decaying breath on my face, I realized that just when things seemed like they couldn't have gotten any worse, they had. A lot worse.

"A month in solitary," came his whisper. "If the rats don't find a way to kill you, then the madness will. And if you make it, if by some miracle you're not a gibbering wreck when we pull you out, then the wheezers can have you. And that's when the fun truly begins."

Both Zee and I were crying now. We remembered Donovan's stories of solitary, of what it could do to you. We were going to die in there, in the most slow and agonizing way imaginable. Surely this couldn't happen, surely the outside world had to know something bad was going on in Furnace? Except I had no idea if the outside world even existed anymore. To be honest, I wasn't sure if it ever had. There was only Furnace. It was our world, our grave, our hell.

"Take them away," said the warden, followed by the dull laughter of the blacksuits as they advanced. "Take them to the hole."

THE HOLE

THE MOMENTS FOLLOWING the warden's final command were lost to fear, blotted out by my faltering brain. I could tell you what I saw, but I don't truly remember it. The human mind is a powerful thing in many ways, but in others it's endlessly fragile—it takes only a single moment of pure terror to tear a hole in it, like a finger through a cobweb, leaving you forever just a shadow, a half-person. God only knows how mine was still functioning. It could only be because when things got so bad the emotional side of it simply shut down, making me a machine that could see, hear, think, but not feel. This automatic damage control had saved me from madness many times, but I knew it wouldn't last long, not in the hole.

As soon as the warden had stepped to one side his nightmare posse moved into the space he had left. Like dark water flooding into a vacuum, they crashed and spat around us, the dogs snapping their mantrap jaws so close to our faces I could feel their hot mucus hit my skin, the wheezers convulsing with excitement as the blacksuits scooped us up effortlessly by our overalls.

My feet dragged pathetically on the smooth floor as we were taken through a massive steel door set into the rock. It reminded

me of the vault door back in the prison, only this one was half
the size and looked like it had been pounded by a couple hundred mortar shells. There wasn't a fraction of its surface free
from dents, and it hung off its hinges like peeling skin after a
vacation. I thought for a moment that someone had broken their
way out of it, only it was hanging inward, the scars covering the
outside.

Someone had broken *in*.

It had to have been the creatures I'd seen in the cavern, the *rats*
as the warden had called them. If they could do that to a meter-
thick metal door, what would they have done to me?

We turned corner after corner, the footsteps of the guards
echoing down too many corridors to count. These passages all
seemed to blur into one another, a labyrinth of mottled, flesh-
colored rock brought to life by the flickering lamps embedded
in the ceiling. There were openings in the walls too, shadowed
portals that led to nothing but darkness—eyes that seemed to
watch us pass with disapproval. I ignored most of these just as I
did everything else, but there was one time when I snapped out of
my numbness and managed to focus on the world around me.

I was being pulled past an opening in the rock much wider
than the others, the word "Infirmary" stenciled in faded white
paint. This one was emanating a fierce crimson light that turned
the blacksuits and their dogs into blood-drenched ghosts. I peered
around the body of the brute who held me, trying to get a better
look at where the doorway led, but it was sealed off by a curtain
of thick plastic strips—the same kind you see in a butcher's
workshop.

The wheezers split off from the rest of the group here, walking one by one through the drooping slats like some nightmare

factory line. Last to go was the blacksuit carrying Gary, the boy's
body sliding through and vanishing into the light.

And then we were past it, reaching a T-junction in the corridor
and turning right. It was here that the guard dropped me uncere-
moniously to the floor, rolling me onto my back with his giant
foot and pinning me there.

"The hole's just down there," he said through a grin as wide
as any I'd ever seen, his eyes glinting like a cat's caught in the
moonlight. "You killed two of us in that explosion, you know
that?"

I thought back to the moment the explosive gloves in the ceiling detonated, the two blacksuits who had inadvertently shielded
us from the blast. They had both survived, for a few moments, one
trying to take my life and the other saving it. Monty, turned into a
monster, stripped of everything human.

If they catch you, just don't forget your name.

"I said, did you know that?" the guard repeated, pressing down
harder. I nodded, watching my misshapen head bob in the polished black leather of his boot. "If it was up to me we'd feed you to
the dogs right here, but the boss says we're keeping you. Still, ac-
cidents happen, especially when prisoners try to escape a second
time."

I nodded again, then frowned, wondering what he meant. He
lifted his foot, dragging me up, and from behind him Zee was
thrust forward. He slammed into me and I held him, two trembling forms before a wall of blacksuits and skinless dogs.

"Solitary's down there," the guard repeated, his grin never
faltering. "I'd say, what, fifty meters?"

"'Bout that," came a gravel-voiced reply.

"So, a five-second head start seem right?"

Again the voice behind him answered. "Yeah, that sounds fair."

"Then if I were you, I'd start running," the guard said. "Because as far as the warden needs to know, you made a break for it and the dogs got you." I didn't move, wondering if it was a trick, but two of the blacksuits suddenly appeared beside the one who had been holding me, each trying to restrain a monstrous canine. The foaming beasts thrashed against their leashes, the solid metal links looking as if they were about to snap like cotton thread. "Five."

I didn't need any more of a hint than that. We let go of each other and turned, bolting down the corridor as fast as our legs would let us. Seeing us run, the dogs started to bark—bullets of sound that tore after us.

"Four . . . Three," came the count, almost lost beneath the hammering of our feet.

"Did he say fifty meters?" wheezed Zee. "We'll never make it."

There was no sign of anything up ahead, just bare walls that didn't even offer a shadow to hide in.

"Two."

How far had we run? Twenty meters, maybe thirty? The dogs would cover that distance in a heartbeat.

"One."

I didn't hear it so much as know when it had been uttered. With a twin howl of delight the dogs were unleashed, the screech of their eight clawed feet on the rock so much faster than our own labored steps. I wanted to turn around but forced myself not to. One slip, one scuff, is all it would take.

"There!" yelled Zee, pointing down the corridor. I scanned the walls, seeing nothing in their raw red sheen.

"What?" The sound more a pant than a word. I knew the dogs

would have halved the distance between us, driven by madness and hunger.

"The . . . floor."

Sure enough the ground of the tunnel had several steel trap-doors set into it, each no larger than a manhole cover. I don't know what I'd been expecting when I pictured the hole, but I hadn't taken it literally. I thought it would have been a cell, be-neath the prison, sure, but not actually in the ground.

This was no time to be choosy. The monsters were so close I could hear the ragged breaths in their throats. We reached the first of the round doors, skidding onto our knees beside it, twist-ing the lever and lifting the heavy hatch. The space inside—if you can call it space—was like a coffin on its end. There wasn't even enough room for us both to clamber in.

"You take this one," I said, diving across the ground to the next hatch and wrenching it open. I heard the crash of steel on steel as Zee's trapdoor closed, and I made the mistake of looking around. One of the dogs was in mid-leap, its jaws open so wide that I al-most couldn't make out the immense body behind them. With a groan of fear I swung my legs into the hole and dropped.

I was just in time. The dog struck the top of the hatch and its body weight slammed it closed with a clang that made my ear-drums ache. For a moment I could hear it muzzling at the steel and running its claws along the surface. Then came the distant call of a blacksuit and the scuffling stopped.

"Damn shame," came the voice, softened by rock and metal. "Thought it had you there." The dull throb of laughter. "Still, give it a day or two and you'll be wishing they had caught you. Have fun, boys. Don't go mad too soon."

There was the sound of the lever on top of the hatch being

secured, then there was nothing but darkness and the frenzied beating of my own heart.

"Zee?" I called out softly, stretching my arms to gauge where the walls were. To my relief the space was bigger than I'd first thought, although it was at most half the size of the cell I'd had on top.

On top? I shook my head, not quite believing I'd used the phrase to describe Furnace. Already the prison with its light and its mattresses and the sound of its inmates seemed like home.

"Zee?" I called out, louder this time. There was still no reply. I found the wall that separated us and thumped on it with my fist, but the noise was quickly absorbed by silence. I swore, and swore again, cursing with every word I knew as I kept on driving my fist against the rock. Each time it hit, the panic set in a little more, the fear of being alone, of being in the dark, and I could picture the intricate web of my mind unraveling into insanity.

"Zee!" A scream this time, but my cell didn't even grant it an echo.

I collapsed to the floor, found that there wasn't enough room to stretch out my legs completely. Instead I pulled them close, my knees touching my chin, and rocked gently. The blacksuit was right: pretty soon I would be wishing that the dogs had caught me. At least they would have had the decency to finish me off quickly.

This room was a different kind of beast entirely, infinitely more patient and infinitely more terrifying. The hole didn't need monsters to do its dirty work, it had no use for brutes in black suits and their silver-eyed hounds, or wheezing freaks with filthy syringes.

No, all it needed was me, and my fear. Because alone in the silence, in the unfathomable darkness, I knew that my own thoughts would drive me mad. My own mind would kill me.

THOUGHTS FROM THE ABYSS

WHEN EVERY LINK to the outside world is severed, time has no meaning. It ceases to exist other than as a dull memory, a vague recollection of what a minute used to be, an hour, a day. Sealed up tight so far beneath the ground, every single second was stretched out almost to infinity—each one a vast and empty abyss where time used to reign, an ageless aeon barren of significance and consequence.

When every scrap of light and sound has been taken away, reality has no meaning. It too ceases to exist, for what is reality other than the cumulation of senses—images witnessed by our own eyes and the noises that enter through our ears? But when all those senses are starved, then the real world fades away like the last frantic gasp of a television program when the set is switched off.

And when reality goes, sanity has no reason. How can your ability to behave in a normal and rational way still exist when nothing normal or rational remains? As soon as reality breaks, as soon as we are separated from the physical world, the cracks begin to appear in our minds. And through them seeps the madness that has always been there, flowing into your skull like a liquid nightmare.

I couldn't tell you how long I'd been in the hole before the hallucinations began. Starved of sensory input my brain began to concoct its own reality, causing phantoms to peel themselves from the darkness of my cell. At first they had no faces, no bodies, other than a swirl of soft white like silk in water. But then they began to solidify, filling out until they resembled people I half recognized.

The first to take shape was somebody I hadn't thought about in years—Mr. Machin, a teacher I'd had way back in elementary school. He was the one who first made me want to be a magician, back before I gave my life to crime. He performed an impromptu show one rainy lunchtime, and I'll never forget the way he'd always known what everyone's card would be despite the fact they'd been shuffled back into the pack, even my eight of spades, which he picked out with a flourish.

He strode toward me as if from a great distance, his features becoming clearer with every step. At first his expression was gentle, smiling at me with fondness the way he had done back in class. But I knew he was a figment of my imagination, and right now I had nothing good left inside me, just hatred of what I had become, what I had done to myself. So I guess it wasn't surprising when his eyes narrowed and his mouth opened and he started ranting. There was no sound in this trick of the mind, but I knew what he was saying.

You took your life and wasted it, Alex. All the advice I gave you, all that inspiration, all those hours we spent learning. You wasted my time too, and all for what? You make me sick.

I scrunched my eyes closed but the image remained, projected onto my eyelids instead of the wall. Choking on my panic, I swept my hands in front of my face and the hallucination responded, exploding into light and drifting in fragments around the cell. It wasn't long before it started coalescing again, this time forming a short, birdlike figure I knew immediately was my gran. The wraith seemed to struggle to take shape this time, the face twisting to form a nightmare parody of itself that grinned grotesquely at me in a way my mom's mom never would have done.

To think of everything your parents did for you, that we all did for you, and how did you pay us back? By breaking our hearts. How could you do that to your own mother?

I wanted to argue, wanted to plead my innocence. But I was as guilty as they came, and those crimes I never would have dreamed of committing on the outside—assault, arson, even murder when I'd sent that kid Ashley falling to his death—Furnace had brought out of me all too easily. There could be no doubt about it, I was evil, rotten to the core.

My gran's spectral form seemed to nod at my confession, then broke apart by itself. It wasn't long before it swept into focus again, and I turned my back on it, unable to bear any more tirades from the people who had once loved me. But there was no stopping it—how could I hide when the only things that existed to me were my thoughts and the abyss?

I counted ten people in the procession that drifted through my cell, all with variants of the same message. The last three were my mom, my dad, and Toby, my friend from school—my *dead* friend from school—who materialized together and spoke as one. What they said seemed to carve out a little of my soul, and even though I forced myself to forget their words as soon as they had faded I could never get rid of the way they made me feel.

I gritted my teeth, clenched my fists so tight I could feel the sting of nail against palm. It felt like I'd been in the hole for weeks already, tortured by the ghosts of my past for hours on end. But for all I knew it could have taken place in one of those gaping seconds, one single tick of a clock stretched to eternity by the horrors it contained.

Because time had no meaning, reality had no meaning, sanity had no meaning. And when everything else has been taken away, *you* have no meaning. You simply don't exist.

I DIDN'T THINK I was going to survive that first second, first hour, first day. But there must have been a part of my mind that wasn't convinced I was wicked. Somewhere deep inside me, past all the chaos, all the anger, the kid I'd once been still remained, and he wasn't going to let me be consumed by my own nightmares.

Another figure began to form from the spots of white light in my cell, right by my side. I shied away from it, unable to bear another attack, but instead of hounding me with screams and accusations this one seemed to laugh—a gentle chuckle that was so alien to me that at first I couldn't even work out what it was.

Would you look at the state of yourself, the voice said, and I recognized it straightaway. Snapping my head around I saw Donovan crouched beside me, his dark skin now glowing like some corny Christmas angel. Light seemed to spill from his eyes, pushing back the walls of the cell and the heavy curtain that had dropped over my thoughts. *It's a good thing there ain't no windows in here, you look like a dog's ass.*

I laughed, another unrecognizable sound. But it soon died away.

"I'm a bad person, D," I said, my voice slurred beyond recognition but clear enough in my head. "I deserve to be here."

Donovan reached up a hand and slapped me around the back of the head. I couldn't feel it, but the touch seemed to chase even more of the cold shadows from me, leaving a welcome warmth in their place.

If I hear any more of that crap, then I'll give you something to cry about, he said, the grin never leaving his face. *That's exactly how they want you to feel, those are the same thoughts that went through my head when I was down here. This room, this pit, it's designed to suck every last bit of strength from you, every last scrap of fight. Why do you think they've been using solitary confinement in prisons for thousands of years?*

"To punish the guilty," the dark part of me replied.

To make us weak, Alex. To rip out our spirit, to crush our self-worth, to make us feel like we don't have a right to escape. Because if they do that, then they can pretty much guarantee we'll never want to get out. If they break us, if they break you, they could keep you a prisoner in a place with no walls. You're a good kid, Alex.

"And you're a figment of my imagination," I mumbled, but I was smiling.

I know, I know, he replied. *But call me one again and I'll kick your ass. I might not be real, but if I was I'd be saying the exact same things. Don't give in, Alex, don't let them win. You beat them once and you can do it again. Don't let this place break you. Keep your mind busy, keep yourself occupied, find things to do. If you're doing things, then you still exist, right?*

I nodded to his fading form, watched his body dissolve into the darkness like sugar in tea. He was gone, but he'd taken my fear and futility with him. I knew it had been just another hallucination, but it had brought me back from the edge. The voice in my head masquerading as Donovan meant that there was a part of me which understood I didn't deserve to be here, which still had faith in me, which knew I had escaped once and could do it again.

And it was right, if I kept myself busy then it meant I was still here, still flesh and blood and bone. It would keep the madness at bay.

I started immediately, scrabbling up and using my arms to map out the exact dimensions of my cell. I could just about stretch them from wall to wall, which brought a little relief—it meant that I could probably lie diagonally with a little room to spare.

The stone beneath my fingertips was solid, cut as smooth as the walls in the corridors outside. Even to the touch it conveyed a sense of its strength. It would take dynamite to make a scratch on it, and that's probably all it would do.

But there was condensation there, a clammy sheen that felt like sweaty skin. I vaguely remembered Donovan saying he'd survived by licking the moisture from the walls, but I wasn't quite thirsty enough yet—I still felt like I'd swallowed half the river when we'd jumped.

Next I reached up to the top of the cell, which was less than an arm's length above my head. Feeling the ceiling so low threatened to bring back the claustrophobia. But I kept it at bay by trying to work out the exact size of the hatch, the method by which it had been wedged into the rock. It must have been just wide enough for a body and sealed tight, not even the slightest hint of light creeping through the joint between metal and stone.

I remembered how heavy the hatch had been when I'd lifted it—maybe minutes, maybe hours—earlier, and then I'd been pumped with adrenaline. I didn't think I'd have the strength to push it all the way open from below, even if it wasn't locked.

I paused, taking a good few breaths of stale, warm air, then I got down on my knees and started to investigate the floor. Like the walls, it was made of rock, polished flat. It was an unbroken slab, save for one corner where I could feel something metallic set into the surface. Running my hands gently over it, I discovered it was a small grille. I stuck a finger inside, feeling nothing where the floor should be and realizing that this was both my toilet and my air supply. I was grateful—a month doing my business on a watertight stone floor would lead to death by drowning in the most horrible way possible.

I hawked up a ball of spit and launched it through the opening, hearing a distant plop. Then I tried to pull on the grille, but it didn't do much more than rattle. It was far too small a gap to escape through—not that I'd really want to, knowing what was down there—but it might have another use. A weapon, perhaps. I pictured myself trying to bludgeon a blacksuit with a foot-wide iron grille and laughed. It was ridiculous, but it was wonderful— my mind was working, too busy to give the darkness and the loneliness and the madness any room.

I placed my hand on the wall that separated my cell from Zee's, hoped he was doing the same thing, trying to keep busy, trying to stay real. Then I leaned back, ran a hand through my hair, and tried to come up with a plan.

SCREAMS

PANTING LIKE AN OVERWEIGHT DOG, and sweating more than a sumo wrestler in a sauna, I pulled my aching fingers free of the grille and collapsed. It was still in place, but I'd been wrenching it and pushing it and stamping on it and twisting it for what seemed like forever, and its resolve was starting to wane. Another few attempts, maybe, and it would be loose.

I still hadn't thought of a way to use it, but my mind had been busy with other things. I'd sat for what must have been hours going over everything in my head, trying to make sense of what was happening here. Back in Furnace's general population, with all the other inmates, we'd been so focused on getting the hell out that I guess we didn't let ourselves think about the other stuff—the wheezers, the monsters brought back, all bulging muscles and bloody-skinned, then somehow turned into blacksuits. Yeah, those thoughts had been in our heads permanently, but they'd been pushed to the side so we could give everything we had to the break.

Down here there was nothing else to do but think. I started with the wheezers and their gas masks, stitched into faces that looked so old, so decayed, that they could have belonged to corpses—black eyes like coal set into dark pits rubbed red raw. Everything about them was wrong, the way they looked, the way they screamed to each other, the way they moved—all staggered jerks like marionettes being operated by a child.

And the way they injected their prey with darkness.

They had to be human—what else could they be?—but twisted and broken beyond repair. By age perhaps? Or were they demons spawned here in the pits of hell? They certainly looked the part, and why else would they take people kicking and screaming down to the bottom of the world, to the pits beneath the prison? It would explain why those victims returned, morphed into freaks with grotesque bodies and appetites to match. What could do that to a human other than a creature of darkness, a demon? It would explain the warden too, because if anyone reminded me of the devil it was him.

But even as I thought it, it sounded crazy. Besides, the thought of the devil and his slaves didn't fill me with one iota of the terror I felt when I thought of the most probable alternative.

Science.

Shuddering involuntarily I crouched forward again and hooked my fingers through the grille. It rocked back in its socket as if afraid that this time I might pull it free, but after a couple of tugs that almost ripped my arms from my shoulders it remained stubbornly locked in place. I'd heard the grating of mortar on rock, though, and I knew it was weakening.

I wiped the sweat from my brow, trying not to think what my hands must look like after groping the toilet for hours on end. Banging the back of my head gently against the wall, I attempted to analyze the thoughts racing through my skull.

Science. Bad science. It made sense. I mean, what had the

warden called us? *Specimens*. Lab rats for some sick and twisted project. Surely some genetic experiment could be responsible for turning Monty into a creature so muscular it had threatened to burst right out of its stitched skin, so furious that it had broken Kevin into a thousand pieces barely held together by his prison overalls.

But then turning Monty from a monster into a blacksuit?

I could feel the thoughts all tumbling together and shook my head to separate them. Turning to the wheezers again, I wondered if they too had been the result of some kind of gene therapy. We'd covered the basics of biology at school, learned that genes were the building blocks of every living thing, but other than that it was all completely over my head. Although I hadn't been so devoted to my life of crime that I'd missed the stuff on the news about gene maps and all the neat tricks they'd done with mice— giving them diseases, making them be born with a human ear on their back or an extra kidney, even changing their sex.

And if you could do that to a mouse, then why not a kid?

I groaned, realizing that this theory sounded just as insane as demons stalking the corridors of Hades. There was no way they could turn a man, a child, into a monster. It couldn't happen. And what kind of nutcase would want to? Who would go to the trouble of framing innocent kids for murder and dragging them into Furnace just to mess with their genes?

But my mind kept flicking back to the infirmary we had passed, the wheezers all marching through the plastic slats like surgeons going to work.

Taking another deep breath, I lifted the loose end of the grille and wedged my heel against it. Bracing my back against the wall, I pushed as hard as the space would let me, hearing the metal loose a creak of distress. My foot shifted as the grille bent, but my leg cramped before I could finish the job. I lay still, rubbing the knotted muscles beneath my overalls and waiting for the throbbing agony to subside.

Could science explain the creature that attacked me back in the cavern? And the constellation of silver eyes racing through the darkness drawn to the smell of fresh blood? And what about the thing that had saved me? I remembered the touch of his skin, so hot it burned me even through my overalls. Science could change somebody's appearance, certainly, but make it feel like there were glowing embers set under their flesh? Surely that was impossible.

So what were the rats? Why didn't they cluster around the warden like all his other sick freaks? Why were they running like wild dogs in the lightless tunnels beneath the prison? Each time I thought I had an answer a million different questions presented themselves.

The pain in my calf had dulled to an echo, beating in time to my heart. I tentatively flexed my leg, pointing and rotating my foot like we used to do in soccer after a charley horse. The thought inevitably conjured a rush of memories—sunshine on our backs as we belted the ball up and down the field, laughter roared out over the world in celebration. I wondered if my old mates were playing now, wondered who had replaced me at left back, and who was taking Toby's shots up front. This time it felt as if my mind was cramping, bolts of white-hot pain flashing across the back of my eyes.

I growled with anger, a sound that could have come from an animal. Then, suddenly pumped with adrenaline, I began pounding the grille with my feet. After the first dozen strikes my heels were bruised and bloody, but it only took a couple more blows before the rigid metal popped from its frame. The squeal of rending iron was deafening, and the clatter of the grille as it dropped onto the rock reverberated around my cell like a wasp. But that was one advantage of being in such a tightly sealed space—there were no cries of alarm from outside, no stamp of booted feet on the path above my head.

Crouching forward, trying not to put any pressure on my battered feet, I picked up the grille and held it to my chest. It was still useless, but the fact that I'd been able to pry it loose was an achievement that brought a grin to my face—so wide that my cheeks were aching. I would have kissed the bloody thing if it hadn't been covered in crap. Instead, to celebrate, I got to my feet and used the toilet, the sound of splashing below giving the pleasant illusion of space.

I didn't sit down again straightaway, happy to let some blood flow to my legs. While I was standing I swung the grille at the wall between my cell and Zee's. After I had been in the dark so long the spark it produced was like a firework going off in my eye, the clang deafening. I blinked, enjoying the spots of light that had burned my retinas. Then I whirled it around again, harder this time. Another spark, flashing the cell into life for a fraction of a second—wet, red walls like the inside of a stomach.

I stopped, putting my head against the cold stone and waiting for a response. Zee must have heard it—human voices might be too soft to penetrate rock, but I knew sound traveled through solid objects a hell of a lot better than through air. Surely an impact like that must have carried.

But there was nothing, not even a scratch. I swung it again, more from frustration than with any hope of a response. Then I dropped the grille to the floor.

"Zee!" I howled, the volume of my own voice somehow making the panic rise up in my gut. I clamped it before it could get any worse, slapping my palm against the wall before sliding onto my haunches again. A couple of deep breaths calmed me down, and they also brought tiredness—my eyelids drooping as if drawn shut by my last spluttered exhalation.

I lay down as best as I could in the tiny space, wedging my head in the corner opposite the toilet and stretching my feet out. I wasn't sure if sleep would be able to find me here, hidden so well in the rock, so far underground. But it was on me in seconds. Everything we'd been through since we'd tried to escape had drained me of all but the last gasp of wakefulness. And with a sigh even that fled, freeing me—if just temporarily—from my tomb.

THE DREAM, when it started, was more real than the reality I'd just left. I guess it was bound to be—in the hole I was completely cut off. There was no light, no sound, no connection at all to the everyday world, but in the dream my senses were bombarded with fresh information. It was a wonderful feeling, until I realized where the illusion was taking me.

When I did, my hollow groan seemed to settle over me like a thunderhead. I was walking down the corridor of the house where Toby and I had been caught. Although this time Zee was there instead, a few meters ahead of me, running at full pelt. He turned in my direction and the way his face morphed into a grimace of pure fear was like a dagger in my heart.

There was something right behind me.

I started running too, my pace sluggish, the way it always is in nightmares. Zee looked back again, and even though he was gasping for breath he unleashed a haggard, desperate scream.

He reached the door to the living room, now guarded like
Furnace's infirmary by a curtain of plastic slats. With a choked cry
he swung around and vanished through them and I followed without thinking, feeling the filthy strips like pondweed on my face.

On the other side of the curtain was the room where the
wheezer had picked Toby to die and me to be framed for murder,
where the blacksuits had laughed as one of them, Moleface, pulled
the trigger.

Only this time the bodies of a dozen boys hung limp and
bloody from the ceiling, suspended upside down, ancient ropes
tight around pale ankles. They were all dead. And they were all
screaming.

I felt terror grip me, and I mean really grip me, so hard I thought
my insides were being crushed—my heart too constricted to prop-
erly pump my blood, my lungs unable to expand, my vision flickering on and off like a faulty projector.

Zee flew into one of the corpses, the impact knocking him off
balance. He careened to the floor, spinning around to face whatever was behind us. I ran toward him, terrified but knowing that
we stood more of a chance if we fought together. I thought he'd be
grateful, but instead he lashed out at me with his feet, screaming
words that were soundless but which were all too clear.

You're one of them, you're one of them, you're one of them.

I tried to argue, but before I could the figures above me started
to convulse, their drooping hands snatching for my head and their
lifeless eyes burning into my soul. I fought them but there were
simply too many, their cold touch grabbing, tearing, gouging.

You're one of them, you're one of them, you're one of them.

I felt one of the dead boys press something against my mouth,
the sting of a needle in my flesh. I screamed, but all that came out

was a dry wheeze, and when I tried to catch my breath to cry out again I felt poison flood my lungs. The room began to spin, the cadavers spiraling outward like some macabre Catherine wheel. In a second all that remained was their howls, an endless funeral dirge as I tried to rip the gas mask from my face.

I shot up in my cell, the dream fading as the darkness around me once again began to seep into my mind, erasing all that had been there.

Except for the screams.

It was so faint it could have been an echo of my nightmare, but I knew immediately it wasn't. The noise was loud enough to penetrate my cell, dripping down on me like ice water. I felt my skin tighten into gooseflesh, held my breath the better to hear it when it came again.

Louder this time, and closer. This wasn't the same scream I had heard in my dream, although it had obviously inspired it. This sound definitely wasn't human but a frenzied cry devoid of anything but hatred and cruelty. And whatever it was, it was coming this way.

I thought about what the warden had said, about the rats—those creatures from the cavern—coming to get us. But it was fine, I was locked up here, safe from whatever it was. Right?

Except the lock was on the outside.

When the scream came again it could have been from right above me. It still sounded like it was miles away, but I knew it was just a thin barrier of rock giving the illusion of distance. Something hit my hatch hard, and my entire body flinched. Another thump, then the sound of claws against metal. I curled into the smallest ball I could, praying for the noise to stop. Praying so hard I thought my clenched fingers would break.

There was a muted shot, little louder than bubble wrap popping, then a thump as something fell onto the hatch. A second shot followed, then what might have been feet, and a third shot, which I could hear pinging off the metal. I strained my ears to hear more, but whatever had been happening now seemed to be over.

I didn't move, kept my arms and legs bound tight and my head pressed into the warmth of my chest. With nightmares waiting for me when I slept and death here when I woke up, it was all I could do.

COMMUNICATION

I DON'T REMEMBER FALLING ASLEEP, but I must have because I was woken by another noise. I sat up, thinking for a split second that I'd gone blind before remembering where I was.

There was an unpleasant feeling in my gut, like someone had twisted my stomach around then pinched it in place with a bull-dog clip. It was probably hunger—I had no idea how long I'd been here, but it must have been more than a day.

The noise didn't repeat itself, but I could have sworn it had come from the direction of the toilet. I shuffled my body around, too used to the pain to really bother with it, and lowered my head to the opening.

Nothing.

Maybe I had dreamed it. Given what had been going through my head last night (or morning, or afternoon, whatever it had been), another weird noise didn't seem unlikely. I realized I needed the hole for something else, and did my best to squat over it in the darkness. I never thought I'd miss the stained hunk of metal that had been our toilet back in the cell up top, but right now as I tried and failed to hit the target I would have traded my eyeteeth for it.

As I crouched there, wondering what to do about toilet paper, a muffled clank rose up from beneath me. I turned and put my head as close to the floor as I could bear, holding my breath to better hear if the noise came again—as well as for more obvious reasons. It did, another sound like metal on metal.

Without warning, something in my heart lifted. I scrabbled around the tiny floor and found the grille, smashing it as hard as I could against the wall. The noise it made was loud, but it didn't sound like the one I'd just heard. I poked a finger down the hole where the grille had been set and felt a pipe with a ring of iron or steel around its lip. There was another clank, and this time I answered, lifting the grille above my head and smashing it down against the ring of metal.

It hit with the sound of a muffled church bell and I dropped it, putting my hands to my ears to try to stop them ringing. Behind the whine of my eardrums the noise came again, followed by a pause long enough for me to know what to do. I snatched up the grille and struck, softer this time, just once. A few seconds later the sound from the pipe came twice and I echoed it. Then three times, followed by three strikes which I belted out with choked sobs of relief.

"Zee," I said, more to myself than from any hope he'd hear me. "You genius."

He'd obviously managed to pry his grille off too, and had thought to smash it against the iron in the toilet. The sound was traveling down then up again, making it seem like it was coming from right beneath me. I yelled in celebration, and this time rapped out the five notes of "shave and a haircut." Even before the echo had died down in the pipe, Zee's "two bits" burst through it with glorious clarity.

I collapsed back against the wall, giggling helplessly. It seems like a stupid thing to be so happy about, but those tiny taps broke all hold that solitary had over us. They punched through its one power, its only strength—its ability to keep us isolated, locked away from the world. It wasn't much, and we wouldn't be using it to discuss the next World Cup or who our favorite Hollywood babe was, but it was enough. I wasn't alone anymore.

This time, so overwhelmed by enthusiasm, I raised the grille to my mouth and kissed it.

KEEP YOUR MIND BUSY, *keep yourself occupied, find things to do. If you're doing things, then you still exist, right?*

"Right," I said, remembering Donovan's words. Well, remembering the words spoken by the piece of my subconscious that was masquerading as the memory of Donovan to stop me crumbling into depression. It's weird how complicated things can get when you're on the edge of madness.

I'd been keeping my mind busy for what seemed like forever; Zee too, as we tried to work out a system of communication. He'd started by tapping out short clacks then longer ones, and I guessed he was doing Morse code. I'd never gone to Scouts or anything like that, so all I could do was repeatedly bang my grille against the pipe in frustration until he got the hint. It would have been easier if we had a one hit for yes, two for no system, but we had no way of asking questions so it was impossible.

We spent quite a bit of time just tapping meaningless staccato tunes, not really caring that we weren't forming words, just happy to hear each other. At least I was just tapping out nonsense—for all I know, Zee was coming up with a master code that I just wasn't grasping.

There was a moment, sometime after we'd discovered each other, where he did seem to be creating a system of taps. I listened carefully, trying to work out the code. There were five clear taps, followed by five more, then a pause. Next there was one tap, followed by five, another pause, then one and five again. I tried to work out what it might mean, but it was probably something he'd seen on one of his damn documentaries and I didn't have a clue.

After racking my brains for a while, the only thing I could think of was that he was using numbers to stand in for letters. But that only spelled *EEAEAE*, and unless he was being tortured and letting me know he was screaming, it didn't seem to mean anything.

My own confusion gave me an idea. Waiting until Zee had fallen silent I smashed my grille against the pipe eight times, one for each letter up to *H*. I paused, then brought it down five times. *E*. Twice I smashed out twelve dull, battered notes. *LL*. My fingers aching, I finished off with fifteen clear, steady hits. *O*.

Silence. I chewed my nails in anticipation, spitting violently when I realized what I was doing. There was no time to think about it, though, as Zee's response drilled up the pipe with all the subtlety of a homicidal robot on the loose.

Eight. *H*. Nine. *I*. One. *A*. Twelve. *L*. Five. *E*. I didn't need to wait for the twenty-four notes of *X* to chime like clockwork from the pipe to know he'd got it. I let the grille drop for a moment, flexed my weary fingers. Then, from nowhere, I began to cry. They weren't bad tears, I guess. They weren't happy ones either. I couldn't tell you what they were. It's like when you're listening to the radio and all of a sudden a song comes on that really jerks your heartstrings. And it doesn't matter where you are or what you're doing but you can just feel the emotion welling up inside you like a tide. There's no stopping it.

Here in Furnace there was no music, so this was our song. And it was more beautiful than anything I'd ever heard. As Zee hammered out another tuneless verse I let my body heave, warm drops of salt water dripping past my lips onto the rock. When the sobs had subsided I wiped my eyes, even though there was nothing to see, and decoded Zee's message.

Seven. *G*. Fifteen. *O*. Fifteen, again. *O*. Four. *D*. A longer pause. Twenty. *T*. Fifteen. *O*. Another pause. Eight, five, one, eighteen, pause, then twenty-one. *Hear u. Good to hear you*.

I wanted to send back *You're not kidding*, but it would have taken forever, so I settled with twenty-one short notes like we'd been using, then two longer ones. *U 2*. I hoped he'd get it.

U OK, came his eventual reply. I nodded, even though he couldn't see me, then answered with a series of strikes.

GR8. Sound couldn't penetrate the walls, but it seemed sarcasm could.

ME 2.

We went on like that without daring to stop. In a way it was just like texting using a really ancient phone, and we quickly picked up on each other's shortcuts and abbreviations. It wasn't the easiest form of communication in the world, the simplest sentence taking minutes to hammer out. But that was perfect—it kept our minds occupied far longer than a spoken conversation would. Each tap was like the seconds ticking by on a clock, and it forced time back into the room, brought us back to reality. We could hear the minutes passing, our conversations literally devouring the hours.

I replayed Zee's messages in his own voice, although surprisingly I couldn't remember exactly what it sounded like. I knew his accent, though, and after we'd been "talking" for a while it was like he was right there next to me, speaking in my ear.

"Been to the toilet yet?" he asked, his taps becoming words.

"Yeah, but I took the grille off first."

"Lucky you. I've still got my own crap on my fingers."

I laughed, picturing Zee's face on our first morning in Furnace, when he'd been on Stink duty cleaning the toilets. I could see that same gurning expression now.

"Nice," I clanked.

There was a pause while we both gave our tired hands a rest, then Zee started up again.

"Hear that thing last night?"

I didn't reply immediately. I couldn't bear to think about it, especially after finding some scrap of goodness in the hole. The memory of that creature, whatever it had been, clawing and scratching at the entrance to my cell was enough to bring the walls crashing back in, enough to make me feel all alone again. To scare the fear away I banged out a response that I hoped would end the topic of conversation.

"Just noise."

"Sounded like the thing back in the cavern," he pressed. He was right, and there was no doubt in my mind it had been one of the creatures, the rats. When I didn't answer he went on. "Think it'll come back?"

"Heard shots. Must be dead," I said hopefully.

"Maybe. Thought I heard it run off."

I pictured the freak running into the shadows, returning later on tonight, and decided to change the subject.

"How long you think we've been here?"

A pause, then the beat of his response.

"Dunno. A day?"

"Only twenty-nine left to go," I replied, snorting to myself.

"Like being on vacation."

I laughed again, but Zee's question about the rat had dredged up memories that showed no sign of departing. I picked up my grille and smashed out another sentence.

"Any way to lock your hatch from the inside?"

There was no response. I figured he was probably investigating his cell door before answering; maybe he hadn't already done it. I counted the seconds, then the minutes.

"You okay?" I asked. Still nothing. Something had happened. I was about to drum out another frantic message when I heard the bar on top of my hatch swivel around. The shock was so great that my stomach lurched as if on a roller coaster, and I dropped the grille, the sound lost beneath the squeal of hinges as the trapdoor opened.

Light flooded the cell like liquid fire, burning my eyes so fiercely that I doubled over and pressed my face into my hands. But not before I'd seen the hulking shape silhouetted against the inferno, two silver eyes glaring down at me like twin spotlights. It was a blacksuit. They'd heard us communicating, they were here to separate us even further, to take away the grilles. Or maybe just to punish us, to drag us off to the infirmary.

"Bang all you like, you're not getting out."

I eased my head from my arms, squinting against the glow. My heart was hammering hard enough to be heard through the wall, but I forced myself to look up, the blurred shadow of the man hanging over me like a storm cloud.

"What?" I asked.

"Don't let me stop you, though," he boomed, half words, half laughter. "The more you wear yourselves out the worse it will get." He moved, his hand flashing into my cell like lightning. I ducked, feeling something crash down on top of me, all sharp edges. Hot liquid was running down my face and I thought it was blood, but then it dripped into my mouth and I recognized the unmistakable texture of slop—the almost inedible purée of skin, bones, guts, and offal that passed for food in this place.

"I get to eat?" I asked, genuinely surprised. I don't quite know how I'd thought we were going to survive for a month without rations of some kind, but the last thing I'd expected was to be fed.

"Enjoy," said the suit as he closed the hatch, laughing again at the comical expression I must have been wearing. "You're not getting any more for another two days."

VISITORS

I DIDN'T KNOW WHICH WAS BETTER—the fact that I had something to eat, or the fact that we'd already been in here for two days.

Luckily the bowl of slop had landed right side up and with most of its contents still in place, a miracle in this place where Murphy's Law seemed to be an official prison rule. I ate slowly, knowing that if I guzzled down the lot in one go after not eating for so long I'd probably throw it straight back up. It wasn't much, the sawdust-flavored gunk even lumpier than I'd gotten used to in the trough room, but it chiseled away at the dull ache in my gut and left me feeling full.

I finished the last morsel of salty goo then licked the bowl, my stomach gurgling with satisfaction. Picking up the grille, I clanked out a message to Zee. I wasn't really sure what to say, so opened with some small talk.

"Yum."

"Best meal ever," came his reply a minute or so later.

"Didn't think they were gonna feed us."

"Guess they want to keep us alive, make us suffer," he said, a sentence that seemed to take an eternity. "Thought they had us then."

"Me too. We were lucky."

There was a moment of silence. I could picture Zee licking his bowl with the same relish I had.

"Suit said it's been two days," I went on. "Believe it?"

"Impossible to say. Feels like forever."

The guard might have been messing with our heads, but surely if he'd been doing that he'd have told us we'd been there for a few hours rather than a couple of days. No, he'd let it slip without meaning to, trying to torture us by saying we weren't going to be fed for *another* two days without realizing he'd given us hope. Hell, if two days could fly by like that, filled with slow but wonderful conversation, then a month would be no trouble.

"Can you think of any games?" I asked after another period of stillness.

"I Spy?" he replied, making me choke with laughter. "Something beginning with D."

"Donkeys?" I beat back.

"No."

"Dog crap?"

"Probably."

"Dickweeds."

"Nah, they've gone."

More laughter. My arms were killing me where I'd been smashing the grille against the pipe, but I was having too much fun to stop. I found myself thinking back to all the car rides we'd taken as a family when I was a kid, all the times my dad had suggested playing I Spy and I'd been too cool to go along with it. *It's the best game ever*, he'd say, always trying too hard. Right now I agreed with him.

"Donovan," I suggested eventually, struggling to remember

more words that began with D. My memories of the outside world had been fading ever since I'd arrived in Furnace, starved of reference to the things I once took for granted. Sure, I still knew what ducks and daffodils and dragonflies were, but it took me a while to dredge up the images and sounds and smells and thoughts that went with the words. And sometimes I just couldn't manage it. I'd lost the memory completely, I'd never get it back.

Zee hadn't replied, and I wondered if he was thinking about Donovan. The very mention of his name had sparked the hallucinations again. Patches of white vapor no more substantial than sea mist swirled in front of my sense-starved eyes, coalescing into a vague shape before spinning out and unraveling again. Instead of fighting it, blotting it away like I had done that first hour in the hole, I let it come.

Keeping busy, I see, said the image of Donovan, his skin glowing white and red and even green in places.

"Staying sane, yeah," I replied. "Well, apart from the fact I'm talking to a figment of my imagination again."

Don't call Zee that, he joked.

"I meant you, you idiot."

The sound of Zee's grille burst through the illusion, causing Donovan's body to explode into specks like a flock of birds startled by gunshot. The hallucination bobbed around the cell before forming on the other side of me, my old cellmate now tiny like he was sitting some distance away.

"Where do you think D is?" Zee asked.

Right here, I thought about replying, my own words coming out of Donovan's mouth. But only the memory of him existed in my cell right now, and I was pretty sure I knew where the real version was.

"Infirmary," I chipped out, my ears ringing from the echoes.

Gee, thanks, yelled the hallucination, wearing a frown but grinning beneath it. *You could have said on a beach somewhere, eating a burger. Why have you got to imagine me in that place? You shi—*

Once more Zee's response chased the image away. I shook my head, attempting to clear my thoughts. It was difficult enough trying to hold two conversations at once in any situation, never mind one with a hallucination and the other with a guy on the far side of a solid stone wall using a toilet grille and an alphabetic code.

"I hope not," was all his hammer blows said.

This time, when Donovan re-formed, he was right next to me.

Doughnuts, he said. I looked at him—through him really, as his skin was almost translucent—and shrugged. He couldn't have seen it, but he was in my head so he knew what I meant. *Guess doughnuts, you know, for I Spy.*

"That's stupid," I grumbled, but tapped out the word anyway.

"I wish," came the chiming pulse of Zee's reply.

Diana Wilkes, suggested Donovan. *I always wanted to ask her out but never had the guts.*

"I don't think so," I said, having a flashback to school, and to the girl who sat three seats in front of me in math. Diana Wilkes. I'd had such a crush on her, had even written her a couple of notes on postcards. But I'd never given them to her, never said anything. Never would. I wondered who was sitting in my seat now, idling away the lesson by staring at the back of her neck and wondering what it smelled like. I turned back to Donovan and pretended to punch him on the arm, my hand passing right through like he was a reflection on water. "That's my life you're remembering, get your own."

Pretty tough when you're made from someone else's imagination, he said. *Speaking of which, I definitely had bigger arms than these.*

He flexed them, and the hallucination seemed to grow to ridiculous proportions. He nodded approvingly at his biceps, which now looked like rugby balls beneath his glowing shirt.

"Happy?"

Much better.

There was an impatient hammering from the pipe, the clangs adding up to spell "Give up?"

"Never," I replied. "Dinosaurs."

"No."

"Drive-in movie theater," an answer that seemed to take about an hour and left me with a blister at the base of my thumb.

"No."

It's darkness, said Donovan in my head. *The answer is darkness. He can't see anything in there.*

"Duh," I said, turning to scowl at him. "I know that. I was dragging the game out, having a bit of fun. Way to kill the buzz."

Sorry, the apparition muttered. Then he looked up at me, eyes shining like pearls in the ocean. *Dogs.*

"What's the point?" I answered, putting on a mock pout. "You've already ruined the game."

No, listen, he said. *Dogs.*

A growl like jet engines above my head, then the unmistakable bark of one of the warden's mutts. Donovan vanished and I shot to my feet, standing on tiptoes and cocking my ear as close to the hatch as possible. Zee had obviously heard it too, as there wasn't the slightest sound from the toilet pipe.

I didn't hear the dog again, but I could make out the sound of feet on the rock above. It was only a whisper, but they must have been moving fast and hard to have produced any sound in here at all. I held my breath, becoming absolutely silent except for the stammer of my pulse. There was a voice, too deep to make any sense of but obviously urgent. It sounded like an order being given.

The footsteps faded, then broke off completely as a muted shot rang out. It was the same thing I'd heard the other night, but softer this time, which meant further away. Two more followed, so close they were almost a single sound. There was a scream, as faint as a fingernail scraping glass. Then that too died away.

I had the grille poised above the pipe to make sure Zee was okay when the screech came again. This time it was right above my hatch.

The lever grated as it was pushed around, the sound of nails or claws on the metal making my scalp shrink. I dropped the grille, reaching up and trying to find something—anything—to grip. There was a slight lip around the circumference of the hatch, barely enough for me to hook my fingers into. I grabbed it as best I could, practically hanging from it to stop it opening.

The pressure in the cell changed as the seal was broken, my ears popping so hard I was deaf. I swallowed to clear them, but instantly wished I hadn't as the creature outside the hole screamed again. It was a noise of pure rage, so demonic that every muscle in my body lost its strength. It was all I could do to hang on as I felt the hatch shift, something tugging on it from the other side.

It lifted, enough to let in a crack of blood-colored light. I screwed my eyes shut, wrenched the hatch back down. One of my hands slipped off but the other held firm, the steel slamming closed with a jolt that could have torn my spine out. Another shriek, the scrabbling of frenzied claws on metal. Again the hatch was forced upward, this time far enough for me to catch a glimpse of whatever was outside—flesh the same color as the walls, limbs too swollen to be human. But whatever it was had feet—broken and misshapen, yes, but other than that no different from mine.

"Leave me alone!" I howled, the words distorted by my sobs. It only seemed to make the creature more furious, and the hatch was torn up a little further. This time a hooked hand slipped through, the nails sharpened into claws, gripping the edge. It pried the door open a fraction more. Another few centimeters and it would be able to flip it all the way over, leaving me exposed.

I dug my fingers in so hard I felt a nail snap. Ignoring the pain, I jerked my body down again and again, and by some miracle each time I did it the sliver of light breaking through the gap got smaller and smaller. The thing unleashed a gargled roar of defiance, but its strength seemed to be fading. With a crunch the hatch slammed shut, trapping its fingers. Another cry, this one filled with pain rather than anger, and all too human for it.

The creature was cut off mid-scream. One second it was thrashing to try to free its hand, the next there was a dull snap and it fell silent. I pushed its fingers through the gap, desperate to close the hatch before anything else tried to find a way in. They slid out with the sickening sound of grating bones, and I was plunged into the welcoming darkness. I couldn't lock the hatch from inside, I was just grateful it was shut.

But my gratitude didn't last long. Before I could suck in a breath the hatch burst open, and I didn't even have enough air to scream with as a pair of bloody hands ripped me from my cell.

SNATCHED

THE CREATURE'S PAWS WERE LIKE MACHINES, clamping my arms to my sides and hoisting me out of the hole as though I weighed nothing. I thrashed with my legs, but the thing was behind me and my pathetic kicks didn't even seem to register.

Whatever was holding me paused to knock my hatch closed, using a huge leg to swing the lever back into place. The other creature, the one that had been trying to get to me first, was hunched over and lifeless on the floor, its skinless, glistening body facing down. Its head had been twisted around at an impossible angle—its dead eyes open and fading, its toothless maw gaping like an empty shopping bag, as if it was howling silently at the ceiling.

I screamed for help, throwing myself against my captor and trying to wrench myself free from its grip. From nearby there was a bang, so much louder out in the open than it had been in the hole. It was a shotgun; I recognized the sound from the prison. Three more shots followed in close succession, a booming cry from a blacksuit. I wanted to see one of them run around the corner, appear from the dark tunnels behind us, anything. They might have been scary, but they were nothing compared to the writhing monster of knotted muscle and fist that breathed its blood breath on my neck.

It started to run, each giant, pounding leap carrying me away from the passageway I'd arrived through. The hatches in the floor flashed past, too many to count. I called Zee's name, knowing he wouldn't be able to hear me, then the creature turned a corner and solitary was behind us.

We were in another stretch of corridor, narrower this time, and I managed to bring up my leg and kick out at the stone. I made contact, thrusting hard and sending us both off balance. The creature hit the opposite wall, the impact ripping its hand from my arm. I saw my chance, swinging my head back with every ounce of strength I possessed.

Stars exploded in my vision, first light then pain. But it had been worth it. Something behind me crunched, followed by a howl of agony. The other arm loosened and I tore myself free, staggering on the rock before finding my feet.

The corridor was shorter than the one we'd just left, lightless openings on either side. It bent around again at the end, and I could make out huge shadows bobbing up and down. They had to be cast by guards. They'd probably shoot me as soon as they saw me, but that was better than whatever the creature behind me had in store.

I opened my mouth, ready to call out, but before I could a hand wrapped itself around my face. I felt fingers in my mouth, encrusted with dirt, and bit down on them. Another hand swung around my waist and I was lifted again, like a toddler scooped up by a parent. I saw the shadows growing larger, the blacksuits almost on us. But then the tunnel lurched as I was dragged into one of the openings along the wall, and darkness swallowed me.

I knew what was happening. The creature was taking me to a quiet corner where it could eat me slowly, finger by finger, limb by limb. I lashed out again, hoping to flick a foot out of the doorway, one last chance to draw the attention of the guards. It was too strong, and in one leap we were halfway across a pitch-black room, the door nothing but a block of dull crimson light in the distance. Another leap and it had almost completely disappeared.

The creature pinned me to the ground, its hand still clamped against my lips. I could hear the march of booted feet outside and made one last attempt to scream.

"Quiet," came a voice, *its* voice, like a death rattle.

My muffled wail died out, more from shock than anything. Had it really spoken? Being devoured by a monster, a creature with little resemblance to humankind, that was one thing. But there was something far, far worse about being carved up by a beast that could speak.

"Quiet," came the voice again, softer. It was familiar. The footsteps had all but died away, and I felt the weight on me lift. The hand on my mouth was as firm as ever. "I need to know you're not going to call out," the harsh whisper continued. "I need you to trust me."

I lay there for a moment, trembling too much to reply. But what choice did I have? I nodded my head hard enough for it to feel the movement.

"I'm not going to hurt you," it went on, gently removing its hand. I tasted blood, although I couldn't tell if it came from my lips or its fingers where I had bitten them. Gasping for breath, I thought about screaming. Even if I'd wanted to, I doubt I'd have had the strength.

"I'm sorry," said the voice again, the sound of joints clicking as it shifted position. "There was no other way. I only had seconds to get you out."

"You could have just asked," I replied hoarsely, sitting up. I felt a hard surface behind me, metal shelves, and shuffled until I was leaning against them. The creature was invisible in the gloom, and I was still terrified of it. But I had thought I'd have claws beneath my skin by now, teeth in my neck, so I couldn't complain.

"You wouldn't have come," it said. "By the time I'd convinced you it would have been too late."

And then it struck me, where I'd heard the voice before. I suddenly realized how hot its hands had felt on my face.

"You're the thing that saved me, right? Back in the cavern."

A grunt that could have been yes. I could hear something else, a gross squishing sound that reminded me of raw meat sliding into the food grinders in the prison kitchen.

"You okay?" I asked.

"I think you broke my nose," it replied, its voice laced with pain. "But it's healing, just give me a minute."

I'd never known a broken nose that could heal in a minute, but I kept quiet until the noise stopped and the creature spoke again.

"You're Alex Sawyer," it said, and I was about to answer before I realized it wasn't a question. "You broke free."

I nodded, forgetting that it couldn't see me. To my surprise, however, its silver eyes seemed to focus on the movement.

"I thought so. We heard the explosion from down here. Didn't know what had happened at first, but when we saw you in the river we couldn't believe it."

"We?" I asked.

Before it could respond there was another screech from the

corridor outside, more gunfire. Something flew past the distant door, a shadow too swift to make out. I squinted, wondering why it seemed to have been running along the wall, tearing chunks from it as it passed.

"There's no time," the creature hissed. "You've got to get back."

"Back?"

"To the hole."

I started shaking my head but it rested its hot fingers on my arm, snatching them away a second later as if fearing they might burn me.

"Just listen to me. I needed you to know that we're down here, that you're not on your own."

More footsteps drumming out a panicked rhythm as two blacksuits sprinted past the door, little more than a blur.

"What's going on out there?" I asked when the noise had faded. "Are you one of those things? Those creatures?"

"Yes and no," came its answer. "I'll explain later. All you need to know is that there's a war going on down here, and we're on the losing side. We need you, Alex. If you can get out of general population then you can get us out of here."

My head was spinning, the sensation amplified by the darkness. My thoughts were like planets careening out of orbit, crashing together and exploding into meaningless dust. I saw one clearly, snatched at it before it vanished along with the others.

"Donovan. Carl Donovan. Is he down here?"

"I don't know," it said, but I could sense the hesitation in its answer. "There are some kids in the infirmary, including the guy you escaped with."

"Not him," I interrupted. "Another guy, about the same age, dark skin, big."

"There might be." The creature's silver eyes blinked uneasily. "I don't know, I can't tell, they're all . . ."

"What? They're all what?"

"Just forget about them, okay? Forget about him. It's too late. But not for us."

It had been quiet outside since the blacksuits had run past, and the creature stood. I felt its fingers searing through my overalls again as it pulled me to my feet, leading me back toward the door. I wanted to ask it more about Donovan, ask it to take me to him. I wanted my old cellmate to know that I was here, that I hadn't abandoned him. But the creature was the first to speak.

"The guards should be occupied by the north door," it said, mumbling to itself as we walked slowly toward the corridor. With more time to look around I could see that we were in some kind of storeroom, the light from the passageway outside too weak to identify what was in the countless boxes and jars lining the shelves. "That's where the breach took place, where the rats got in. We should be clear back to the hole."

We reached the door and I turned around, ready to plead not to be taken back to solitary. But it grabbed my shoulders and held me tight, kept me facing forward.

"Don't look at me," it said, and I could sense a boundless sadness in its voice, the choked whimper of shame. "Please, don't look at me."

It held me still for a moment, during which a far-off shot whispered down the corridor. Then it pushed me forward, telling me to run. I didn't argue, sprinting back the way we'd come. The passageway containing solitary was clear and we made our way down it faster than I thought was possible, the creature's hands pressing at my back and betraying the sheer power of its body.

Keeping one hand on me to make sure I didn't turn, it swung the lever around and wrenched open the hatch.

"I'll be back," it whispered. "The next time there's a breach, the next time the blacksuits are distracted, I'll be back. Hurry, get in."

I sat, gripping the edge of the hole and angling my feet in.

"Just tell me your name," I said.

"My name?" the creature replied as I dropped, as if unsure what the question meant. I hit the floor, immediately turning my head. The hatch was already closing, but through the shrinking gap I could make out the top half of a monstrous body, one arm as thick and bulbous as a tree trunk, the other wasted away to skin and bone. It raised its scrawny arm as I looked at it, covering itself with a gnarled hand. But not before I caught a glimpse of the face beyond—that of a teenager, little older than me, silver eyes set into gray skin.

"It's Simon," he replied, then the hatch slammed shut, the lever turning, leaving me with nothing but the fleeting echo of the boy.

RECOVERY

FOR WHAT SEEMED AN ETERNITY I stood in my cell staring into the infinite night, giving my body time to remember how to breathe. My heart was struggling as well, its rhythm frantic and forgetful, thumping too hard and too quick and then missing a beat before trying to catch up. The tiny space felt like it was spinning, even though there was no way I could actually tell if anything was moving or not.

I thought I could hear thunder in my ears until my clouded mind focused and I pictured Zee next door. He was banging his grille furiously, waiting for a response. Touching the wall to push away my dizziness, I crouched and used my other hand to reach out, finding my own grille upended in one corner. I wasn't sure what to say, so I simply smashed it against the pipe three times.

There was silence from Zee's cell and I could picture him crashing back against the stone in relief. A few seconds later he started hammering again, his long sentence giving me plenty of time to recover.

"I thought they'd taken you," beat the tuneless notes.

"They did," I answered, taking my time over every letter. Zee was responding before I'd even finished.

"Where? Who?"

I tried to think of an answer, an explanation, but my mind drew a blank. Just so Zee didn't think I'd gone AWOL again I gave him a very brief summary of the last few minutes—they'd seemed like hours—the creature that had opened my cell, then the boy who had killed it and dragged me out. I told Zee where we'd gone, and what he'd said.

"Not alone?" Zee responded. "Who are they?"

"I don't know," I replied. I truly didn't. From what I'd glimpsed of the kid, Simon, he looked like a monster. The way the skin of his arm had bulged, stitches encrusted with blood and dirt and threatening to tear loose, reminded me more than anything else of Monty, cut open and packed so tightly with something else's flesh that he looked like an overripe, flyblown fruit about to burst. He had the same silver eyes too, those of a wolf caught prowling in the moonlight.

But why hadn't Simon acted like a monster? Why had he ripped me from my cell and then given me hope, rather than smuggling me into the darkness and feeding from my squirming torso? He could have killed me in the time it took to open my mouth to scream, yet he hadn't.

"It said it needed me," I went on, fragments of the conversation coming together in my head like a jigsaw puzzle. "To escape."

"Escape?" Zee said, and I could sense his excitement by the eagerness of his taps. "You think there's a way?"

Not a chance in hell, I thought. I mean, we were cocooned in a cell the size of a coffin, miles of rock in every direction except one and a big chunk of reinforced steel there to make up for it. Not only that, but we'd been pushed even deeper into the stinking bowels of Furnace.

Down here there was no chance of salvation. Even if we made it out of solitary, if we found our way back into the labyrinth of tunnels and passageways that made up the guts of the prison, we still had *them* to contend with. The rats with their eel-like mouths and endless rows of needle teeth, their infected claws, which looked like they could slice through skin as if it were tissue paper, their soulless voices screaming through wet throats as they started to feast. I banged out another sentence if only to keep my mind busy.

"How can there be?" I said, regretting it as soon as I'd smacked out the last word. In the hole, keeping up our spirits was the most important thing we could do. Even though I could literally feel the weight of the world pressing down on my shoulders, I knew I should at least try to sound positive.

"I'm not sure," I hammered out, contradicting myself. "Maybe there's a way. Gotta wait for the kid to come back, next time there's a breach."

Zee didn't reply, and I knew his blistered hand must have been as sore as mine.

"Gonna get some sleep," I lied, just so he didn't worry if I was silent for a while. I wasn't sure how to sign off, so ended with "Speak soon."

I wasn't tired, there was enough adrenaline pumping around my system to keep me awake for weeks, but I needed time to think. What the hell was happening down here? If I could just figure it out in my head then maybe I stood a chance of avoiding the same twisted fate as Simon and Monty and God only knew how many others. Staring off into pitch black I thought about my old cellmate, and sure enough after a couple of blinks he strolled toward me, forming as he went.

You're getting good at this, said the hallucination, taking a seat on an invisible chair on what should have been the other side of the wall. I wished I was as insubstantial as my own conjuration, able to float up past the hatch, through a mile of rock, and keep on going—soaring into the calm blue sky until all the world was at my feet. *You wish*, he went on. *You couldn't get your fat ass off the ground, let alone drift up to the surface.*

"Ha ha," I replied dryly. "You're in my head, you should be nice to me."

You obviously know me too well, Donovan said, leaning forward and resting his elbows on his knees. *So what do you want, anyway? I'm not sure I like it when you drag me down here.*

"Just someone to talk to, I guess," I replied, the sound of my voice alone in the cell making me feel foolish even though I knew nobody could hear it. "Someone to help try to make sense of what's going on, what happened to that kid Simon."

Sorry, kiddo, we share the same brain at the moment. What you know, I know.

"You could at least pretend to help," I pleaded.

Fine, fine, he said, cupping his head in his hands like someone deep in thought. *I think this is all some big reality television show, being broadcast right now to the whole nation.*

"Gee, thanks," I said, smiling despite myself. "Seriously, D, what is going on here? Those things, those creatures, they were human once, right?"

Yeah, Donovan replied, staring at the floor. His face was a mass of shimmering white, but his eyes seemed to be glistening even more than usual. *You'd better not be picturing me crying, Alex, or I'm gonna pound you into the middle of next week.*

This time I laughed, and he laughed with me for the fraction of a second it took our faces to fall again.

Yeah, they look human. Look like they were once, anyway. But they're not anymore, especially not the rats. They've had every last scrap of humanity torn out of them. They're animals now; monsters, demons, whatever you want to call them.

"Specimens," I said aloud. Donovan nodded.

I think you're right, it's gotta be some kind of experiments. Some sort of genetic crap. Real nasty. Maybe they're trying to create super-soldiers or something. Those blacksuits could kick some serious ass. You should try to find the real me, I'll know the answer.

"Why would you know any more than me?" I replied. "We both know I'm the clever one."

Donovan just snorted, peering up at me with eyes made from moonlight.

Because whatever happened to Simon, to those freaks, is happening to me right now.

"No," I said, a groan that lurched into a sob. I couldn't bear to picture him in the infirmary while everything recognizable was flayed from his body, everything good was sucked from his soul. I put my head down, staring at the abyss beneath my feet, and when I lifted it Donovan had gone.

"No," I shouted after him. "I won't let it happen. I'll come for you, D, I promised I would. Just hang on."

I steeled myself, clamping down on the emotions, letting the logical thoughts creep through. If Simon and whoever else was out there needed me to help them escape, then I'd give them what they wanted. Somehow I would get us out. But only if they led me to Donovan, and only if he was still alive. Come hell or high water, he was leaving with us.

"Just hang on," I repeated. "It won't be long."

And I was right, it wasn't long at all.

THE WAR

THEY CAME BACK WHILE I SLEPT. I heard them in my dreams again, the sound ripping me from nightmares of hanging limbs and plunging me back into the hole. It was only the faintest echo of a scream, but it left me wide awake, senses heightened, my heart pumping more adrenaline than blood.

This time it was excitement rather than fear that drove me to my feet. I was still terrified, don't get me wrong, but at least I had an idea of what lay on the other side of my cell door, and that gave me some control. Not much, admittedly, but enough to keep me standing, fists clenched at my side, instead of cowering in the corner praying for peace.

I stood on my tiptoes, put my ear as close to the hatch as I could. For what seemed like hours there was no sound except the rush of blood in my head, my pulse like the ocean crashing against a stony shore. Then I heard it again, a squeal, distant even through the solid metal.

I was concentrating so hard on the sound that a sudden hammering from Zee's cell scared me half to death.

"Take me with you," he tapped out patiently.

I had my grille raised to tell him "Okay" when the bar on my hatch squealed, metal grating against metal as it was unlocked. I shifted the heavy grille over my shoulder, ready to swing it up into the face of anything that wasn't Simon. But when the door lifted and I blinked away the burning light of the corridor, it was him I saw, silver eyes peering shamefully out at me from behind crooked fingers.

"Quick," he said, his voice like that of an old man who'd smoked a hundred cigarettes a day all his life. He offered me his other hand, the skin taut and smooth like ancient leather, criss-crossed by stitches. "Quick!" he repeated, more urgently. I placed both my hands in his and with no effort at all he hoisted me from my cell, then slammed the hatch shut.

He started to run, heading toward the storeroom he'd taken me to before. I didn't follow immediately, skipping over my hatch to the one that sealed Zee's cell. I had my hands on the bar, straining to open it, when I heard Simon whisper in my ear.

"What are you doing?" Breath as warm as desert dust on the back of my neck. "There's no time."

"He's coming with us," I said, my weakened arms unable to swing the lever more than a hair's breadth. "Help me get this open."

I heard the beginnings of a protest swell up in the kid's throat, but he swallowed hard then barged me out of the way, sending the bar crashing around with a single sweep of his oversized arm. He wrenched open the hatch, revealing a pair of eyes in the darkness so wide and so white that they seemed to be glowing.

"Alex?" came Zee's voice, a flutter no louder than a bird's wings. He didn't have time to say anything else before Simon plunged his hand into the shadows and pulled him out, dropping him on the floor. Simon kicked the hatch shut and locked it, then started sprinting again.

"Stupid stupid stupid," I could hear his voice with every thunderous footstep as he swung around the corner into the smaller corridor. I grabbed Zee's hand and followed, ignoring his cries of confusion until we'd ducked through the opening in the wall and stumbled blindly into the storeroom. There was a moment of panic when I couldn't see Simon, but then I spotted the twin moons of his eyes blinking at us from a far corner.

"What's going on?" whispered Zee. "Is that him? That kid?"

I didn't answer, concentrating on avoiding the shelves and boxes that were nothing more than shadows against shadows in front of me. I heard the scratch of matches ahead and was bathed in a warm amber glow.

"Hurry," said Simon, holding the match as far from himself as he could. He squinted at the light through the fingers of his other hand as though he were afraid of it, and after a couple of seconds tossed the flame to the floor. We trod carefully around a metal shelf and sat beside Simon, the match flaring up in an arc of deep orange—like a dying breath—before it was overrun by the darkness.

"That was stupid," his voice snaked up from nowhere. "Every time I come for you I risk my life. Blacksuits are everywhere; they'll shoot me on sight."

"Sorry," I said. "But Zee and I work together, we're a team. You want me to help then you're gonna want him too."

"Help?" said Zee. "You mean escape?"

Simon's silver eyes bobbed up and down as he nodded. I looked over my shoulder at the storeroom door, the corridor deserted and silent beyond.

"Where is everyone?" I asked. "The blacksuits?"

"Breach took place on the other side again, the north door. Guards're all up there. Will be until they can secure it."

"Secure it against what?" said Zee. I heard Simon utter a grunt of frustration.

"You don't need to know. It's not important, not now. You need a clear head, Alex, you need to help us find a way out. If you knew what was going on, if you knew what they were doing . . ."

"I need to know everything," I cut in. "*We* need to know everything. If we're going to get out of here, then we have to know the truth."

Simon was probably right, I'd be better off not knowing, better off using every scrap of brain power I had looking for an exit. The truth, the unthinkable horrors of Furnace, would only sink into my consciousness like a poison, clouding my mind. But right then it didn't matter. I just wanted to know. The kid sighed, the sound of a breeze kicking leaves along the pavement.

"The rats, they're people," he said, his voice shaky. "They're boys, like you, like me. They've just"—he seemed to choke on his own words—"they've just gone wrong."

"What do you mean, 'boys'?" said Zee, his voice rising. "What's happened to them? Why are they down here?"

"The warden, the wheezers, they bit off more than they could chew," Simon went on. "They were messing with forces that they couldn't understand, couldn't control. Ever since this place opened they've been using us. I can't tell you why, I can't tell you how. All I know is they take us from our cells down to that infirmary, and they . . . they *change* us."

"That's crazy," muttered Zee, although I knew from the way his voice trembled that he believed it. How could he not? We'd both seen the wheezers picking their victims, watched in horror as they pumped them full of darkness. We'd seen the kids return, barely enough left to identify them with as they howled and pounded their way through the prison. It *was* crazy. Even with the evidence right before us it was insane to think that something like this was happening with the world going about its business on the streets over our heads. But it was true.

"I would have thought it was insane too," said Simon, the emotion drained from his voice. "Until it happened to me."

There was another flare of light as the kid sparked up a match. I screwed my eyes shut against the brightness, then eased them open to see Simon sitting before us, hands held out to his sides to give us a front-row view of what they'd done to him.

The first thing I noticed was that the overalls hanging off him were the same as the ones Zee and I were wearing. They'd been torn to shreds, sewn up and tied where possible, but were unable to conceal the body beneath. Every visible patch of skin had been sliced open then stitched back up, the lumps that I'd spotted earlier angry swellings that made me think of infections. Something strange had happened to his torso. It looked like it had been sculpted by a child from Play-Doh, stretched too far and allowed to slump back on itself. I could see lines around his stomach where the skin had been pulled taut, patches translucent like a balloon too full of air.

I lifted my gaze to his face, blinking away the tears. It was still that of a boy, maybe sixteen, only now I noticed that the cheeks were swollen, charcoal-gray veins outlined on the pale surface. His eyes flashed in the weak light as if forged from steel, and I thought I could make out scars dripping from each one like teardrops. I gagged, but then the match flickered out and the feeling was snatched away along with the image.

"Jesus," breathed Zee. "Why?"

"You think they tell us?" Simon spat back. "Hell, most of us never even know it's happening, we're so doped up. It's only when something goes wrong . . . when they dump you . . ."

"Dump you?" I said, ignoring the burn in my chest.

"Their experiments don't work on everyone. Sometimes it just messes them up, like me. If that happens, they dump you, throw you out. Most times that happens they chuck the bodies in the incinerator. Not always, though."

"But what do they do to you?" I asked. "I mean, what do they do to you that can change you like that? It's impossible."

He didn't answer, and a second later I realized why. Something was moving out in the corridor, the slap of bare feet against the rock and the wheeze of a breath. When Simon spoke again his voice was so low I could barely hear it.

"I don't know, only the wheezers do, they're the ones who run the infirmary, the labs. All I know is they try to change you into a blacksuit. They make you strong, Alex, they make you fast, but they rip out *you*, your personality, everything that was good inside you." I felt a finger tap me gently on the chest, leaving behind the imprint of its heat. "You can't fight it. It's like your head is flooded with darkness and anger, and the only thing that will make it go away is if you forget who you are. I can't explain it."

"But why us, why kids?" was all I could manage.

"The warden talked about it." His whispered voice was laced with impatience but he continued. "The procedures only work on children. Our bodies, our cells, they're still tough enough to be ripped apart and put back together without serious damage. Try it with an adult and they die."

The slap of feet outside was getting louder, and I looked over at the door. Faint light from the corridor was creeping in, but there was no sign of anything else. Not yet.

"How did you survive?" asked Zee.

"They dumped me, and I would have burned like the others, except the rats got into the compound, gave me time to escape. They've been through the same experiments too, you see, only they've gone too far. They're not humans like us anymore, and they're not blacksuits either. They're something much worse."

He was speaking quickly now, as if he knew he didn't have much time. There was a growl from outside the door, like an injured lion.

"They live in the tunnels outside of Furnace, the rats, but they're always trying to get back in. Nothing can keep them out, not the doors they keep putting up, not the guns, not the blacksuits. They force their way in and they tear everything they see to pieces."

"Why?" I asked, unable to believe what I was hearing.

"For food, mainly. For revenge too, I guess, even though their brains are too messed up to know it. You can see it in their eyes, though: pure hatred. Somewhere in their heads they understand what they've become, and they can't stand it."

"And that's the war you mentioned?" I pressed. The growl outside got louder.

"Keep your voice down," Simon replied. "Yeah, that's the war. If you thought things were bad up in the main prison, in gen pop with the gangs, then you're in for a nasty surprise. The wheezers created something evil, something deadly, and they've filled these tunnels with it. It's raging out there, this war—the brute force of Furnace's elite guard against the filth that they unleashed. And we're stuck smack bang in the middle."

Something flat and hideously ugly poked its head around the door, sniffing the air with two ragged holes in its face that might once have been a nose. It didn't have silver eyes, in fact it didn't seem to have any eyes at all, and when it shuffled forward on all fours it knocked clumsily into the wall.

"It's blind," I said, and the creature tilted its head as if homing in on the words. A throbbing snarl rose up in its throat again as it eased its way into the room. But it couldn't have been a dog, not with a body like that, not walking on its knuckles. It looked more like an ape.

"The breaches are happening more regularly," Simon whispered. "The rats are getting hungrier, they've tasted human flesh too many times, and they know they're winning. I'll come back for you soon, then we can find a way out."

I saw my chance and took it, ignoring the dull slaps of the beast as it closed in on us.

"I'll help you find a way, I'll get us out of here, but I'm not going without Donovan."

"The guy in the infirmary?" Simon replied. "No way, we can't go in there, it's impossible."

"It's either all of us or none of us," I said. "Your choice."

I heard him swear under his breath, then he nodded.

"You need to run back to your cells. I'll come lock you in so the blacksuits don't suspect anything. Just bolt and don't look back, okay? Don't look back."

The creature was halfway across the room now, nothing but a humped shadow framed in the light from the door. We'd have to squeeze right past it if we were going to get out, and I prayed that it actually was blind. I braced myself, taking on a sprinter's start and tensing my muscles.

"Alex?" came Zee's uncertain cry. But it was too late to say anything.

"Go!" screamed Simon. I sprang, seeing the creature rise up before me and howl as it sensed its prey on the move. It lumbered onto its back feet, towering over my head and swinging its long, loose limbs in wild circles. There was a crunch from my side as Simon leaped onto a shelf, then I felt wind on my ear as the kid flew over me. He struck the creature with a thump, sending them both crashing across the storeroom and clearing a path to the door.

"Go!" yelled Simon again, and we obeyed, speeding toward the rectangle of light and the relative safety of the corridor.

I know I shouldn't have looked back, but I did. It was too dark to make out much, but there was no mistaking what was happening in the shadows. I could see the ape-like beast on the floor, pinned down despite its size. It was no longer growling but whimpering, thrashing pathetically at the air while Simon perched on its chest. The boy had bent down and bitten into the beast's neck, the sound of tearing flesh filling the room. The whimper became a low moan, then faded altogether, replaced by a wet noise that sounded like frantic gulps.

Two silver coins peered from the mess, watching me, and I saw them shake softly from side to side. *Don't look back.* Then Zee grabbed my overalls and pulled me into the light.

PREPARATION

WE SCRAMBLED BACK TOWARD OUR CELLS, gripping each other's overalls, too frightened to let go, stopping only once at the bend in the corridor to make sure the coast was clear. There wasn't a living thing in sight, the rock walls so still that time could have stopped, the air silent except for our hoarse breaths.

"You're not thinking of getting back in the hole?" Zee whispered frantically. "We should go now, make a run for it while there's no one here. We might not get another chance."

"We can't go," I replied as calmly as I could. "We don't know where we're going, and we're dead if we run into a blacksuit or . . . or one of those things."

"We're dead if we stay," Zee shouted back, too loud. He broke his hold. "I'm not getting back in there."

I ignored him, knowing that someone could appear at any minute. Compared with what I'd heard, what I'd seen, being torn to shreds by shotgun pellets was a pretty good way to go, but I wasn't ready to give up yet. Jogging up to the first hatch, I kicked out at the stubborn lever with my heel, managing to spin it enough to unlock the cell. Zee was still talking at my back but I shut him up with the fiercest look I could muster.

"Zee, you have to trust me. This is the only way. The warden's given us a month down here and nothing else is going to happen until that time is up. Right now the hole is the safest place we can be." I thought about the rat that had tried to break into my cell but shoved the image from my head before it could take root. "If you make a run for it now you're as good as dead. We've got to come up with a plan, find a way out, then we'll go together. *Trust me.*"

"I trust you, Alex," he said, walking up to the cells. "It's that thing I don't trust, that boy. We don't know anything about him."

"We know he's one of us," I replied. Then, as if to try to convince myself: "He *is* one of us."

I bent down and grabbed the lever, straining to lift Zee's hatch. After a couple of seconds he appeared at my side and grabbed the lip, and together we managed to haul the solid steel manhole cover open. We did the same with mine, then stood in silence staring into the infinite blackness of solitary confinement.

"I can't spend much more time in there," Zee said eventually. "I'm seeing things, you know, things that aren't there. Things that come out of the walls. I think . . . I think there might be bugs in my cell."

I looked up at him and for the first time I noticed how thin he was, how frail—his eyes watery, his skin gray and loose and streaked with dirt like unwashed laundry. He caught my glance and mirrored my expression. I knew I must have looked just as bad. For a second he smiled at me, nothing more than a glint, and I snorted a laugh.

"Don't we make a pretty picture," he said.

"Yeah, but it's good to have a conversation without beating the hell out of my toilet," I replied, offering another dry hiss of a laugh. He nodded, then leaned forward and gave me a hug. It was unexpected, but the feeling of contact after all this time was euphoric. I returned it, slapping him on the back a couple of times like I'd seen my dad do to his male friends, then we separated.

"Tell anyone we did that and I'll deny it," he said as he sat on the edge of his cell. He dropped in, disappearing like a rock in a tar pit, his voice muffled. "Just find a way, okay; get us the hell out of here. And soon."

I nodded, pulling on the hatch until it got caught by its own weight and slammed shut. The lever wouldn't turn all the way, but with another few kicks I managed to slot it back into its casing. I sat on the edge of my cell, the floor invisible beneath me, and wondered if Zee had been right. Maybe we should have made a break for it while we still could. Maybe it was the height of stupidity not to have gone when our cells were open and the corridors were abandoned.

But my gut was telling me we'd be dead in minutes if we fled. As ridiculous as it was, I knew we had to lock ourselves away before we could set ourselves free.

Grabbing the edge of my hatch, I tilted it forward until it was vertical, then I slid into my cell, pulling it behind me. It fell like a ton weight, the change in pressure making my ears ache as if I had dived too deep in the pool. I swallowed, twisting my jaw, until they popped, then leaned back against the wall.

"Honey, I'm home," I said to myself, followed by a noise that could have been a giggle but which was laced with an edge of madness that chilled me to the bone.

FOR A WHILE I did nothing except stand against the wall staring into the dark, letting the night seep into my head and snuff out the thoughts that were squabbling for attention. It worked, and for maybe a minute or so I found the closest thing I'd ever got to peace in the hole.

Then I heard hurried footsteps on the ground above me, the sound of the lever on my hatch being pulled tight, and Furnace forced itself back in.

I pictured Simon fleeing along the corridors, heading back to some dark tunnel where he was safe from the rats and the black-suits. How long had he been down here? I wondered, the first of hundreds of questions that swooped and called in my head like a flock of seagulls. His stitches looked fresh, his skin bruised as if he'd only just escaped from the wheezers. But the way he spoke, the way he acted, was far older than his years, and made me think he'd been trapped in the underbelly of the prison for a long time.

I shuddered as I pictured what he might once have looked like, a year or two older than me and slimmer too. Had he been locked up in the hole first? Tormented by his own demons, reduced to a shivering husk of a human before the wheezers got to have their way? It made sense. I mean, that was one way to avoid going crazy in solitary—just forget who you were, forget all you had ever been.

Is that what was happening to Donovan right now? Everything that once defined him being stripped away like wallpaper, covered up with a new personality, the psychotic menace of a blacksuit? I felt the anger swell inside me, making my muscles heavy and my head pound, but there was nowhere for it to go so it just fizzled out into the shadows of my cell.

Anger was quickly replaced by fear as I wondered what our own fate was, Zee's and mine. Were we doomed to be carved up inside and out, body and mind, to become blacksuits? Or would we fail to make the cut and be dumped, incinerated? Or, worst of all, would we somehow survive and become one of *them*, the rats, stalking the passageways feeding on the flesh of the guards, of the kids who'd once been our cellmates?

It wasn't exactly a great menu of options.

I tried to change the channel in my head. I thought about when I'd been up in my cell on top, watching the blacksuits and the wheezers and occasionally the warden emerge through the vault doorway from the passages beyond. I'd had no idea—none of us up there had had any idea—that below our feet a battle was raging, that the calm, wicked faces that peered up at us in our cages had been fighting tooth and nail with the very freaks of nature they had created. I wouldn't have believed it if somebody had told me. Hell, I barely even believed it now and I'd seen the evidence with my own eyes.

Feeling the ache in my legs I slid down the wall and stretched them out before me, rubbing my skinny calves. I must have lost a ton of weight since I arrived in Furnace, and I didn't exactly have pounds to spare when I got here. My mom would have loved it, she was always trying to slim down. If I did get out, if I ever reached the surface, maybe I'd send her the recipe for Furnace slop. A bowl of that once every two days and she'd be a size zero in no time.

I wanted to laugh again, but I couldn't find the energy. Even the thought of eating slop seemed like a dream, one that made my guts feel as though they'd been compressed into a solid lump that sat in the pit of my stomach. I wasn't hungry, I was *too* hungry to be hungry, but I knew I was starving. Another tactic to wear us down, make us weak, force us to forget who we were. Next time I was in that storeroom I'd be sure to check if there were supplies inside.

I swallowed, the inside of my mouth like cotton wool. Shuffling around I ran my tongue up the wall, feeling it soak up the little moisture that was there. I felt like a cow licking its salt block, and "mooed" softly, giggling to myself again. Yup, there was no doubt about it, I was crazy.

It must have taken me half an hour to slake my thirst, after which my tongue felt numb and swollen from the rock. I lay down diagonally, staring at the patch of black where the ceiling should have been, and tried to bring some order to my thoughts.

Escape. It was almost too painful to even think of the word after everything that had happened. We'd been so close, allowed ourselves to believe we were free, only to be snared again. It had broken our hearts, snapped our spirits, and the thought of trying it again sat on me with greater weight than the mile of rock above my head. Even if we did find a way, who's to say it wouldn't just lead us right back to where we were now?

And what were the odds that, even if we did make it out of our cells, the rats wouldn't get to us? The idea sent a chill running up my spine, and, more to chase it away than because I genuinely thought I could escape, I attempted to think of a plan.

I started by trying to get a mental picture of the prison's underbelly. From what I'd seen of it when we were escorted to the hole it was a labyrinth of corridors, all chipped doorways and shadowed rooms. I knew the infirmary was one of them, and a few must have been storerooms where they kept weapons and food and probably plenty of black suits. We'd rarely seen the guards go up in the elevator that led to the surface when we were in gen pop, which meant they slept down here too. How many were there? Maybe thirty blacksuits? It was impossible to tell because they all looked so similar. They probably each had individual rooms in another stretch of the basement, the wheezers too.

What else did I know? It was pretty clear that they got their fresh water from the river. I mean, how stupid had we been, thinking that the warden hadn't known it was there? The river had probably been one of the reasons they'd built the prison here, one less link to the surface. Knowing about it now wasn't going to help us, though, as throwing ourselves back in would be nothing more than a death sentence.

I felt the claustrophobia start to set in, the weight of the world so great that I was convinced I was breathing it, darkness pouring into my lungs and making it impossible to find oxygen. For a second, panic gripped me, so hard that my entire body tensed and I could feel the blood rush in my head, then I screwed my eyes shut and forced it out.

Urged on by the frenzied beating of my heart, I tried to pick out what else I knew. This section of the prison was basically built in the tunnels and caverns of the earth, the exits sealed off by heavy steel doors like the one we'd passed on the way in. It had looked thick enough to withstand a nuke, but the rats had pulled it off its hinges as if it were tinfoil. No doubt we could find our way out into the subterranean world beyond, but what then? There was obviously no exit that way, otherwise Simon and whoever else was there would have been long gone. And I really didn't fancy being out there in the dark with those things on the loose.

Think, I mentally screamed at myself, lifting my legs up to try to get some blood to my aching back. *What else?* There had to be an electricity generator somewhere, probably connected to the river somehow. I didn't know much about it, but there would need to be a hell of a power source to light up the prison. Even if we found it, though, what good would it do us? Especially as the blacksuits and the beasts with their silver eyes seemed to be able to see in the dark. There was an incinerator too, Simon had said, which wasn't a fat lot of good for anything unless we found some marshmallows to toast. What did that leave?

I was halfway through a spluttered sigh of desperation when I heard the lever on my hatch start to turn. I staggered off the floor, pumping myself up for another trip out of the cell. Maybe I'd get a better idea of the prison's layout this time, maybe I'd get that whiff of fresh air, see the silver thread sparkling off toward an exit.

But when the metal circle swung open it wasn't Simon's face I saw there, it was a blacksuit's. He looked down at me, surprised at my determined expression and my purposeful stance. It was all I could do to stop myself saying, "Oh, it's you," but instead I let my gaze drop to the floor and did my best to look dejected and broken and empty. The guard snorted, then slid a bowl of gunk into my cell. It hit my shoulder and spun, decorating the walls with slop.

"Enjoy," the blacksuit growled, kicking the hatch shut before he noticed my lips curling up into a smile.

THE INFIRMARY

I WOKE WITH A SCREAM, the nightmare of needles in my cheeks so fresh I could still feel the sting. I pictured the bodies of the boys hanging upside down, their arms reaching for me, the gas mask pressed against my face. Panicking, I lashed out, my knuckles cracking against something solid and the pain chasing the last few scraps of dream away.

"Christ!" I slurred, welcoming the darkness around me like an old friend. I ran my hands along the stone, and only when I'd covered every surface with a trembling touch did I relax. I slumped back down, rubbing my temples and cursing my brain for betraying me while I slept.

I'd always had occasional nightmares, like anyone else, but most of the time I'd forget them as soon as I'd woken up, their horror nothing more than a bad taste in my mouth.

The ones I had in Furnace, though, they were unlike anything I'd ever experienced before; terror on a completely new level. The visions of a glass prison I'd suffered so many times in general population, with my reflection that of a wheezer. And now this same recurring dream I had night after night in the hole. I could understand the fear. I mean, if dreams are a reflection of what's plaguing your subconscious then I'd obviously be spending my nights in the company of the prison freaks. But why did I always see myself as one of the enemy? I tried to ignore the obvious answer but it spilled into my brain.

Maybe it was a glimpse of my future.

"Enough," I said, the volume of the word after so much silence scaring the last few flecks of dream away. To keep myself busy I felt the floor of the cell, looking for any slop I'd missed. I'd got most of it before falling asleep, licking the tasteless slime off the stone. It had made such a mess when it landed that there had to be specks here and there. My stomach made a noise that sounded like an earthquake, my guts squirming in pain as they cried out for food.

"I'm doing my best," I told them, feeling a fleck of something suspiciously close to the toilet that was probably better left alone. I moved my search to the other corner of the cell and discovered a splotch of slop congealing in the angle between the wall and the floor. I took my time with it, savoring the minuscule amount and pretending I was stuffing my face with eggs and bacon and whatever else I used to have when my dad made a Sunday fry-up.

I was enjoying the memory so much that I didn't hear the lever on my hatch until the light was already seeping in. I snapped my head up, feeling like a rat that had been caught gnawing on trash and was now cornered. For a second there was nothing but a dark silhouette against the searing light of the corridor, but then color began to seep into the shape and I saw that it was Simon.

"You look like you've seen a ghost," the boy said, offering me his hand.

"I was just trying to enjoy a quiet breakfast," I replied as he pulled me out of the cell. "Here I am, thinking I'll have a nice holiday in the hole, won't get disturbed for a few weeks, but it's like Piccadilly Circus in there, what with you and the blacksuits and Zee banging away on his toilet."

Simon flashed me a puzzled look, then lowered my hatch quietly and jogged over to Zee's. Seconds later he was out, the cells were secured, and we were all sprinting down the corridor again. We turned the corner, pausing for a moment to check that it was deserted, but to my surprise we passed the storeroom and ended up swinging through another door.

"Blacksuits check the storerooms more frequently now after finding the remains of that rat," Simon explained in his soft sandpaper voice as he walked across the room. It was pitch-black in here, but I guessed from the echo that it must have been empty. We hunched over in the far corner, a stone's throw from the door. "We got lucky today, the blacksuits are all busy."

"Another breach?" asked Zee.

"No, a riot. A whole bunch of the inmates up in gen pop tried to smash their way through Room Two to get to the river. Fifty or sixty of them from the sounds of it, mainly Skulls. It had been sealed off but they all just went for it."

"How do you know?" I said, excitement making my whisper louder than it should have been.

"The blacksuits," Simon replied. "I heard them talking. They've pretty much all gone up there, except for a couple guarding the north door. They're not too pleased with you right now."

"Me?" I said.

"Yeah, they're blaming you for giving hope to the other kids. There have been a couple of attempted breakouts, although nobody's managed it yet. Except you, that is."

"I thought the warden told them we died," said Zee.

"Guess that don't matter. No one cares if you survived or not. The important thing is that you got out, one way or another. You made it real, the idea of escape. For them and for us, down here."

I wanted to ask who else was with him but he started talking again.

"Speaking of which, we need to get started, we need to think of a plan, make the most of it before the blacksuits come back down."

"Okay," I said, trying to sound more confident than I felt. "So where do we begin? The tunnels? The doors?"

Simon's eyes narrowed, slivers of steel caught in the light from the door. They darted left then right as he shook his head.

"We start with your friend. We start in the infirmary."

"No."

I said the word without meaning to, so loud that it reverberated around the room like a pistol shot. I clamped my mouth shut, ignoring Simon's shocked silver eyes and Zee's—invisible in the darkness but burning into me with just as much heat.

"What?" asked Zee. "It's Donovan, Alex, he needs our help big time."

"I know," I snapped back. "It's just . . ."

Just what? That I wanted to focus on the task ahead, try to find a way out before we risked going in for D? No. That I needed to get a better idea of the layout of the prison, just in case we were rumbled trying to break him out and had to make a quick getaway? Yeah, right.

Truth was that I was terrified of the place and the mere thought of going anywhere near it made me want to curl up and die, made me want to pretend I hated Donovan, or that I'd never known him, to forget all about him for the rest of my miserable life just so I didn't have to find out what lay behind that plastic curtain. That was more like it, that was the real me, the coward.

I shook my head, too ashamed to try to come up with an explanation. I was grateful for the darkness, which concealed my blazing cheeks, except Simon could see me like I was lit up by a million spotlights. He knew exactly what was wrong. He knew I was afraid. I could tell by the way his head shook that doubts were starting to form.

And if he decided he didn't need us, then we'd be trapped in the hole until the warden came.

"What about the wheezers?" I asked, trying to bury my terror beneath logic. "Aren't they always in the infirmary?"

"Not always. They have to sleep too. We should be fine."

Should? I managed not to question it out loud, instead saying, "And the rats? Won't they be making the most of the fact the blacksuits are up top?"

"There's always that danger, but I wouldn't worry too much. I haven't seen them all day. Besides, they never go in the infirmary, ever. They're scared of the place. It's where they got turned into what they are. We'll be safe once we're inside."

So long as the wheezers don't wake. So long as the blacksuits don't appear. So long as the warden doesn't find us.

"When we go in, Alex, you take the left-hand side, Zee the right. Find your friend. I'll keep watch. There are plenty of hiding places if things go wrong, but we really, really don't want to be there if the wheezers wake up. Okay?"

"Okay," said Zee, more tremor than voice.

"Okay," I said eventually, realizing all eyes were still on me. "We'll go get Donovan, then find a way out of here."

Simon was on the move before I'd even finished talking, his shadow flitting silently back across the room. For a moment I didn't think my legs were going to function, as if they were locked up and bolted to the rock. But Zee tugged on my overalls, pulling me after him.

We flew past the solitary cells, up the passageway where Zee and I had been chased by the dogs, turning left at the junction ahead. Thirty meters of growing terror and I saw the opening in the wall, the stenciled letters. It was like being punched in the gut, and I struggled to claw in my next breath. I thought about Donovan, about my promise that I'd come back for him. I tried to remember the times he'd been there for me, but my mind drew a blank. Had he ever truly been a friend? Or had he just been using me to escape? Surely the latter. I mean, why would a guy like Donovan choose to hang around with a kid like me?

I hated myself right then, hated what I was thinking. But better to hate yourself and survive, right? Like I've said before, so many times before, I'm not a good person, I'm not a hero. I'm a criminal, a liar, a cheat, a killer. It was them or me and I wanted to live.

Then we stopped running and Zee turned to me, placed his hand on my shoulder, and that simple action knocked my cowardly train of thought off the rails. He managed a weak smile.

"Remember, all for one, Alex," he said softly.

"And let's get the hell out of here," I replied. He squeezed my shoulder, then dropped his hand. Simon was waiting by the curtain, staring through the translucent plastic at the blurred shapes beyond. Nothing seemed to be moving, but I could hear the relentless beeps of several heart monitors like some artificial dawn chorus. My fear still sat like a brick, weighing me down, but at least the voices had stopped; the hatred, the self-loathing. I was here for Donovan, just like he'd be here for me. He *would* be here for me.

"We have to be quiet," Simon whispered. "And we have to be quick. Remember, take one side each. If you hear me give the alarm, then we go, no hesitation. Ready?"

No, I almost barked again, but I kept my mouth closed and settled for a nod. Zee returned it, then Simon, and with a collective sigh of fear shuddering from our lips we pushed our way through the curtain.

To come face-to-face with a wheezer.

I would have cried out, but Zee's legs crumpled and he fell back, slamming into me and stealing the air from my lungs. I straightened my back, grabbed hold of Zee, kept him standing, desperately trying to repair the shattered pieces of my brain to come up with a plan.

Any second now the filthy creature was going to lurch forward, stick its needles into our necks. The first thing that crossed my mind was that it was a trap, that Simon had set us up, led us to the infirmary. I looked up at him, waiting for the kid to pounce, to pin us down while the wheezer pumped us full of poison, but to my surprise he simply held one bony finger to his lips and motioned us forward with his head.

I stared back at the wheezer, noticed that its eyes were closed—the lids as scarred as the rest of its hairless, weathered face but mercifully concealing the shriveled-raisin eyes within. It was breathing slowly, rhythmically, and I traced the pipe of its gas mask to see that it was connected to a socket in the wall. Every now and again it spasmed, jerking wildly, but other than that it was still.

"It's asleep?" I whispered as quietly as I was able. Simon nodded as he passed it, his deformed body tensed, ready to pounce if it showed any sign of waking. Zee was still pressed against me and I pushed him gently forward, navigating around the silent specter.

"Why don't you just kill it now?" Zee asked.

"Too risky. Blacksuits would know it wasn't a rat, they'd know we'd been here."

The wheezer didn't shift as we entered the room ahead. It was vast, long rather than wide, the flesh-colored walls rising to a ceiling so high it was lost in shadow. Countless lights hung down on long cords, like spiders, swinging gently even though there was no breeze. The glow emanating from each one was so thick, and so red, that it could have been raining blood. At the far end another door led away into darkness. But our attention was gripped by what was before us.

Lined up along both sides of the room were two seemingly endless rows of screens made up of steel frames and white cloth curtains—the kind you see in hospitals to provide privacy. But a hospital ward usually contained perhaps a dozen well-spaced beds; here there must have been a hundred of them, so close to each other they were almost touching. All the curtains were drawn tight, but I knew that behind each one was a bed occupied by some poor kid who had been stolen from Furnace.

I didn't want proof but it was there anyway. Pitiful groans rose up from hidden faces, quiet sobs tore at my heart, a symphony of distress almost lost in the chirrup of the monitors, the pump of some hidden machine and the endless wheeze of the sleeping monster by my side.

Simon waved his hand, snapping me back to attention. Donovan was in here somewhere, and we didn't have long to find him.

I darted to the left-hand side of the room, took a deep breath and pulled back the cloth of the first screen.

Empty.

There was a bed, metal sides and a thin mattress with pillows but no sheets. Beside it was a machine that I didn't recognize, all polished steel and rubber tubes. Two red lights on a monitor blinked at me as if wondering who I was, and I let the fabric fall back just in case somehow it could see me and sound the alarm.

One down, fifty or so to go. I peered over my shoulder to see Zee on his third screen, moving fast, his determined expression making me pretty sure those ones had been empty too. Simon was standing behind the wheezer, each as motionless as the other.

Come on! I screamed at myself, moving to the next screen and pulling back the curtain. It was deserted too, except for a stripped bed and another strange machine, this one dead. The next was the same, and the two after that, and by the time I'd reached the sixth cubicle my sense of dread was fading.

I should have known not to let my guard down.

I wrenched back the screen of the next compartment and had to rest my hands on the foot of the bed beyond to stop myself keeling over. Lying on the mattress, held in place by several thick leather straps, was Gary Owens. His top half was bare, several wires taped to his chest linking him to the machine by his side. It bleeped away softly to a heartbeat that was slow and unsteady, like a clock in desperate need of being wound.

Looming above him were three skeletal poles, each with a transparent bag hooked to it. One was filled with a dark red substance that had to be blood, another the color and consistency of crap. But there was one more, packed with something that didn't look liquid or solid, that seemed to be both dark and silvery light at the same time. Specks of color swirled inside it as if caught in some hidden current, or as if impatient to flow down the tube into one of the needles lodged in Gary's arm.

Aside from the IV drips, he looked untouched. Bruised and cut from the river, yes, but with none of the stitches and swellings I'd seen on Simon or Monty or the other freaks.

Except for his eyes.

His head was tightly bandaged, the gauze layered from the bridge of his nose to the top of his forehead. And there were two crimson circles right where his eyes should be, like that part of his face had been drawn in crayon by a toddler. Even as I watched I could see the circles spreading outward: too much blood for it to be a graze.

The scene blurred and I realized I was crying. I turned to look at Simon, hoping he'd be able to do something to make this all better. But he had his back to me, his gaze never leaving the wheezer. Zee too was focused on his job, a quarter of the way up the room already and a hell of a lot paler than he'd been a few minutes ago.

I wiped my eyes, let the curtain fall. Gary hadn't heard me, he certainly hadn't seen me. I doubt he'd even been conscious, especially if he'd just had surgery on . . . I couldn't even think about it. I moved toward the next compartment. What else could I do? *If there is time, if we can find a way to make it work, then I'll take you with us, Gary*, I thought silently. And even though I knew it wasn't true, it made me feel better.

There was a cry behind me, a muffled retching. Spinning around I saw Zee stumbling away from a screen, hand to his mouth. He tripped over his own feet, falling, and too late I noticed the trolley of equipment in his path.

"No!" hissed Simon, propelling himself across the room so fast I barely saw him move. He dived to catch Zee but didn't make it, and with a crash that could have woken the dead the two boys slammed into the cart. It exploded across the room, shedding pans and scalpels and things I didn't recognize before grinding to a halt on its side.

The reaction from the wheezer was instantaneous. It came to life like a clockwork toy, its movements staggered and exaggerated, its cry wet and weak before breaking free of its throat as a scream.

"Hide!" shouted Simon, pulling Zee across the floor by his collar and vanishing behind a screen. I half turned, half tripped across the room, knowing I should have ducked into one of the cubicles on my side but unable to bear the thought of being on my own. I risked a glance as I ran, saw the creature starting to turn, its pipe popping free of the wall with a hiss. Then I was past the curtain, Zee and Simon by my side. Surely out of sight.

At least that's what I thought until the wheezer shrieked again, the crunch of its boots growing louder as it headed our way.

SPECIMENS

NO NO NO NO NO NO NO NO.

The voice in my head never got the chance to break free from between my lips. I was too scared to find the breath to speak, my shell-shocked brain forgetting how to form words. It was happening again. I was trapped and powerless as a wheezer approached just like on the night before we made our break. I pictured it stopping on the other side of the screen, its piggy eyes lighting up when it sensed us trembling inside. Visitors. Intruders.

Specimens.

I felt a hand on my shoulder, hot fingers singeing my skin. Simon was there, a finger on his lips and the rest of his face a mask of fear. I turned to Zee, so pale he could have been transparent against the white curtains that separated us from the rest of the infirmary.

The wheezer's steps grew closer, scuffed against the smooth rock of the floor. I heard the sound of it convulsing, the needles strapped to its chest clinking and its leather coat flapping. I wanted to check the cubicle for something we could use as a weapon, but I knew that if I turned away for a second I'd look back to see it

peering through the curtains, the stitches of its gas mask straining as its face split open into a smile.

A shadow sprouted up from the bottom of the screen. I could
make out the dome of its head, the curve of the pipe once more
fastened into a tank on its back. The dark shape grew as the
wheezer came to a halt on the other side of the curtain.

A meter, maybe two, separating us from it. It took a long,
ragged breath, its asthmatic hiss like an ancient, scratched record-
ing of a string quartet. Then it unleashed its hellish cry, so loud
that the sound was like a dagger in my ears.

Something answered it. I thought at first it was an echo, but
the distant scream repeated itself and the wheezer in the infirmary returned the call. It reminded me of vultures announcing
the location of a new corpse on which to feast. Or three, in this
case.

I glanced at Simon again, hoping he'd take on the wheezer with
the same fearlessness with which he'd tackled the rat. But he was
petrified, his eyes stretched so wide they were more vein than
anything else—veins that pulsed black rather than red. Right now
he didn't look like he could tie his own shoes, let alone take down
the wheezer.

Correction, *wheezers*.

I heard the second freak walk into the room. It must have
come from the other door, its footsteps hurried. The silhouette
before us made a noise like it was choking, which morphed into a
wet gurgle, almost a purr, and seconds later we heard it in stereo.

The longer we waited the more danger we were in. If we moved
now we might just make it past the first wheezer, and the second
was approaching from the far side of the room. I'd never seen

them move faster than a stagger, I was pretty sure they couldn't sprint. If we just started running, surely we could make it?

But my muscles were carved from stone. I might as well have been strapped to a bed for all the good they were doing me. I could no more take a single step than start singing "Jailhouse Rock" at the top of my voice.

The shadow on the screen moved, coming closer, a hand reaching out for the curtains ready to draw them back.

Only it never did. Instead the wheezer made another noise, halfway between a gulp and a murmur, its unsteady arm pointing down. Then it turned, becoming smaller, fuzzier around the edges as it shuffled away from us. I could just about see it bend over, long limbs reaching for the equipment that littered the floor, then it moved on again and vanished.

The three of us waited for what must have been a full minute before daring even to take a breath. Only when the sound of the wheezers' boots had retreated to the other side of the room did I give my lungs permission to work, sucking in so much oxygen the world started spinning.

Simon nodded his head toward the side of the cubicle. There was a slight gap between the screen and the back wall, easily big enough for us to squeeze through. If it was the same all the way down, then we should be able to sneak back to the infirmary door without being seen. I checked Zee to make sure he knew what we were doing, but he was staring behind me, his eyes wide pools that shimmered in the rusty light, the corners of his mouth turned down so much it was as if they'd been caught by invisible hooks.

I didn't want to turn around. I didn't want to see what Zee was looking at, what had sent him reeling across the room minutes ago. But I did anyway.

At first I didn't recognize him. He wasn't in a bed like the other kids I'd seen. He was strung up in some kind of coffin, a sarcophagus of black metal tilted back against the wall at a forty-five-degree angle. The straps that held him in place weren't made of leather but of steel, as wide and as thick as my fist, and manacles bound his hands and feet like something from the Middle Ages.

It was easy to see why. Donovan had been big before, but now he was enormous. Well, parts of him were. His torso looked like a rag doll that had been overstuffed, his stomach and chest swollen up so much that the stitches that ran from his navel to his sternum, and across from armpit to armpit, looked like they might tear loose at any minute. The muscles beneath flexed with a life of their own, their shapes bulging through his weakened skin.

One of his legs was also much larger than the other, the size and color of a tree trunk. The sutures here were fresher, droplets of blood still winding lazily toward the floor.

His face was just how I remembered it, although grayer. Even though his brown eyes were now silver, staring blindly up at the shadowed ceiling, it was unmistakably him.

"Donovan," I breathed. I reached up, rested a hand on his arm, only to pull it back a split second later because of the heat that radiated from him. Simon was tugging at my overalls, desperate to pull us away, but for a moment even my fear of the wheezers paled as I called out his name again, still a whisper but louder this time. "Donovan."

"Come on," came a breath in my ear, both ears, actually, as Simon and Zee had spoken the same words at the same time. I ignored them, reaching out and touching Donovan's arm again. This time he seemed to stir, his head easing around then lolling against his chest, his silver gaze finding me for a moment then slipping away. His mouth opened, it seemed like it opened too far, and a long, low groan slid out. It changed at the end, becoming a word.

"Alex?" Too soft to be heard by the wheezers, but loud enough to break my heart. "That you?"

"Yeah," I replied, my grin stretching from ear to ear but the tears still falling. "Yeah it's me, and Zee too."

"Hey, D," said Zee, stepping up.

"You came back," he said, his voice soft and slurred. "You came back for me."

"I told you we would," I said. "We're going to escape, Donovan, all of us. I promise. We'll get you out of this thing."

I'd already started pulling at the steel buckles when I felt Simon's hand on my arm, more insistent this time.

"You can't take him," he said.

"We can pull these loose," I argued as quietly as I could. "Or pick the locks. We can get him out."

"It won't do any good," Simon went on. "It's too late."

"It's not too late," I snapped, too loud. The sound of feet from the other side of the room kicked up again, that chilling purr like a cat with a throat full of blood. I froze, but my outburst seemed to have gone unnoticed in a fresh round of groans and sobs that emanated from the hidden infirmary beds. "It's not too late," I spat into his ear. "He's coming with us, so help me open these chains."

"It's not the chains," Simon explained, pointing to the side of the sarcophagus. I hadn't noticed the IV drips there, another bag of blood and two more filled with darkness and light, the mixture reminding me of space and the galaxies that spiraled in the abyss. I followed the tube, saw where it entered Donovan's neck and arm, the arteries there pulsing black beneath the sheen of his dark skin. "If you stop the feed now, then he'll die. After everything he's gone through, after the surgery, that stuff is all that's keeping him alive."

"We getting out of here or what?" Donovan said, his voice so weak it sounded like a radio with poor reception, fading in and out. "I feel like battered crap."

"We can take it with us," I said, talking to Simon. "Take that feed, whatever it is."

"It won't be enough," the kid replied, looking nervously behind him to check the wheezer hadn't made its way back to the screen. "He needs to stay. Trust me, I know what I'm talking about."

"So why did you bring us here?" I asked, my temper almost fraying again. It was all I could do not to scream my frustration at him, wheezers or no wheezers. Simon sighed, then looked down at the floor.

"Because I wanted you to know that it was too late for your friend. I wanted you to focus on getting us out of here. I'm . . . I'm sorry."

Something in my chest seemed to wither up, pushed into my throat where it sat there as uncomfortable as broken glass. I wrenched my arm free of Simon's grip and tried once again to unclip the metal straps that held Donovan's legs. They didn't budge. Somewhere in the infirmary a pair of curtains were drawn back, a dry wheeze broken into what sounded like soft chuckles. Too close.

"Alex?" said Donovan again. "You just gonna stand there?"

"Listen to me, Donovan," I said. "We will get you free, okay? But we can't do it yet." I remembered what Monty had told me.

"Don't forget your name, okay? Carl Donovan. Just hang in there, we'll be back for you real soon."

"Hang in there," echoed Donovan, smiling. His metallic eyes swung back and forth before finding me again, and I realized he was probably doped up on painkillers or something. "Good one, Alex. I'll just hang around, right here."

"Just think about that burger, okay big guy?" I went on. Simon was already squeezing between the back of the screen and the wall, Zee hot on his heels and beckoning me on. I followed, Donovan's smile fading as he watched me go.

"Alex? Don't leave me."

"I'll be back, I promise. We're just down the hall, we're not going far." I reached the wall, Donovan trying to twist his neck around to watch me. This time it felt as though my heart had been crushed, but I had no choice. "On my life, I swear to you, I'm not going anywhere without you."

Then I ducked past the screen, Donovan's great, heaving sobs following me all the way.

ABANDONED

I DON'T KNOW WHAT WAS MORE OF A RELIEF—the fact that there was enough room for us to pass through the dozen or so cubicles without difficulty, or the fact that only one of the beds was occupied. It was the next but one from Donovan's, a kid a few years younger than me. He was awake, and uninjured—his body strapped down and covered with a sheet—but his mind was obviously in a better place than this, his pale blue eyes barely even acknowledging us as we passed by.

I wanted more than anything to free him, take him with us, take them *all* with us. For a fleeting moment I pictured myself running out and fighting the wheezers, tearing off their masks, felling the blacksuits with a single blow, then smashing my way up to the surface with all the lost boys of Furnace in my wake. But even as I thought it I realized how pathetic it sounded, and instead followed Simon and Zee as they eased around the bed, my body slumped, heavy, useless.

Not before I noticed another trolley of equipment, however, a torturer's kit of stainless steel lying by the boy's bed—all sharpened blades and hooks and clamps. Instinctively I lifted a scalpel from the tray, sliding it into the waistband of my overalls as we squeezed through the gaps left by the last few screens.

We emerged against the wall we'd come in through, the main door visible maybe five meters away. Simon crept to the end of the screen, easing himself around the corner to check the infirmary before turning back to us.

"Wheezers have gone," he whispered. "Must be in the cubicles or something. Follow me and keep quiet."

We did as we were told, jogging across the polished floor. The plastic curtain of the infirmary slapped shut behind us, imitating the soft patter of our feet as we made our way back to solitary. It was as we reached the junction that led back to our cells that we heard voices, too deep, too loud to be anything other than black-suits. Simon cursed, his pace quickening.

"I thought we'd have more time," he said, bending down to flip open Zee's door as if it weighed nothing. "Get in."

Zee looked reluctant but he didn't argue, vanishing once again into the gloom. The voices were getting louder, and I recognized the growl of the dogs too. I didn't particularly fancy another eter-nity locked in the hole but there was nothing else for it. I nodded at Simon as he held open my hatch for me like a butler, then I jumped in. He paused before closing it.

"I'm sorry about your friend," he said. "I hope you understand why I did it. He's gone, Alex. He's turned. Next time I come, we focus on getting out, okay?"

He didn't wait for me to reply, just eased down the hatch then slowly slid the lever across. It was only seconds after the sound of his feet faded that I heard the familiar stomp of the blacksuits. There was the squeal of a lever, and I thought I could make out a shout of distress, then a dull thump. Someone else must have been brought into solitary, some other poor soul banished to the hole to be tortured by his own demons. I wondered who it was, whether I knew him. It was probably a gang member from gen pop, one of the Skulls or Fifty-niners, punished for trying to break out. I listened to see if I could hear anything, but the solid walls did their job well, immersing me in lightless silence.

I slid the scalpel from my overalls and tentatively felt the blade. It was wickedly sharp, the faintest touch leaving a hairline cut on my skin that wasn't deep enough to bleed but which stung nonetheless. I didn't really know what I could use it for—it was too small to leave more than a scratch on a blacksuit and sure as hell wasn't going to let me tunnel my way free—but it felt good to have it, made me feel a little less feeble in the face of Furnace.

Tucking it in the corner of my cell where I wouldn't accidentally slice my hand off, I curled up on the floor, too exhausted to do anything else. We'd only been in the infirmary for a few minutes, but it seemed like hours, every sick detail carved into my brain.

I saw Gary, knew that when those bandages were removed he too would have eyes of cold silver. And I saw Donovan, his body morphed almost beyond recognition, his soul trapped inside a casket of mutated flesh and growing weaker with every second. If we didn't do something soon, then he would be gone forever, a prisoner inside himself as he became a monster, a blacksuit.

It took me a while to notice that I wasn't alone in my cell. Tilting my head up, I made out a familiar cloud of white that seemed to hover above me. I blinked and it swirled into a rough shape—that of a boy sitting against the wall, knees curled up to his chin—but it didn't seem to want to focus. I knew why, and the thought of it made me wish the shape away, pray to be left alone. But my imagination was adamant that I had company.

That's charming, Donovan's voice ebbed around the cell. Or at least it ebbed around my head. *A little cosmetic surgery and you can't even stand to look at your old mate.* I tucked my head into my arms, screwed my eyes closed, but he was still there. *Not laughing at my jokes anymore either, I see.*

"They've killed you," I said, speaking the words aloud even though I knew I didn't need to.

Whoa! he shouted back. *Not yet they haven't. I'm still in there somewhere, I just look a little different, that's all.* His voice became urgent. *Don't give up on me yet, Alex.*

"I won't," I said, sitting up and staring at the blurred shape, a figure on the other side of frosted glass. "I'm not. I made you a promise, I'll get you out."

Good, kid. Because I really didn't look too hot back there.

"I don't know, it's more effective than going to the gym," I replied with a twitch of a smile. The image seemed to solidify for a moment, its chest exploding outward, stomach hardening to a grotesque cluster of cramped muscles, one leg swollen up like a victim of elephantiasis. Donovan's eyes glinted back, half metal and half moonlight, and he flexed his arms.

You've got a point there, he said. *Hope they do my arms too, though, or I'm gonna be as lopsided as your new mate Simon.*

"Yeah, he's got a pretty unique look." We laughed, but it was forced. Donovan's body deflated like a balloon, returning to its original size. It didn't stop there, continuing to shrink as the hallucination spoke.

Find a way, Alex. Get us the hell out of here.

"What if I can't?" I asked the figure, now nothing more than a thread of light that hung from the invisible ceiling like a spider's web.

You can, was all it said. Then it was gone.

I wasn't feeling too positive about escaping, but some part of my mind seemed to be holding out hope. Somewhere deep inside my subconscious I must have had faith in myself, and why not? I mean, I *had* found a way out of Furnace. Okay, it hadn't got us very far, but we'd got out of gen pop. We'd beaten it. I tried to remember how I'd felt standing on the lip of the chasm in Room Two, the rock still smoking, the river raging beneath us like our own private expressway home. For all we knew we were about to die, but we'd done it, we'd cracked the prison open like an egg and, for that moment at least, we'd been free.

The memory of those feelings was still there, a faint and insubstantial ghost of an emotion rather than the real thing, but I could still taste it. I wanted it again, I wanted to be standing on the edge of freedom knowing that all it would take to get out was one simple step. And I *would* find a way. I swore to myself right then and there that I would split the prison open once again, and that this time there would be no doubts, no uncertainty about our fate. There would only be the outside world and us in it, drenched in sunlight and warmth and gulping down burgers by the beach.

"You've got me started now," I said to the empty space where Donovan had been, imagining chunks of salty beef and thick mayo and moist bread and burnt onions sliding down my throat, the wind in my hair and the sound of gulls as they dived for our scraps.

Oh yes, I'd do it. The next time Simon came I'd find our way out.

Only Simon didn't come.

I WAITED PATIENTLY, so patiently, counting the seconds as they passed, the minutes, then the hours. At one point I heard footsteps again and got myself ready, hoping that the hatch would open and Simon's face would appear. But they passed overhead and vanished.

I kept counting, rocking my head back and forth with each passing beat to try to keep track of the time. It was just about the most monotonous thing I'd ever done in my life, but it kept my mind busy, kept the bad thoughts away. And I was counting toward something, I knew it wouldn't be long before the kid reappeared. At least I thought I knew.

I lost count at somewhere over 15,000, thrown off stride by the sound of Zee from the next cell. I calculated the time even as I decoded his message, the clank of his grille against the pipe knocking out even more seconds. Four hours. It had seemed like forty.

"Think D's okay?" he asked. I wondered why he'd waited so long to get in touch. Maybe he'd been asleep.

"He will be," I banged back, the wounds on my hand opening up again as the grille smashed against the toilet. "When we're out."

"Hope so," came Zee's reply. "You okay?"

"Just dandy," I struck, laughing as I did so. "Waiting for Simon."

There was a pause, then the muted metallic thuds started up again.

"Suppose he's been caught?"

I'd been trying not to consider that possibility. Of all of us Simon was the most at risk, spiriting through the passageways of

Furnace's underbelly where the blacksuits or the wheezers or the warden could find him at any time, then retreating to whatever hole he'd found, praying that the rats didn't sniff him out. Like he'd said, his life was in danger every time he came to release us. I was amazed he'd lasted as long as he had.

"He'll be back," I replied eventually, ignoring my own doubts. "Won't be long."

But it was. I started the count from scratch: 3,600 seconds in every hour, 3,600, 7,200, 10,800, after which I drifted off, dreaming of Donovan in the infirmary screaming numbers at me as if they were a combination to unlock the restraints that held him.

The sound of the hatch woke me and I sat up, my heart lifting, waiting for Simon to appear. But the door didn't open. Something was scratching at the lever, something with claws rather than fingers, something that panted and growled as it tried to dig its way to me.

It was a rat, all bloody claws and lamprey-mouth.

I scrabbled for the scalpel, luck letting me grab it by the handle as I shot to my feet. There was a thump, the thick metal hatch buckling inward a fraction. Another impact, another dent. It wasn't much but I knew the door couldn't withstand an onslaught like this for long. I prayed for the blacksuits to appear, to shoot the thing that was trying to get in, but I soon regretted it.

The sound of scratching became the unmistakable racket of a scuffle—a grunt followed by a scream and then a crunch as something else slammed onto the hatch. I stood there, scalpel by my side, fear for my life the only thing keeping me upright.

I heard the lever grinding open, then the hatch was ripped outward. For a fraction of a second I thought I saw the outline of Simon, the pinpricks of his eyes so bright they looked like holes in his head where the light was streaming through. Then the outline lashed out, catching me around the head with its clubbed fist. Fireworks exploded in front of my eyes, and my legs gave out. That probably saved my life.

The rat lunged into my cell, its clawed arms like some living combine harvester that churned the air. I curled up as tightly as I could, hands over my head, the scalpel dropped and lost. Warm spit and a retching growl dripped down on me and I waited for the next blow, the one that would finish me. But it never came. Instead I heard the throb of thunder, the booming laugh of a blacksuit.

"What do you think?" came the voice, so thick, so powerful that it cut right through the squeals of the rat. I risked a look up, saw the creature halfway into my cell, its mouth so wide that its jaw looked dislocated, rows of teeth like broken glass embedded in its gums. It saw me watching it and lunged again, but something was holding it back. A fist, locked tight around its throat.

My eyes drifted past the thrashing beast, saw the immaculate suit beyond, the shark's grin. The blacksuit loosened his grip and the rat sank deeper, its claws so close I could smell them, like trash left too long in the sun.

"No one would ever know," the blacksuit went on, pulling the rat back then dropping it in again. "Everyone knows the vermin like to get in the cells, help themselves to some fresh meat. This one would have had you already if I hadn't come along."

The rat tried to squirm around, biting at the gloved hand that held it. The blacksuit simply bunched up his other fist and struck out, the blow causing the creature's head to snap back, blood dripping. It shook itself, obviously stunned, then resumed its efforts to reach me.

"So, should I drop it in? Let you get to know each other? Who knows, you might have been friends already, up in gen pop."

More laughter, like a storm was raging above my cell. The blacksuit lowered the rat even further and I felt a searing heat on my arm where its claws had drawn blood. There was a snap like a bear trap inches from my ear as its jaws closed in.

Then it was gone, hauled out of the hatch back into the corridor. I peered up through trembling fingers, saw the blacksuit wedge his shotgun into the rat's waist then pull the trigger. The corridor flashed for a second, the lightning once more followed by a dull rumble.

"The warden wants you left alone for a month," the guard said, leaning over the opening. "But he doesn't call all the shots around here. Next time, you might not be so lucky."

He kicked the hatch shut. For once I was thankful for the darkness, which hid the crimson beads that pattered like gentle rain to the floor of my cell.

LOST BOYS

I'M NOT ASHAMED TO SAY that I almost lost it after that. Lying there—the echo of the shot still gunning through my skull, the sting of the rat's claws making my arm pound, the grin of the blacksuit as he dangled my own death over me seared into my light-starved retinas—I felt myself start to unravel. I could picture my body unwinding into threads, then flooding down the pipe into the toilet with all the other waste.

I know it seems strange that I was thinking about death with the same anticipation and hunger with which I was clinging to life only hours earlier. But the two were one and the same right then. My existence was a living hell, fraught with the knowledge that the hatch could be opened at any time and my nightmares would climb inside with me. And death promised a new life. Whether it was in the afterlife my mom had always told me about, or as a ghost wandering Furnace for all eternity, or even just the wonderful oblivion of nothingness, it meant freedom.

And now I had the means to get there.

A shudder passed through my body as I realized what I had thought. But it was difficult to ignore the obvious. I mean, something had made me take that scalpel, even knowing that I could never hope to use it as a weapon against the legion of giants and gas masks that dwelled down here. Maybe a part of me, a part so far inside me I could barely hear it, knew the real reason I'd want a blade in my cell.

And it would be so easy. Two clean cuts and I'd be out of here, I'd have my escape route. No more guards, no more wheezers, no more warden. No more responsibility for saving Zee and Donovan and Simon. I smiled, picturing the next blacksuit to come and torment me as he realized I was free, that I'd slipped out from right between his fingers.

Yeah, because you'll really be showing them, won't you. Talk about cutting up your wrists to spite your fate.

Where had that come from? It hadn't sounded like me, or like Donovan for that matter. I wondered how many voices there were living in my head, and how they could all have such different opinions. Not that I wasn't grateful. If it hadn't been for that chirruped burst of sarcasm somewhere in my subconscious, then maybe I would have just picked up that scalpel again and finished the job.

Instead, I located the blade with my fingertips and pushed it across the cell. It hit the lip of my toilet pipe and stopped, as if imploring me to think about what I was doing. But I was, and with a prod I sent it tumbling toward the sewage below. I know, I know, I should have kept it. It was a weapon, and however small it was it could have at least given me the element of surprise if I found myself in a skirmish. But you have to believe me when I say that down here that blade was the closest thing to the exit key I had, and sooner or later I would have used it.

Dumping the scalpel seemed to take some of the weight off my shoulders, although the fear was still perched on my chest like a demon. What had happened with the blacksuit and the rat hammered home once again how vulnerable I was here.

And there was still no sign of Simon.

For the first time since I'd been thrown in the hole, the bad hallucinations started. I saw a figure start to form from the strands of gossamer strung web-like across my cell and somehow I knew it wasn't going to be Donovan this time. I was right. Neither was it my old friends and family, who would have been welcome even if they were screaming at me with hatred and anger and sadness. It wasn't even the freaks of Furnace.

No, this was something else, something I couldn't quite identify. A figure shrouded in black who sat on the fringe of my vision and shifted whenever I tried to focus on it. It didn't do anything, didn't say anything, just sat and stared at me. Like it was waiting. Like it was waiting for me to die.

I felt panic grab hold of my guts and I swung around, the figure always one step ahead of me. I slapped the walls in frustration, then started punching them, imagining that the hooded creep was laughing at me, urging me on. I was yelling at it, swearing at the top of my voice, challenging it to show itself. But the angel of death—because I knew that's what it was—hung back, content to watch me suffer.

Eventually I must have passed out, vertigo sucking me up like a tornado, the cell spinning. I cracked my head as I fell, knowing even in the pitch black that my vision was failing. I waited to drop from this waking nightmare right into a cruel dream, but it seemed that my mind had grown tired of tormenting me, switching everything off and letting me rest in peace—if you'll excuse the expression.

I don't know how long I was out for, but it took the sound of my hatch being unlocked to wake me. I didn't even bother to sit up, too exhausted to try to escape my fate. But when the door swung open it was Simon I saw in the dull light. He grinned lopsidedly, then offered me a hand.

"Miss me?"

WE RAN SILENTLY ALONG the corridor, Simon taking the lead and Zee and I treading on his shadow. I asked him where he'd been and he shut me up with a steely look, glancing nervously at the deserted passageways.

"Got to be quiet," he whispered as we reached the T-junction that split off toward the infirmary. "Blacksuits everywhere."

I bit my tongue, saving my questions for later. We turned left, and for a minute I thought we were heading back toward Donovan. But although we slowed down as we passed the plastic curtain, we didn't stop. Doors flashed by, gaping black mouths in the red walls, and I could make out voices from inside more than one—deep chuckles, guttural snarls and at one point even a high-pitched, tuneless song that sent shivers up my spine.

We reached another junction, one I didn't remember from before even though we must have passed it the day we were first dragged to the hole. I glanced right and felt something inside me run cold, as if I'd just stepped into a freezer. There was nothing there, nothing I could see anyway. The stretch of barren stone was deserted. But all the same something seemed to hang in the air, a dark presence that tried to hook itself into my soul as we ran past.

"Warden's quarters," Simon hissed in explanation. Then he turned left and the feeling vanished. I glanced back once as we sprinted the other way, invisible eyes boring into my back from the ever-growing shadows behind us.

Two more openings, one on either side of the corridor, no sign of life from inside, then we reached the massive vault door that separated the prison's underbelly from the caverns beyond. It still hung off its hinges like a broken limb, its thick surface pocked and scratched. Simon motioned for us to stop, edging around the corner and flashing his silver eyes into the cave beyond. I could tell from the way his gray face was suddenly illuminated that the spotlights were on, but there was obviously nothing else there, as after a moment or two the kid darted off again.

I followed, keeping my head low as we entered the huge cavern where we'd been caught. It was empty save for the lights, and we cut right across it, past the tunnel where Zee and I had thought we'd seen sunlight, toward the far end. Here the ceiling drooped as if unable to hold up the vast weight above it, leaving a crack between its jagged edge and the floor that was too narrow for even the halogen beams to penetrate.

"Hurry," Simon hissed, grabbing my arm and steering me toward the ugly strip of darkness. He glanced behind him and I thought I saw movement from another of the fractured corridors that led from the cavern. "Suits," Simon explained. "They patrol around here. Hurry!"

I ducked under the uneven lip of the ceiling, finding myself in a small pocket of air surrounded on all sides by rock and jagged piles of rubble. I wasn't sure where to go, but Zee was soon in and Simon too, and the bigger kid began to scramble up the wall opposite, vanishing into the gloom.

"Where are you going?" Zee asked. "I can't see a thing."

"Just follow me, it's easier than it looks."

He was right. The wall was full of cracks we could wedge our feet into and hooked lumps that served as handholds. The higher we climbed the darker it got, but it was easy enough to feel our way ahead. After a good ten minutes or so of slow progress the acoustics of the space changed, and soon after that the wall leveled out. Simon grabbed me, pulled me up the last little bit, and while he waited for Zee I tried to get a better sense of where we were.

That's when I heard the noise up ahead. A click that could have been the chattering of teeth or the dry voice of some giant insect.

"You hear that?" I asked, wondering how fast I could get back down the wall if I had to make a quick exit. It was so dark I couldn't even work out where we'd climbed.

"It's okay," Simon called from the shadows. "They're with us."

They? He took hold of my overalls and guided me forward, steering me gently around a post of rock before angling sharply right. We'd taken a few more twisted turns before I heard the spark of a match. The world flared and I was shocked to see a pair of frightened faces only a few paces ahead. They scattered back like startled mice.

"It's me," Simon said, his voice louder but still cautious. "I brought him . . . them."

There was a soft pop and a flashlight fluttered on, the light weaker and more uncertain than the match in Simon's hand. We were standing in a small cave, barely larger than one of the cells up top, the ceiling arched above us. There were two other kids in the space, their bodies so hunched and distorted that they looked for a moment like crude paintings on the wall. One stared at us with silver eyes as large as saucers, while the other, the younger, blinked at me through pools of watery blue. I thought I recognized him from Furnace: one of the kids who'd been taken during the blood watch, dragged off by the wheezers.

The boy with silver eyes ducked his head and I saw that he was eating something, gnawing at it with animal ferocity. My stomach seemed to turn itself inside out with excitement at the thought of food, until the splintered bone caught the lamplight and my stomach turned for a different reason.

"Is that . . . ?" I asked, pointing. Simon followed my outstretched finger, his stance suddenly becoming defensive.

"We have to eat," he snapped, but his face twisted into a mask of shame before dropping to the floor.

"You Alex?" asked the kid with the blue eyes. As far as I could tell he'd escaped the wheezer's blades. His overalls were rust-colored in places but other than that he just looked like he'd stepped from his cell in gen pop. "I remember you. You used to hang with Carl Donovan, right?"

I nodded, unsure what to say.

"And you can get us out?" said the figure in the middle of the room. Like Simon he'd been cut open and stitched back up, although only his torso was affected—a bloated sack from which skinny limbs stuck out like spider legs. This time I didn't respond. The kid shuffled forward as if to get a better look at me. "We heard the blacksuits after you escaped. Man, they were pissed." His throaty laugh was contagious, spreading to the blue-eyed kid and to Simon.

"Alex, Zee, meet Pete." The mutilated teenager nodded a welcome. "He used to be a Skull but he's okay now."

"Better than ever," Pete said, laughing again.

"The kid there is Ozzie."

I smiled uneasily at them both as Pete continued to grind his teeth down on whatever it was he was eating. It was good to see some friendly faces, but part of me had been hoping that Simon commanded an army up here, a band of fifty kids or something who were ready to storm out of Furnace. This ragtag bunch of children didn't look capable of escaping from the cave we were in, let alone fighting their way to the surface. Not that I could talk, I suppose. I don't know what they'd been expecting of me, but right now I looked like a walking skeleton only held together by the tattered remnants of my overalls.

"How have you survived down here?" Zee asked. "Why haven't the blacksuits found you?"

"They would have," Simon answered, picking an upturned IV bag from the floor and offering it to me. It was full of clear water, probably from the river, and I drank deeply, the cool liquid putting out a fire in my gut that I hadn't even noticed was raging until now. I passed it to Zee as Simon continued. "The dogs have followed our scent a few times but there's no way they could get up that wall, the suits neither. They probably just think they're picking up a rat's trail."

"Getting pretty bored, though," said Pete. "It's been, what? A few months at least."

"Just weeks for me," said Ozzie. "Feels longer though. Glad you're here. You know a way out?"

I shook my head and, sensing my discomfort, Simon slapped me on the shoulder.

"Not yet he doesn't, but I know exactly where to start."

THE STEEPLE

OZZIE CAME WITH US as we crossed the cave, exiting through a narrow cleft at the back. Pete did his best, but he had barely taken a couple of paces on his wasted legs before they crumpled.

"Damn them," he said with another forced laugh as he passed the torch to Simon. "They could at least have given me the limbs to match this body."

"You wait here, keep an ear out," Simon said over his shoulder, taking the lamp and pressing on. "We won't be long."

"Is there a way out up here?" Zee asked as we shuffled sideways along a passage that was barely big enough for any of us. It sloped down, sometimes so sharply that I thought I was going to tumble into the darkness below.

"We're not sure," Simon replied. "I've searched all these tunnels, trust me. Been through them again and again and again, tried every crevice, every hole, every damn shadow in the ceiling. Nothing. They're all dead ends, blocked by rock falls, or they just plummet straight down. But then we found the steeple."

"Steeple?" I asked, sliding on a carpet of loose stones and clinging onto the wall to stay upright.

"I called it that," came Ozzie's voice, muffled by the shadows. "Reminded me of a church."

The flickering light from Simon's torch did little to pick out the route ahead, which seemed to close up the farther we walked as though it was trying to force us back. Just to help ward off the fear, I kept the conversation flowing.

"So how long were you in Furnace?" I asked, directing the question forward. But it was the younger kid behind me who answered again.

"Just a year," he said, then laughed. "I say *just*, it felt like a life-time. Got sent down for murder after my parents were killed. Not by me, I might add."

"Blacksuits?" I asked.

"Yeah, blacksuits. Framed me."

"Same here," I said. "I'm supposed to have murdered my best friend. What about the others?"

"Guilty as charged. Pete got locked up during the Summer of Slaughter, with the Skulls and all. Doesn't really say much about it. Simon . . . well, he'll tell you."

"Thanks," Simon's sarcasm echoed off the walls as he tried to squeeze through a crack in the rock. He vanished with a pop, his voice filtering back with the weak light. "Yeah, I was an idiot. The gang fights had finished but me and my mates got locked up for hitting a jewelry store. Things got out of hand, the owners had a gun." His voice faded as he walked off, and I sucked in my breath to press myself through the gap. "The guy threatened to use it, we fought, the gun went off and the rest, as they say, is history. Watch where you walk."

We'd emerged into another vast cavern, Simon's voice suddenly swallowed by the immense weight of darkness. His lamp revealed that we were on a narrow ledge, which dipped away into an ocean of pitch that seemed to have no end. The wall we'd come through stretched up, the dark canvas above us like the night sky and just as cold. The jutting rock narrowed as it climbed, like a needle. Like a spire.

"Well, this is it," said Simon, gazing up at the invisible ceiling far above our heads.

"That's it?" Zee said, emerging from the hole and brushing the dust from his overalls. "That's our way out?"

Simon flashed another defiant look our way but it didn't last, and after a second his face fell. I wasn't sure what he wanted from me, from us, but I didn't see anything that resembled a way out. There wasn't even a glimmer of hope in my mind. It was just another cavern, and a pillar of rock that stretched toward nothing.

"It's all we've got," said Ozzie as he joined us. "Don't look like much, I know, but it's the only part of this whole system that goes any higher. Like Simon said, all the tunnels dead-end or go deeper. But this one looks like it could stretch up to the top."

There was no way of telling. The light from the lamp clawed its way maybe ten meters into the heavy shadow but there it stalled.

"I think this is part of the gorge, the one they put the prison in," explained Simon, holding the lamp above his head but failing to illuminate any more of the steeple. "It could lead to the surface."

"Ever seen any sunlight up there?" I asked, knowing the answer already.

"No. But that doesn't mean there isn't any." Simon shifted his gaze to the chasm at our side, as deep as the space above us was high. "It has to be, Alex. Because there is no other way out."

"Even if it was, how would we get up there?" asked Zee. "We'd need ropes, spikes. Nobody would be able to make that climb bare-handed."

The mood was sinking fast and the darkness seemed to sense it, pressing down on us.

"We *could* climb it," Simon said, unwilling to give up. He sounded like the child he was, almost stamping his foot to emphasize the point. "Anyway, you're here now. You can help us find a way, come up with something. You did it before."

The rock of the steeple was rough and cracked, like the slope we'd climbed a moment ago, and there were splits that looked big enough to rest on. But Zee was right, it would take someone at the peak of their physical ability to scale the steeple, which none of us could claim to be right now. And even if we got there, reached the top, who's to say it wouldn't just end at the cavern roof, leaving us stranded on a rocky pillar with no way down. I realized everyone was looking at me, and that I was shaking my head.

"I'll think about it," was all I could find to say. "There might be a way. If one of us could scout it, maybe, take a rope. I don't know."

I could hear the doubt dripping from my voice, but for Simon the mere mention of an idea seemed enough. He grinned, and for a moment I thought he was going to throw his hulking body forward and hug me.

"I knew you'd be up for it," he said. "It doesn't even matter if we all can't make it—like, I can't see Pete getting up there with his legs, you know—if just one of us can get out we can find some help."

I stared up again, and for a moment I could see it—the steeple pushing relentlessly toward the surface, the ancient rock breaking through the crust of the earth and leaving enough room for us.

I imagined my hand pushing through the loose soil, gripped by sunlight, which pulled me out from my grave, laid me down on the warm grass.

"See, you feel it too," said Simon, and I realized my cheeks were aching from the grin they were holding up. "There's something about this place. I come here sometimes, lie on the ledge and look up, pretend that it's the night sky up there. Sometimes it's so real I can see the stars, feel the breeze. It's gotta be our way ou—" His last word was snapped off early and he tilted his head, listening to something I couldn't hear. Then he walked past me, back to the wall. "Come on, it's pretty safe here, but the rats'll home in on any sound and I don't fancy being stuck on this ledge if they show up."

"We're staying with you, right?" I asked his misshapen back as he vanished. "In the cave?"

"No, we need to get you to your cells."

Zee and I protested with the same cry of alarm but he was still talking.

"If you go missing, then the blacksuits'll start to suspect something. Especially if there's no blood. Right now they don't know anything about us, but if they come looking for you then they might find us too. We can't take that risk."

"I don't know how much longer we're gonna stay alive in there," I replied, the rock against my chest and back weakening my words. "Blacksuits will kill us whether the warden wants it or not."

"Just another day or so," said Simon. "Till we can think of the best way to get up the steeple."

I was about to keep arguing when I realized what was going on. Simon didn't trust us—not completely, anyway. He was scared we'd make a run for it, find a way out and leave them behind. And if he kept us locked up then he knew we couldn't go anywhere without him. It seemed pretty harsh, but then Furnace doesn't exactly inspire trust.

"Why haven't you tried to climb it yet?" came Zee's voice from behind me.

"I did," Simon replied. "Couple of times. Didn't get far before I started to panic. Couldn't find a way to get up there safely. Then when we heard the blacksuits talking about the bust up top we figured we'd wait, see if someone actually made it out, see if we could follow them." I heard him breathe a sigh of relief as he pushed himself out into the cave. "Now we've got you, and I know you'll think of something. I was never bright, never did well at nothing on the outside. But you came up with the plan, blew the walls."

"Yeah, you've gotta tell us how you did it," said Ozzie as we all filtered out into the tiny space.

"Another time," said Simon, walking past the expectant face of Pete. "Right now you've got some thinking to do."

THE TRIP BACK INTO FURNACE wasn't half as easy as the trip out, and several times I found myself pleading for Simon to let us stay with him. I should have put my foot down, given the order.

Yet the truth was I was scared of him. His silver eyes were always on me, glinting as if he knew something I didn't. I couldn't help but be reminded of one of the guards, which chilled me to the bone. On top of that I'd seen what he could do. I'd never forget the way he'd taken down that rat, then ripped out its throat. *Bitten* it out. If he wanted, he could tear me limb from limb as easily as a blacksuit or one of their dogs could. And something about him, something about the intenseness of his stare, made me think he was right on the edge of sanity, that he could drop off into madness at any time and take us all down with him.

Who can blame him? I thought as we lurked in the shadows beneath the cavern's low ceiling, waiting for two distant blacksuits to disappear into the tunnels. Whatever I'd been through, he'd had it a million times worse.

We were about to move when another guard appeared from a tunnel to our right and walked through the battered vault door, dragging a bloody corpse behind him. It left a red trail as he vanished, a crimson stream that seemed to glow in the spotlights.

"Is that a rat?" I asked when the figure was gone. "Where is he taking it?"

"To the incinerator, probably," Simon replied, his body tensing, ready to make a run for it. "They burn them, make sure they don't feed on each other, make sure they don't, you know, decide they aren't dead and start roaming around again."

Both Zee and I looked at Simon but he had already leaped up. I ran behind him, clumsily sprinting across the cavern floor and wishing once again that the heat on my face was daylight rather than halogen.

We skidded past the vault door, following the slick trail up to the first junction. One path split off toward the warden's quarters. The feeling of dread I'd got last time I'd passed was gone, but we had to duck into a darkened room while two more blacksuits strolled past. My heart was pounding so high up in my throat I could taste it, but they obviously didn't suspect a thing, the military rhythm of their footsteps fading after a few seconds.

A couple of cautious sprints later and we were back at the cells. My heart dropped right from my tonsils to my stomach as soon as

I saw them, but it was too late to argue. Simon held mine open like he was tucking me in, and when I was once again gripped in its smothering fist he winked at me.

"I'll come again after your next meal, if I can. That should give us plenty of time to do this."

I reflected his expectant nod, but I couldn't bring myself to imitate his wide—too wide—grin as the hatch once again slammed shut.

BREAKING AND ENTERING

MY NEXT MEAL came a few hours after Simon had locked us back in, and when the blacksuit wrenched open the door and chucked in a bowl of slop I was surprised to see the warden standing alongside him. He'd obviously come to see how I was faring in the hole, and his mere presence outside the hatch made me double over. Even then I could feel his gaze boring into the back of my skull, transmitting images that I could make little sense of but which were always composed of a palette of reds and dirty whites.

I made out a rasping laugh, each breath of which seemed to hammer the pictures deeper into my head, forcing them to take shape. Not that I could tell you what I saw. Those images were so twisted, so terrifying, that they slipped right out again, each one stealing a little more of my sanity and leaving filthy traces in its place.

"Almost a week in the hole and you're still breathing," said the warden, although I couldn't hear his voice, I could only feel it like needles sliding into my ears. He laughed again and it was all I could do not to scream. "I'd save your breath, Sawyer," he said, as if he could read my mind. "There's a long way to go yet and there are so many more nightmares to face. Enjoy your food."

The warden continued to talk as the hatch was closed, but each word hurt more than the last and I did my best to shut them out. Some filtered through, wrapped in razor wire and sinking right to the heart of my consciousness—*perfect subject . . . the Chamber . . . harness his fury*—then the hatch was sealed and the voice faded. Slowly, very slowly, the poison from the warden's mind ebbed from my own, leaving me with a throbbing headache and a nose-bleed. I lay on the floor, pinching the flow and trying not to think about the blood that dripped pleasantly down my throat. It had just started to ease off when I heard Zee tapping a message from his cell.

"Think we can do it? The steeple?"

"No idea," I replied, sitting up to better hammer out my response. "Might not even go anywhere."

"Yeah, thought that too." There was silence for a few minutes. "Worth a try, though."

"Worth a try," I repeated, rubbing the blisters on my hand and wishing there weren't so many letters in the alphabet.

"Any ideas?" he pressed.

I didn't answer straightaway. Instead I ran my hand across the cell floor, scooping up the slop and stuffing it into my mouth— too hungry to care about where it had been or how dirty it was. To keep my mind off the texture I tried to picture the steeple, tried to imagine how an escape might work. There was nothing to do but climb, it didn't take a genius to see that. And to do it we'd need some equipment, otherwise sooner or later we'd all take a fall, plummet past the ledge and down into the bottomless pit of the gorge.

I was pretty sure there wouldn't be any climbing gear in Furnace, not unless the wheezers liked a little recreational rappelling when they weren't working in the infirmary. The thought brought a smile to my face. I pictured them jerking and twitching as they bobbled from a ledge, their piggy eyes wide with excitement as they eased their way down, suture clamps wedged in the wall and scalpels strapped to their feet for grip.

Thank you, brain. I sat up, feeling the familiar rush of inspiration. It was so obvious. The infirmary had been full of hooks and straps and hammers and pins that could double as a climbing kit.

The euphoria was so intense that it blocked out what little rational thought I had left, banishing logic to some dark part of my brain where its protests couldn't be heard. I didn't question the fact that the equipment wasn't made for the stresses and strains of climbing and would probably break. I didn't worry that I'd never climbed before in my life. I didn't even acknowledge the thought that in order to get our hands on it we'd have to go back into the infirmary where the wheezers were waiting. No, all I could see was us scaling the steeple with ropes of rubber tubing and leather, pulling ourselves up with forceps and bone saws until we clawed our way into the world outside.

I know, it sounds utterly ridiculous. But when you've spent days inside a black hole in the center of the earth, then even the craziest escape plans become gloriously real. And I mean nothing was as crazy as filling rubber gloves with gas and using them to blow a hole in the floor, right?

Simon showed up some time later and I was telling him my plan even as he was lifting me out of my cell. He gestured for me to keep my voice down, telling me in a panicked whisper that there had been no breach or riots, and that the blacksuits could be anywhere.

"Nice idea," he said as we freed Zee, his enthusiasm bubbling up through his caution. "We're so close, I know we can do this."

His confidence was contagious, giving us strength as we stealthily made our way down the corridor, hovering by the dark doorways for cover before sprinting down the next stretch. I wondered if we should be searching the rooms for anything we could use, but Simon shook his head.

"Most are empty," he said as he peeked around the corner of the junction that led up to the infirmary. "Shelves, boxes with nothing in them. Nothing there that will help us climb. Everything we need is in the infirmary . . ." He paused, and even though his features were as white as parchment, I thought they paled another shade or two. "Or beyond, where they do the surgery."

We rested, breath locked in our lungs, as the sound of footsteps rose up from somewhere close. It was the tread of a blacksuit, and we prepared to flee back to solitary if we needed to. But they began to recede again, leaving the corridor beyond clear. Simon sprang, bolting toward the infirmary doorway, and we struggled to keep up with him. I was so scared that the adrenaline in my blood felt like acid. I was used to it, though. I'd forgotten what it was like to live a life where every waking moment wasn't filled with terror.

We skidded to a halt outside the door, our backs pressed against the stenciled letters as Simon took a look through the plastic curtain.

"Can't see any movement," I thought I heard him say, although it was too quiet to be sure. He turned to face us. "Head right, back to the screens we were in before. If you see a trolley grab anything you think might be useful. Clamps, bandages, stuff like that."

"What about the wheezers?" Zee's voice fluttered past my ear.

"We'll just be careful," was his less than reassuring reply. "Get the hell out of there if there's any sign of trouble."

Simon eased a finger between two of the plastic slats and glanced inside. It must have been clear because with a flutter his bulbous body vanished like it was sinking into dirty pond water. I realized I'd been holding my breath and exhaled slowly through my nose. I knew if I waited any longer my courage would desert me completely, so after snatching a mouthful of air I pushed myself through the curtain and ducked right, sprinting behind the first screen without even checking to see if the infirmary was empty.

There were no wheezed cries of alarm, no sound of shotguns being pumped and fired, no screams of anger as Zee sped in, almost tumbling over the empty bed in his haste to be in hiding. All I could hear were the pitiful cries of the patients and our own gasping breaths.

"Let's go," said Simon, leading the way between the screen and the wall to the next compartment. This too was empty, and the half dozen or so after that, but when I followed him through one more gap, I realized it was where I'd stolen the scalpel. The boy who'd occupied the bed was now gone, sheets stripped and a stained pillow the only evidence he'd ever been there. But the trolley was still in place, the rack of stainless-steel equipment glinting red in the intense light of the room.

"Zee, help me with these," said Simon. "Alex, you keep looking."

I nodded, grateful that he was letting me go on. Picking up equipment wasn't the only reason I'd been hoping to return to the infirmary. Donovan was up here, just two screens away. At least I prayed he was. I pushed through the next compartment a little too quickly, entering Donovan's cubicle to see the weird metal sarcophagus still in place.

He was suspended inside it just as before, only now both his legs matched his grotesquely stretched torso. It was like he was slowly being filled with air, his body puffed up and his limbs swollen to bursting point. His arms, which had seemed enormous when we were up top, now looked like twigs stuck into a giant sack of dough.

I walked around to face him and almost cried out. His face wasn't his anymore. I mean, I could still recognize him, but it was distended and scarred like an over-roasted pig's. His jaw was enormous, something writhing beneath the skin and making it look as if he was chewing gum. His silver eyes were those of a statue, sightless and full of death.

"Donovan?" I whispered. "Are you still in there?"

It seemed a stupid thing to ask, but it's all I could come up with. It was as if someone had taken my friend and packed him inside someone else's body, pasting so much flesh over him that he could no longer remember who he was. *Please God, let him be in there somewhere.*

"Don't get too comfortable, we're still getting out of here," I said.

His head swung from side to side for a moment like one of those toy dogs you put in cars. It would have been funny if it hadn't chilled me to the bone. I said his name again and his gaze dropped, almost finding me, straying off to the side then sliding back. I saw his eyes focus, then his lips peeled apart, the stitches straining as he smiled.

I staggered back. It wasn't an expression of welcome; it was that same blood-curdling shark's grin that the blacksuits all wore. He held it for as long as he could, then his cheeks started to spasm and his face fell. Seconds later his mouth opened again and he spoke a string of soft words that didn't make any sense.

"Donovan?" I talked over him, loud enough to be heard from

outside the compartment. "You remember your name, right? We're still getting out. We've found a way. Think we have, anyway. It won't be long, I promise."

He was still ranting, specks of spit and blood flying from his lips as he hissed out the same sequence of words. I leaned in, close enough to feel the heat from his body against my face, and his choked cries suddenly made sense.

"Donovan is dead," he whispered, his metallic gaze sweeping the curtain, trying to find something. "Donovan is dead. Donovan is dead. Donovan is dead." Over and over, louder and louder. I saw the side of the screen twitch, two faces appearing.

"What are you doing?" Simon asked. "We came to get equipment, not to see him. You're going to get us all caught."

"Donovan is dead, Donovan is dead, Donovan is dead."

I wanted to put a hand on his arm, try to calm him down, but he was too hot to touch. Simon walked up and started hauling me away toward the next cubicle.

"The wheezers are going to hear," he was saying, more to himself than to me. He was right, and fear made me follow without objection. It was only as I was slipping past the screen that Donovan's mantra stopped. I turned, saw that his face was locked on mine again, his soulless Cheshire Cat smile engraved in my head long after it had disappeared behind the curtains.

A wheeze fluttered up from close by, increasing in volume and pitch like a siren. My heart was pounding too hard, I couldn't make out which direction the sound was coming from. I realized I was gripping Simon with the same white-knuckle strength he was holding me with, Zee already backing off the way we had come.

The wheeze trailed off into another of those gargled purrs, a noise that could only be a cold chuckle. I heard the sound of curtains being pulled back, a cry like that of an injured bird.

"Where is it?" I asked, my mouth practically up against Simon's ear. He shook his head, not daring to move in case the armful of equipment he held gave him away. It sounded as though the wheezer was between us and the main door, out in the aisle that separated the two rows of beds. Surely we'd be fine as long as we stayed out of sight.

Another set of curtains pulled back, a tuneless whisper like a broken accordion.

"Go," muttered Simon, nodding back toward Donovan's cubicle. Zee went first, gently easing himself between the screen and the wall. I followed, and it was just as Simon emerged behind me that a shadow rose up on the screen. The three of us froze like this was a game of musical statues and the music had just stopped.

But to my horror Donovan started laughing, a cold, booming chuckle that could have come right from a blacksuit.

"You're ours now," he said through a grin.

Then the curtain was ripped open and death lurched in.

THE CHARNEL HOUSE

THE WHEEZER SHOWED NO HINT OF SURPRISE, no sign of hesitation. It took one giant stride across the cubicle and before I could even blink its gloved hand was around my throat.

I'd assumed the wheezers were weak, and slow. I thought that's why they needed the blacksuits to carry away the prisoners they picked when they came up top on the blood watch.

I'd assumed wrong. The hand that held me was like a vice, crushing my windpipe so hard that I couldn't even draw a breath. It pulled me toward it and I could do nothing but stare at its mottled face, the rusting gas mask sewn into its leathery skin, two eyes as dull as coal but somehow gleaming with sick pleasure.

The edges of my vision were clouding, flecks of black lightning leaving dark scars and threatening to plunge me into unconsciousness. The wheezer threw back its head and called out, a twisted scream that tore my soul in two.

There was movement to my side, Zee running forward and crying out defiantly. The wheezer's head twisted unnaturally and it extended its other arm. It was too late for Zee to change direction and he flew right into it, the gloved hand locking around his neck and holding him there even though his legs were off the ground and shaking like a rag doll's. The monster cocked its head and looked at us as though it couldn't believe its luck. I couldn't see its mouth because of the contraption over it, but I knew it was smiling. It called out again, and something distant answered it. Then something else, a chorus of wet cries that flooded into the infirmary.

We were dead. I knew it. I kicked out at the freak that held me, but its flesh felt like porridge beneath its jacket and it didn't even seem to feel my blows. One of my kicks caused a pair of syringes around its chest to explode and its expression changed, the eyes narrowing and its wheeze lowering in pitch, like it was warning me to stay still.

It didn't have to. What little strength I had was long gone, totally drained. I tried to suck in some air but the fingers clamped around my windpipe wouldn't let me.

It screamed again, the noise fading into that mucus-filled growl of delight. My mind was snatching at the last few strands of consciousness, like someone sinking into quicksand grasping for a fistful of weeds. I looked at Zee, saw him staring back, his tear-stained face a perfect reflection of my own.

Then the fleshy noose around my throat loosened and I fell to my knees. For a moment my lungs couldn't remember what to do, then they expanded, air flooding in and purging the darkness from my vision. I thought that maybe the wheezer had suffered one of its spasms, or had thrown me down in order to stick me with a poisoned hypodermic.

But it was staggering back, the silver handle of a scalpel protruding from its shoulder like a military epaulette. Zee was on the floor next to me sobbing and gasping for breath. I looked around, saw Simon standing close by, his face a rictus of shock and repulsion.

The wheezer was stunned but not badly injured. It unleashed another cry, one I'd never heard before, which echoed around the room like an arriving fleet of demons. It reached up and pulled out the scalpel, releasing a spurt of putrid, oil-colored blood. Then it threw itself at us.

Still on my knees, I did the only thing I could think of. I threw myself forward, bunched up into a ball, praying it wouldn't notice me. I felt its boots crunch into my side and thought it was kicking me until I sensed its body tripping over mine, crashing earthward. For a moment I was lost in the folds of its coat, its graveyard stench enveloping me. Then it was on the floor, twisting and writhing like a beetle on its back.

"Quick!" yelled Simon, throwing himself on the wheezer despite his obvious terror. He was still holding the equipment he'd stolen from the trolley and with a cry he plunged another scalpel into its chest. It bucked, trying to stand, kicking the side of Donovan's metal sarcophagus loudly enough to be heard up top. I glanced at the doors on either side of the infirmary, knowing the blacksuits would be here in seconds.

"Help me!" Simon called again, sticking something else into the freak beneath him. I scrabbled around, looking for a weapon. The creature lashed out, catching Simon on the jaw and sending him reeling across the cubicle.

Trying not to think about what I was doing, I slammed my body onto the wheezer's chest, pinning it. Zee was by my side throwing ineffective punches. One hit the creature's gas mask and it howled in pain as two of the stitches split.

"The mask," I heaved, throwing a punch of my own. Pain shot up my arm as my fist connected with the metal apparatus, but four more of the ancient stitches snapped loose. The wheezer knew what we were doing, its body spasming and rocking with such force that I was almost thrown off. Simon reappeared, kneeling on the wheezer's arm then placing his massive hand over the gas mask. Zee bundled onto its other arm, holding it down with all his strength, and together we punched and pulled and ripped at the wheezer's face.

The mask came loose with a sound that turned my stomach inside out. There was the snap of wire, loud enough to be a pistol shot, then the sickening tear of split flesh and the sucking noise of a pressurized seal coming loose, like the sound a sink plunger makes. The mask fell to the floor and I immediately felt the strength vanish from the wheezer. We got off it, barely managing to stay upright as we huddled on the other side of the compartment.

It was still thrashing, but made no attempt to stand. Its hands were held up to its face, desperately fumbling for the mask that was no longer there, its mouth flopping open, huge and toothless. It screamed, but all that came out was a hoarse croak. It tried to take one more breath, its eyes now wide with panic as they searched the cubicle for its attackers. But before they found us it was dead.

There was no time to think about what we'd done. We bolted, sprinting past the screen into the infirmary and making for the door that led back to the cells. A savage bark stopped us in our tracks, a howl that I knew only too well. It was a dog, somewhere out in the corridor beyond, and by the sounds of the throbbing voices that yelled alongside it the creature wasn't alone.

"Blacksuits," Simon said, cursing, then doubling back, heading for the door on the other side of the room. The door that led even deeper into the prison's medical facility. "Come on, follow me."

We did, trying not to look at the dead wheezer as we passed it. The cries were still flowing into the room and I expected to see more of the gas masks lurching in at any moment. Christ, wheezers in front of us, blacksuits and their dogs behind us. We were as dead as all the other kids buckled down in their beds in the infirmary.

Part of me wanted to stop, wanted to just wait here for the blacksuits. I mean, they were scary, but at least you could talk to them. Whatever the wheezers were, it was something age-old and rotten, the kind of evil you could never bargain with.

And we were running right toward them.

Simon reached the doorway, this too covered with a curtain of plastic strips. He didn't hesitate, just threw himself into it and disappeared with a flap. Swearing under my breath, I lowered my head and pushed through, feeling Zee's breath on my neck as he followed.

I should have kept my eyes forward, but you know what it's like when you're running, when you're terrified, and you're convinced there's something right behind you. I stopped, peered back through the dirty plastic, saw the blacksuits pile in through the door opposite—one, three, seven, all scanning the room for the wheezer that had screamed and for whatever had attacked it.

But the dogs already knew. Two sets of silver eyes blazed right through the curtain at us, and when the creatures howled I knew it was because they had our scent in their muzzles.

I realized Zee and Simon were still running and I sprinted after them. We were in another long corridor, which thankfully was empty, although I knew from the screams that echoed off the blood-red walls that the wheezers were close. I didn't realize how close until we passed the first of several rooms hewn out of the rock.

Inside, sealed by a thick Plexiglas door and protected by an electrical lock that looked far too modern for Furnace, was a small operating theater. And in the room, midway through a procedure, was a wheezer. It had its filthy hands in a figure laid out on a steel table, a boy whose eyes were closed but whose peeled chest rose up and down slowly.

I staggered past the door, knowing that if I didn't start running then it would be me on that table, me being dissected then put back together like a kit model.

I barely noticed the other rooms to my left and right, each with the same electrical door. Most were empty, but some had wheezers inside, their raisin eyes too engrossed in their specimens to notice us run past.

"Where are we going?" I heard Zee hiss, he and Simon still hurling themselves forward up ahead.

"I don't know," Simon answered. "I've never been this deep before, no one has. At least, no one who has survived."

They stopped at a junction, giving me a chance to catch up.

"Which way?" asked Zee.

"Didn't you just hear me?" the kid snapped. "I don't know." He glanced right, then straight ahead, then took off to the left.

"The screams are coming from that way!" Zee said, stretching out a hand after him. But Simon was gone, the muscles beneath his warped skin visible as he pounded down the corridor. Zee turned to me. "What do we do?"

"Just go," I shouted, taking off after him. The passage kinked up ahead and I heard Simon swear when he looked around the corner, throwing himself back against the wall.

"Wheezers," was all he said.

I ducked down, knowing that the blacksuits and the dogs

would burst in behind us at any moment, and inched my head around the corner.

There must have been thirty of them, packed into the long corridor and coming this way, called by the scream of their dying comrade.

I fell, scrambled up again, and ran back to the junction. Something in my fried mind told me that if the left-hand turn led to the wheezers' quarters then the right-hand turn was probably a dead end too. I hit the crossroads and swung left, darting down a short corridor that ended in a metal door.

A howl behind us, the shout of the blacksuits. I grabbed the handle, prayed that it wasn't locked. Then the latch lifted, the door creaked, and swung open, and I wished that it had been.

Before us was a charnel house. I thought at first that I was looking at more red stone walls, rougher than the others we'd passed and decorated with strips of torn clothing. Only it wasn't rocks that lined either side of the large room, stacked in piles as tall as I was.

It was corpses.

IN HIDING

THE SOUNDS BEHIND US were getting louder, the blacksuits and the dogs and the wheezers closing in. I don't think I could have brought myself to enter the room if Simon hadn't shoved us forward, pushing me and Zee into the meat locker before stepping in himself and closing the door quietly behind him.

I realized I was shaking, my whole body trembling uncontrollably. I couldn't figure out which emotion was causing it. There was fear, yes, and disbelief. But there was anger too, surging up from my gut like molten rock, making my blood feel like it was on fire.

How could they do this? How could they get away with it?

I didn't want to look but I couldn't stop myself. Most of the bodies were rats, deformed limbs and faces that looked wild and vicious even in death. Their silver eyes were open and staring blankly into the room, and I could almost forget that they had once been human, been kids like me and Zee.

Almost.

It was less easy to pretend with the other bodies scattered around. I saw pale limbs, untouched by the wheezers' scalpels, the hint of a cheek or a tuft of mousy brown hair. *Specimens* was the only word that came to mind. These were the ones that had gone wrong, that had been dumped.

The emotion flared for a moment, then it dulled, leaving me numb. I know why—if it hadn't, then my mind would have shattered right there, broken into pieces so small and so damaged it could never have been put back together.

I caught sight of a suit and frowned. In one corner, half buried under the bodies of a couple of smaller corpses, was one of the guards. His jacket had been torn open, the shirt stained black. He must have died fighting the rats, I realized. I didn't quite know why, but there was something even worse about the way he'd been discarded here by his own people than there was about the other dead. What kind of monsters would do that?

Then again, the blacksuits were just more specimens, and if they died they were no more useful to the warden than the kids they'd once been.

"It's the incinerator," said Simon, the sound of his voice startling me after the stunned silence. I'd been so busy looking at the corpses that littered the floor that I hadn't noticed the hulking metal doors on the other side of the room. They were open, an enormous crematorium oven visible behind them with walls smoked black and a thick carpet of ashes. "This is where they burn them."

"No," said Zee, echoing my own thoughts. "They can't. It's just . . . wrong."

"Is there anything about this place that isn't?" replied Simon softly.

A muffled bark from the doorway reminded us of the freaks on our tail and we all looked left and right for a way out. But the room only had one door and an incinerator.

"We've got to hide," I said, hearing the thump of boots on rock getting closer against a backdrop of angry screams from the wheezers. Nobody knew where we were, but it wouldn't take them long if they opened the door and spotted us standing like statues in the middle of the room.

"Where?" asked Simon, looking at the incinerator. "I'm not getting in there. What if they turn it on?"

I scanned the room. There was nowhere else. Not unless . . .

"The bodies," I said, my voice so weak it barely left my mouth.

Simon and Zee were shaking their heads, but the noises outside were growing in volume every second. I walked toward a corner of the room, my body still shaking but my mind blank, all the emotional receptors switched off. There were five or six corpses here, all rats, slumped over each other and motionless like a tableau of some grotesque wrestling match. I reached out, grabbed an exposed arm, then immediately pulled back.

The body was still warm. Not just warm, it was hot.

I checked for a pulse but there was nothing. I scanned the pile. None of the creatures were breathing, their chests all locked tight. I heard a shout from behind the door, the noise of approaching feet. Taking a deep breath, and trying to ignore the smell, I grabbed the arm again and pulled the corpse away from the wall. Then I lowered a foot into the gap I'd made, nestling myself down between the other bodies.

I let the topmost cadaver fall back on me, its dead weight pushing my head uncomfortably to the side. Fortunately there were no flies this deep beneath the surface, but the stench of decay was so pungent I could almost see it rising like a heat mirage off the crumbling flesh.

There was a choked cry from across the room and I peered

through the gap between an arm and a foot to see both Simon and Zee clambering into their own hiding places. I wasn't sure who had made the noise but they were both sobbing gently as they pulled scraps of clothing or stiff limbs over themselves.

The latch clicked, a mournful creak filling the room as the door swung open. I heard the soft growl of a dog, followed instantly by a whine of protest.

"Get in there," said a blacksuit. There was more whimpering, as if the dog was reluctant to proceed. I didn't blame it; its animal instincts must have sensed the death in this place from the other side of the infirmary, warning it to stay away. I realized it had probably followed our scent here, but I knew the corpses would shield us from the dogs' noses as well as they would hide us from the blacksuits' eyes.

"I'll do it," said another voice, just as loud and just as deep. A dark shape strode into the room, although from the angle I was crouched in I could only make out a pair of suited legs and polished boots. I closed my eyes, tried to stay as still as humanly possible. Any minute now I was going to feel a powerful hand on my shoulder, wrenching me out and tossing me to the dogs or into the incinerator.

But after a few seconds the guard turned and disappeared back through the door.

"Rats must have bolted back out of the compound before we arrived," I heard him say as the door swung shut. "Can't have got far; see if the dogs can pick up the scent from outside. And get those wheezers back to their cells."

IT WAS ZEE WHO ESCAPED FIRST, pushing his way free and gasping for air. I waited a moment, too scared to move in case the blacksuits came back, but there was no more sound from outside, not even the wail of a wheezer. I pushed upward with my legs, the corpses resisting for a moment before tumbling loose. I stepped from the coffin of rotting flesh, walking to the center of the room where the three of us stood for a minute in silence, trying not to think about what we'd just done.

"We have to get you back to solitary before they realize you're gone," Simon said eventually. "They obviously think the rats are to blame. And if they suspect the rats have started breaking into the infirmary then security is going to double." He swore, stamping his foot. "We don't even have any of the stuff we came for."

"How will we get back?" asked Zee. "Won't there be wheezers and blacksuits everywhere?"

"Sounds like the suits have gone off on a rat hunt," Simon answered, brushing his hands down his body as if trying to rub off some invisible mess. I felt itchy all over as well, like death was contagious. "There might be one or two but we'll have to take that chance. We can't stay here."

The thought of stepping through that door, coming face-to-face with the wheezers again, turned my legs to water. But Simon was right. What was the alternative? Sit around until they fired up the incinerator?

I realized nobody was moving and steeled myself, walking back to the door. Putting my ear to the warm metal revealed no sound from outside, and with my pulse drumming in my ears I lifted the latch and eased it open.

A wheezer was making its way down the corridor beyond, but it had its back to us. It took a couple of steps then stopped, its body shaking wildly, its head snapping back and forth like it was having a fit. Then it reached one of the electronic doors and vanished.

I willed my legs to work and it seemed to take a mammoth effort to make that first step. But once I'd started moving, momentum took over. We flew down the corridor, the Plexiglas doors flashing by on both sides. I didn't look inside, knowing that if I did I'd see a wheezer gazing out, ready to sound the alarm. But nothing happened, and we'd almost reached the door that led back into the infirmary when I heard Simon call out softly. By the time I'd turned he had disappeared into one of the operating theaters, and I would have assumed he'd been pulled in if Zee wasn't standing relatively calmly half in and half out of the doorway.

Cursing, I doubled back, peered inside to see that it was empty. Simon was standing over a trolley snatching up suture clamps and bone pins. He'd already slung a coil of surgical tubing over his shoulder.

"Take what you can," he said, and Zee and I responded without thinking. I grabbed hold of a hammer with a hooked end, pulled another length of thick rubber hose from a rack on the wall. There wasn't anything else on the trolley that looked remotely useful for climbing, so I headed back to the door and out into the passageway.

In the room opposite a wheezer was standing over a metal table, scalpel held in one unsteady hand. I moved on before it noticed me.

Seconds later we were peering through the plastic slats at the back of the infirmary, wondering whether it was good luck that the room ahead was deserted or whether it was a trap. For all we knew there could have been blacksuits behind every set of curtains, shotguns locked and loaded, waiting to gun us down.

But we'd made it this far . . .

We ran, legs lined with lead, lungs wrinkled up into prunes.

We ran, straight down the middle of the room, straight out through the filthy curtain, straight down the corridor beyond. We ran, and by the time we'd hit the junction leading back to the cells and still hadn't been detected, we were giggling insanely, sheer relief rushing like pure, clear water through our veins.

The hatch locks were still in place; nobody had checked to see if we were there. Zee went in first, then I handed Simon the kit I'd stolen and leaped into the black hole of my cell, too exhausted from what had just happened to even care that I was being buried alive again. It was only when Simon moved to close my hatch that the laughter faded.

"You are coming back, aren't you?" I said.

But Simon didn't answer. Instead he let the door close and pushed the lock back into its casing, leaving me alone in the dark with the gut-wrenching fear that we'd never see him again.

DOUBTS

IT WAS AS IF THIS TIME the darkness had weight, substance. It pressed down on me, making my arms and legs and neck feel like they were cased in concrete. I let myself drop, then sat there in the corner of the tiny cell waiting for feeling to return to my limbs.

Part of me couldn't believe what had just happened. It was easier to think that the whole thing had been in my head, that I'd been stuck here in my cell all this time fighting imaginary enemies. Except I could still feel the wheezer's grip around my throat, fingertips on my windpipe. I knew that if there were light and a mirror in here I'd be able to see the bruising on my neck, like someone who'd been hanged on the gallows.

My entire body still throbbed, but the pain was a welcome diversion from my thoughts. I shifted on the uncomfortable stone, licked some of the moisture from the wall to quench my thirst. I wondered again whether Simon would return, or whether he'd already be making his way up the steeple.

He hadn't needed us at all, not really. It was he who had found the rock, who had made the assumption that freedom lay at the top. And he'd probably already thought of using the medical equipment to help him climb it. All he'd wanted from me was reassurance that his plan would work even if I didn't think it would. He'd gotten that, and there was no other reason for him to come back for us.

The lightless air seemed to thicken, filling up the cell and closing over my mouth. I choked, tried and failed to draw breath. My lungs burned, a high-pitched whistle began to ring in my ears. But it was just panic. I knew enough to recognize it, and inhaled twice through my nose, breathing out slowly and feeling the oxygen hit my veins like a drug.

Knowing Simon was up there, that he'd be coming back for us, had given us the illusion that we were free. It lessened the power of solitary purely because we weren't trapped, we weren't isolated, we weren't alone. With him gone, however, the cell became a tomb.

And that wasn't the only reason I felt the panic gnawing at my stomach again. Deep down I knew Simon's plan wouldn't work. It *couldn't* work.

Yes I'd had the flash of inspiration about the climbing gear, but it had never been serious. I'd been clutching at straws, and only saw it as a real possibility because, well, I was desperate, delusional. Simon too had only gone along with it because he had nothing else. And when reality denies you the tools you need for survival you grab them from wherever you can.

And if we couldn't get out, then what? We'd probably live, but we wouldn't be alive, not in the way we were now. We'd become rats who devoured the living, or blacksuits who terrorized them. We'd be demons, the living dead, and the thought was unbearable.

I wished I'd kept that scalpel.

I stared into the darkness, hoping that my brain would conjure up some company—someone, anyone, to help me pull free of this cloud of depression. I saw the strands of silk suspended in the distance, as if there were no walls between them and me, and sure enough they began to coil into a body. But the image wouldn't solidify, shimmering above the invisible ground like a heat haze.

"Donovan?" I asked the ghost, hoping to see a familiar face. But something in my head wouldn't let him form. Either I'd forgotten what he really looked like beneath his monstrous new flesh, or I knew he was dead. I called his name again and the figure replied with white noise, the voice lost in static.

"I'm sorry," I said, reaching out for him. "I'm sorry I couldn't save you."

The image didn't change, as blurred as the reflection in a disturbed puddle, but suddenly the voice became clearer, like a radio being tuned.

It's not too late, he replied. *You don't have to free me to save me.*

I frowned, but the phantom was dissolving like salt in water. I tried to bring him back, tried to picture his face, but I couldn't recall it. All I could see was what he had become—the monstrous visage, the cold eyes, that face-splitting grin. And right then I knew that I'd never be able to remember him the way he was.

I'm not sure how long I cried. Just minutes, probably, but it could have been hours. At first heaving sobs racked my exhausted body, but after a while they softened to pathetic whimpers, mewls better suited to a kitten. I wrapped my arms around myself, pretended they were my mom's, or my dad's, or Donovan's, or Zee's, or anyone's. But they carried no warmth, no comfort. Not here, alone, at the bottom of the world.

I straightened up, feeling my spine crack, then picked up the grille. I smashed it against the toilet pipe, the clang of metal on metal shaking the sadness from me, helping my mind pull itself back together.

"What now?" I asked.

There was a pause, then Zee's muted reply.

"Wait for Simon."

"And if he doesn't come back?"

Another pause.

"He has to." Even through solid rock, with staccato words, I could hear the unvoiced question at the end of Zee's statement. I started hammering out "why" but then changed my mind, realizing that it was pointless. Instead I smacked out a question.

"Any other ideas?"

"Nope," came his reassuring reply. "You?"

The last of Zee's echoes almost concealed footsteps above me and I held my breath, wondering if I'd been wrong about Simon. Maybe he was back after all, about to pull open our hatches and take us back to the steeple. At least that way we could die trying to do something, trying to save ourselves. I heard the creak of a hatch opening, but it wasn't mine. There were more scuffled footsteps overhead, but none of the scratching and snuffling of a rat. I waited to hear the hatch slam back down, but nothing happened.

"Zee?" I hammered out. There was no reply. I tried again, cursing him for having a name that began with a Z. Still nothing. I felt my heart sink into my stomach, stewed in acid.

"Come on," I said, smashing the grille against the pipe randomly in the hope I'd get a response. I thought I heard something from outside, a cry of pain, but the ringing in my ears was too loud to be sure. "Zee!" I yelled, knowing he wouldn't be able to hear me. Had they taken him? Jesus, had they taken him to the infirmary?

Something whacked against the pipe in Zee's cell, hard enough to sound like a bomb going off in my head. It struck again, even louder than before. What the hell was he doing in there? Trying to tunnel his way into the sewer? I put the question to him in a series of frantic strikes with my own grille. No reply. Then the deafening clangs came again. Twenty-three, eight, one, twenty.

"What?"

My heart lifted, still adrenaline-fueled but not on the verge of giving out as it had been a moment ago. It was such a relief to hear him that I just sat for a moment smiling at the wall. Then I started hammering out another message.

"Thought I heard something." It took forever.

"Nothing," he replied, the sound of his strikes loud enough to make my brain vibrate. I wondered if maybe he'd knocked his toilet pipe loose or something, if that could explain the increase in volume. After waiting an age for him to say something else, I picked up my grille again and spoke.

"Sure nothing's wrong?"

"Nothing."

"Zee," I struck. "You're acting weird."

No response.

"Zee?" I rubbed my palm, prepared for more blisters. "Zee?" If we ever did get out of here I was making him change his name.

The blows from his cell began again and I listened carefully.

"Alex," the message started, the strikes still too loud, too powerful. "What makes you think I'm Zee?"

CHOICES

EVEN BEFORE THE LAST CHIME FADED I knew what had happened. Despite the heat in my cell, the sweat that poured down my face from smashing the pipe, I felt my blood run cold, gooseflesh erupting on my skin.

Zee was gone. The blacksuits had taken him.

It had been them trampling above my cell, Zee's hatch opening. It was probably one of the guards in there right now. I could picture them grinning as they led me on, their dull laughter fading into the passageway as they carted Zee off to his fate.

I tried to think. Had they heard anything that could give us away? Anything to indicate we were planning to escape? No. We'd been talking about Simon but that was before the footsteps above me. I doubt they'd heard our plans, and even if they had they probably wouldn't have decoded it. Still, it wouldn't be long before Zee was forced to talk. It was difficult to keep secrets when the freaks of Furnace were asking the questions.

Maybe it would be better if they knew. Maybe I should even tell them, try to make a deal with the blacksuits. Would they let us live if we told them about Simon and the other lost boys? They wouldn't release us, but they might send us back up top, to the relative luxury of gen pop with its daily slop and comfortable beds and cool showers. They might let us go home.

Home. I was stunned by the fact I'd thought it, but there was nothing outside anymore, nothing for me. Furnace *was* my home now, and I wanted to be back there.

"Hey!" I shouted, pounding on the hatch. "Don't hurt him. I've got information you want." It seemed like the first time in years that I'd raised my voice and my throat was instantly raw. It didn't stop me. I smashed my fists against the metal even harder, knowing that the sound would barely even reach the floor above.

Nobody came. I punched the hatch one last time and screamed with frustration. Why had they taken him and not me? It didn't make any sense. Not that anything did here. I knew well enough that there was no system to the atrocities in Furnace, no logic. The warden and his monsters did what they wanted whenever they wanted, anarchy disguised as regimented control.

I felt like crying again but forced the emotion away. Zee was in trouble, and me blubbing my eyes out in my cell wasn't going to do him any good at all. I needed Simon. I needed him to come back, to let me out.

"Come on," I said, trying to project the thought through the stone, down the tunnels and up the slope to where the lost boys were hiding. "Come on, don't leave me here."

I kept saying it, kept thinking it, kept picturing it being transmitted right into Simon's head. There's no such thing as psychic power. If you ask me, it's all a load of horse crap. Which is why, when I heard the lever of my hatch grind open, I couldn't quite believe it. Crimson light flooded in like blood and I peered through the mottled glow to see a familiar face above me, teeth like broken piano keys in a goofy grin.

"You look surprised," the kid said softly, offering me his giant hand. "Think I was gonna leave without you?"

"Never," I replied, feeling the muscles in his arm tense as he hoisted me out. Zee's hatch was still open, and a quick glance inside told me what I already knew. Simon saw the look in my eye and shook his head.

"I couldn't get back in time," he whispered. "I was on my way, the suits nearly caught me. They were coming here, coming for him."

"But the warden wanted us in here for a month," I said, eyeing the passageway warily. "They shouldn't have taken him."

Simon shrugged, walking down the corridor toward the junction that led to the infirmary. He hadn't bothered to close my hatch this time and I didn't either. I wasn't coming back, no matter what.

"Never enough specimens," he muttered sadly. "Wheezers are always after fresh blood. Can't believe they let you live this long."

"But the warden . . ."

"Doesn't always get his own way," Simon replied. "Now we've gotta move."

"We're going after Zee, right?" I asked, trotting to catch up and knowing what his answer would be. He spun around, silver eyes burning into my own.

"You've got a choice to make, Alex," he said, the voice too old for his face. "And you've got to make it right now. You either go after your friend, and you die—die inside, anyway—or you cut loose and come with me. We've got a shot at this, a real good one I think. Once you're outside you can come back, with the police, the army, everyone. But if you try to help Zee now, or Donovan, or any of them, then you're as good as dead." He looked over his shoulder, ear cocked. "We need to go right now, so make your choice."

I felt like I'd gone back in time, promising feverishly to Donovan that I'd come back, bring the authorities before the warden could do anything to him. I'd failed, and if I went with Simon, who's to say I wouldn't fail again, leaving Zee to rot?

But what would happen if I went after him? I pictured myself walking into the infirmary, trying to find Zee, trying to fight off the wheezers as the blacksuits laughed at me. Feeling them lift me up, the darkness flooding my veins even as they strapped me to the mattress.

And I made my decision. Not because I knew I could escape and return with the cavalry. Not because I thought it was the best—the only—way to help Zee. But because I could still smell the stench of the wheezer on me, and I couldn't go back.

Some hero.

"Let's go," I said, the words barely making it out of my mouth I was so ashamed of them. "Let's get out of here. We'll come back, with help."

Simon nodded, then sped down the corridor. We reached the junction, the path leading off to the main prison dead ahead, the infirmary off to our left. We'd have to pass it to get out, and for a moment my brain pictured Zee inside, staring at the plastic curtain as we ran past, calling out silently to our backs. It was almost too much.

"Clear," said Simon, running again. I didn't look as we sped past the door, closing my ears to the sounds of screaming I could hear from inside—so high-pitched that I couldn't tell if it came from the wheezers or their victims. I didn't think about anything other than putting one foot in front of the other, and somehow I managed to stay upright, to keep Simon in my line of sight. The sound of the blacksuits seemed to be everywhere, deep voices that chuckled from inside the rooms we passed. But by some miracle they didn't see us, didn't hear us.

I just kept running. Because surely if I didn't look back I didn't have to think about what I'd done.

It was the sound of a phone that stopped me. The shrill, old-fashioned ring was so out of place here that I almost tripped over my own feet and had to brace a hand on the wall to stop from falling.

We'd reached the junction that led up to the vault door. To our left was the final stretch of tunnel before the cavern. To our right lay the access to the warden's quarters. The phone was ringing from that direction, the same place where I'd sensed something wrong before, where I thought I'd seen . . . what? A cloud of some-thing, something bad. Simon had bounded ahead, skidding to a halt only when he noticed I wasn't with him.

"Come on!" he hissed. But I couldn't move. The phone was like an invisible hook that kept me in place, that tugged on my mind, threatening to reel me in. Every time it rang the corridor seemed to grow darker, the walls pulsing and stretching like a living thing, some vast intestinal tract. A pain was growing right in the center of my forehead, but inside my skull, not outside. With each shrill cry the sensation spread, as though beneath my skin I was crum-bling into dust.

There was a door in the rock halfway down the corridor, the phone's ring emanating from there. It seemed like it had been going on forever, a siren that had become an entity inside my own head. Simon was behind me, I could feel his hand on my arm, but I couldn't hear him. The only thing that existed was the phone.

Then it stopped, and the pain exploded. I made out a voice and I knew it straightaway. The warden. It was faint but at the same time it was like he was screaming in my ear.

"Yes, sir," he said. Two syllables like dynamite. "I understand, sir. It will be done."

I couldn't hear who was on the other end, obviously. But I could *feel* it. After everything I'd witnessed in Furnace, the horrors I had endured, this was so much worse. Because whatever it was didn't scare me, it called to me. And even though I knew it was rotten, evil, I found myself moving toward it, my limbs jerking like a puppet's, something coiled around my brain, soft and rancid.

Then I felt the corridor flip upside down, felt Simon's misshapen body beneath me, felt the wind rush past my ears as he fled. Each clumsy step carried me farther from the voice, from its dark call, until all that was left was a gentle whisper that echoed like the last breath of a dying man.

We flew through the vault door, the cavern ahead deserted. Simon didn't put me down until we reached the cracked rock where the ceiling dropped to the floor, and then only because we couldn't squeeze through together. He let me go first, hand on my head to make sure I didn't bang it, then he was in after me.

He waited, panting, the harsh light of the halogens following us through and giving his scarred, patchwork skin a weird translucent sheen. I stared at him, wanting to thank him but unable to quite recall how to talk.

"Just give it a minute," he said. "The first time you hear it you feel like you're going to die. It takes a while for the sickness to go."

He was right, something was sitting in my gut like a spiked ball, as if all the pain that had been in my head moments ago had sunk there, waiting to be digested. I rubbed my stomach, trying to settle it, and only when the nausea had ebbed away did I dare speak.

"What was it? The warden?"

Simon emitted a laugh, but there was no humor in it.

"Him? No. He looks the part but he's nothing. He's just another employee." He stopped as the sound of rocks hitting the ground seeped through the crack. It could have been anything, but we were still a little too close to the compound for comfort. I could just about see him scuttling up the rough slope ahead of us like a spider. "Don't worry about it, okay? Let's get up to the steeple."

I followed, far less graceful than him but able to manage the handholds easily enough despite the dark. We emerged in the tunnel at the top, taking a few jagged turns to get back to the cave. It was empty.

"They're waiting for us there," Simon explained, leading the way through. I questioned him about the voice again but he didn't respond, and it was only when we squeezed through the last crevice and found ourselves back in the immense gorge that he answered me. "Maybe it's best you don't know, okay? At least until we're out in the open. We need to focus on this, or we're all gonna end up dead. And we've sacrificed too much to mess it up now. Forget about it, Alex. Forget about everything you've ever seen down here. Just think about getting out."

He turned away, called out softly into the darkness. Almost immediately a torch blinked into life. It did nothing to illuminate the cavern, but it did pick out two dirty faces huddling by the wall.

"You made it," said Ozzie. "What about the other one?"

"Suits got him," Simon replied bluntly. "We got Alex though."

Both Ozzie and Pete nodded at me but I didn't acknowledge them. I couldn't stop thinking about what I'd felt outside the warden's quarters. The phone, the voice, the hooks in my mind. Even when I noticed the equipment piled up beneath Pete's crooked body—the clamps that had been twisted into hooks, the thick tube pierced by pins—I couldn't clear my head. All I could focus on was the warden, and the person he had been talking to.

And the fact that I'd left Zee in there alone.

"He okay?" I heard Ozzie ask, a small voice right on the edge of my consciousness. I felt their eyes on me but didn't look up. Not even when I heard Simon's whispered response:

"I don't know. He just heard the warden on the phone. He just heard him speaking to Alfred Furnace."

THE ONLY WAY IS UP

SIMON WAS RIGHT. I couldn't afford to be distracted. I'd made my choice, I was here, so the only thing to do was make the best of it. If somehow the vast steeple of rock that towered over our heads led to the surface, or at least to a higher set of tunnels that connected to the outside world, then I could get help. I could come back for Zee and for Donovan. It wouldn't be too late.

And however crazy the idea sounded, however much I doubted it could work, it felt good knowing I'd never have to return to the hole, or to the infirmary. Not without a goddamned army behind me. No, it was either climb to heaven or plunge to our deaths. There was no other way this was going to play out.

I soon discovered I wasn't the only one who had to leave a friend behind. Pete's spindly legs and arms could never hope to drag his overstuffed torso up the wall. He could barely even walk. The kid cheered us on, talked us up as we got our kit ready, but his voice was cracked and filled with desperation.

"I'm coming back," Simon must have told him a dozen times in the space of a few minutes. "I promise you, you have my word. I won't leave you here."

It was like a mirror image of my life, and for the first time I wondered how many other people had tried to break out of Furnace, saying the same words to their cellmates and friends and brothers. I'll bet it was far more than I realized, far more than the warden and the blacksuits ever revealed. It was a strange recognition, and even though I knew that nobody had ever made it out, that nobody had ever kept their promise and returned, it filled me with hope.

Maybe we *could* do this.

The plan was that Simon and I would make our way up the steeple, Ozzie keeping watch below with Pete. The younger kid had wanted to go, but he was more scared of heights than he was of the nightmares in the prison and knew he'd never make it. Besides, he didn't have the heart to leave Pete on his own.

We had two twenty-meter coils of surgical tubing. It was thick stuff, but even so Simon had doubled it up and twisted it into a spiral. The bulk of it would hang between us, and we both had a shorter length to hammer into the rock at regular intervals. Whoever was ahead would fix one strand of makeshift rope every fifteen meters or so, ensuring that if either of us fell we wouldn't go far.

Not unless the tube snapped or the pins slipped out of the wall or the rock came loose or our knots failed.

"Ready?" Simon asked, scaring the doubts from my mind. I looked at him, at his lopsided smile, and wondered why I had ever questioned his motives. He'd come back for me, risking his life even though he could have scaled the wall alone.

"Nope," I said, my voice trembling. I took a deep drink of water from the IV bag they had brought with them, relishing the strength it lent to my muscles.

"Me neither," he replied, his silver eyes flashing. "So let's do it."

He handed me a pair of clamps and I toyed with them. They were like scissors, only with a wide, blunt end instead of blades. They were sprung so that when you squeezed the handles the two prongs expanded—designed to keep wounds and ribcages open during surgery, but equally useful for wedging into small cracks in the rock. Next came a handful of long, tough bone pins and one of the hammers with a hooked end which I looped onto my overalls.

Simon took a minute to say goodbye, hugging the other two kids, the three of them sobbing. I stood by awkwardly, then waved a farewell once they had parted.

"We'll see you again," said Ozzie. "Real soon."

"Not too soon, though," joked Simon.

They laughed, wishing us a final good luck. Simon tied the flashlight to his overalls with a small section of tube, and for a moment we stood side by side, heads craned back as we stared at the steeple—the rough, red rock disappearing into an endless night above us.

"Here goes nothing," I said.

"Here goes everything," he answered.

And we started to climb.

IT WAS HARDER THAN I'D IMAGINED. Much harder. The fissures in the pinnacle were jagged and uneven, and before I'd climbed a couple of meters blood was threatening my grip. My muscles, weakened from lack of food and stripped bare by adrenaline, struggled to lift me, and each time I straightened a leg or tensed my arms I thought they were going to fold. The only thing that gave me any comfort was the fact that the rockface angled inward rather than hanging out over the gulf of darkness below. This meant that when I felt myself losing strength I could rest my body against the slope without fear of tumbling off.

Simon had already taken the lead, his massive arm pulling him up while his smaller limb wedged him tightly in place. Each time he moved, the flashlight swung, making the shadows on the wall dart and stretch so that it was impossible to work out which holes were big enough to support me.

One of my feet slipped from a narrow scar and for a moment I thought I was a goner. We weren't yet ten meters off the ground but that was plenty far enough to break a leg or two. I grabbed the rock like it was my best friend, cheek pressed flat against its warm touch. My heart was trying to thump its way out and I didn't blame it. I mean, how many meters are in a mile? There was a long, long way to go.

But I wasn't complaining. We were climbing, we were escaping. I pictured the blacksuits coming to pull me from solitary, the shock on their faces as they realized I was gone. They'd probably assume I'd been eaten by a rat, but they'd never know for sure—not until I stormed back in with a rocket-propelled grenade and blew the bastards to pieces.

I shuffled up another few meters, Simon pausing as he waited for me to catch up. I glanced down, saw that the light from his flashlight no longer reached the ledge. But there were two silver pennies glinting up at us that I knew belonged to Pete. I would have waved if I thought I could do it without killing myself.

"We should start roping," he said as I drew level, and I was relieved to hear that he was panting too. "High enough now to do some serious damage if we fall. I'll plug while you climb, then when you reach the end of the rope you plug, I'll pull loose and we'll step up. That make sense?"

"Yes," I lied, wishing we'd gone over it on the ledge below. I figured I knew what he meant though, and while he pushed a bone pin into his end of the tube and started hammering it into the rock I kept on climbing. It was tricky without the light, but I took it slowly, feeling my way up the steeple and testing every nook and cranny twice, three times, before trusting it with my full weight. After a few minutes I felt the length of rope connecting me to Simon go taut and I braced myself against the rock, slipping loose the section that dangled from around my waist and pushing a pin through it. A couple of hammer blows later and I was secured to the wall. As secured as I was ever going to be, that was.

"It's in," I yelled, looking down at Simon in his bubble of golden light. He pulled his tube free, knowing that if he fell now my length of rope would hold him, and clambered up. His breathing was ragged when he reached me, but he was still smiling.

"Great idea for the ropes," he panted.

"Great idea for the climb," I replied. Then he was off again, overtaking me and scuttling up at speed. I made the most of my rest, relaxing my muscles and stretching my neck, hearing everything crack in protest. There was a tug on my waist as the rope reached its limit again, then the chime of metal on metal.

"Your turn," he called down.

I rammed the hammer's hooked handle into the crevice where I'd wedged the bone pin. It was pretty tight, but after a couple of twists the tube popped free and hung limply by my side. This was actually working! I started climbing again, buoyed up by our success. And it was only when I lifted my head to throw Simon a grin that I noticed something was wrong.

"Turn your light off," I yelled. He looked down at me, shadow throwing his face into a frown.

"What?"

"Just do it, turn it off. Look." I couldn't point but I nodded, gesturing further up the steeple. He grumbled but clicked off the flashlight, plunging the entire chasm into darkness.

Well, *almost* the entire chasm. Maybe ten meters or so above Simon's head I could make out a soft glow emanating from the rock. It would have been easy to mistake it for daylight, the warm glow of a sunset, but I wasn't going to fall for that again. We were still way too deep. I carried on climbing, taking care not to make any noise. Simon obviously sensed my fear, waiting for me to reach him before speaking.

"What do you think it is?" he asked.

I shrugged, the motion knocking loose a pebble from the wall. It seemed to take a long time to hit the ledge below. The light could have been something from the prison, as we must have reached the level of the yard in general population by now. I pictured it on the other side of this slab of solid rock, the inmates running around inside like ants with no idea that we were scaling the wall, that we were gunning for freedom.

"Maybe they knocked a hole in one of the chipping rooms," Simon went on. "Maybe your explosion blew out the wall."

Maybe, but not likely. Whatever the light was, it didn't look strong enough to be coming from any of the rooms in Furnace, and even as I watched, it seemed to flicker like a cinema projector.

"Let's take it slow," I said. "And keep it quiet."

We did, easing up the wall together, too nervous of drawing

attention to ourselves by hammering in the pins. We'd covered maybe five or six meters by the time we noticed the gap in the rock ahead. The steeple was broken: a massive chunk of it was missing. The pillar of rock rose up again above the gaping crack, but there was no way we were getting past it unless we could scale the walls inside the cave.

That's where the light was coming from. And not just light, I realized, but noise—a wet snuffling that could have been a vacuum cleaner held under water. I felt my stomach turn as I recognized the sound, but I refused to believe it.

We eased up toward the split, the noise getting louder every second. The light was shaking now, trembling up and down and back and forth. I heard something tear, and the beam vanished altogether for a second before snapping back on, gold tinged with red.

Three meters, two, one. We were there.

It sounded like there was a party going on just above our heads—stamping feet, grunts, snaps like somebody tearing chicken wings. I looked at Simon, grateful that I couldn't see his expression of fear and wishing that he couldn't see mine. We didn't speak, just nodded, tightened our grip on the wall and peered up over the lip of rock.

The first thing I noticed was that the light came from a flashlight, being held by an arm clad in black. But the arm itself wasn't attached to anything. It was being eaten by a naked, grotesquely muscled creature that looked like it might once have been a monkey or a chimp. It was squatting on its haunches in the middle of a small cavern, too engrossed in its meal to notice us.

Behind it, on the floor, was the rest of the blacksuit. What remained of him, anyway. Even that was rapidly disappearing. Six or seven shadowed forms just as twisted as the first were stooped over the carcass, taking it to pieces like some living food processor. Every now and again one would turn to the walls and growl at the constellation of stars assembled there—silver eyes blinking on and off as they watched the carnage. Twenty of them, thirty maybe.

Rats. A whole nest of them. Smack bang between us and the way out.

RETREAT

IT WAS ALL I COULD DO not to let go of the wall. I sank back down, Simon still by my side. We didn't speak. We didn't *dare*. One word might be all it took to bring the horde down on our heads.

I took another look at the steeple, which rose on upward toward the roof of the cave. It was too far away to reach. It curved around to either side of us, the rock as smooth and slippery as ice. We had a choice between charging into the nest, climbing to the ceiling then somehow angling back around to continue our ascent, or retreating. It wasn't a choice at all.

Something shrieked in the cave, halfway between a monkey's cry and the howl of a kid in pain. We slipped and scrabbled in the dark, our fingers barely able to hold us in place as we desperately searched for footholds beneath us. Only when we'd put some distance between us and the rats did Simon risk clicking on the flashlight. With its soft glow enveloping us the descent was much easier, but we still kept our thoughts to ourselves until the ledge appeared from the black tide. As soon as we were close enough I dropped, my legs and arms cramping the moment I struck solid ground. I cried out, slumping against the wall.

Simon fell beside me, his face twisted into an expression of agony—although whether from pain or from our failure I wasn't sure. Moments later I heard the scuffle of feet and Ozzie and Pete were there, small hands on my shoulders and their shrill questions too loud.

"Dead end?" asked Pete. "I knew it. I knew it was too good to be true."

"Keep it down," said Simon, sucking down air between each word. "Not a dead end. Rats."

Both the other boys swore in unison, looking up into the darkness. From here the flashlight wasn't visible. Either that or the rat had finished its sick meal and had tossed the bones away. We sat in silence for a while, heads back and eyes on the sky for any sign of the creatures. My entire body was a wreck, my hands locked into cruel talons that wouldn't straighten out no matter how much I pressed on my fingers.

"So it's no-go?" asked Ozzie eventually. Simon shook his head, his face expressionless.

"There must have been dozens of them in there," he muttered. "No wonder the blacksuits haven't been able to find them."

"Can't we wait for them to go, wait for a breach?" the younger kid went on. "We could tell the suits where they are, let the guards deal with them."

"Feel free," Simon said.

"It wouldn't do any good, I don't think," I added. "There's a massive section of the steeple missing. Even if the cave was empty I'm not sure we could pass it."

"And we don't even know if it goes all the way to the top," said Pete with a weary sigh. "Well, I guess it's back to our apartment for now."

"It would have worked," snapped Simon. "It still could work. What, one little hitch and the whole thing goes up in smoke?" He looked like he was going to say more, but the volume of his voice dropped and all that came out was a string of muffled curses. I didn't listen. Something was nagging at the back of my mind, something important.

"What do you think, Alex?" asked Ozzie, but I shut him up with an impatient wave.

"Give me a minute," I said, scratching at my fragmented thoughts in order to try to find whatever it was that had called for my attention. Something in what Simon had just said. I almost had it, an idea flashing before my eyes so fleetingly that it was gone before I could identify it.

"You got something?" asked Pete, and this time it was Simon who told him to be quiet, his silver eyes wide and impatient.

"I'm not sure," I said. "I thought . . ." There it was again, like one of those stupid 3-D pictures where you have to squint to see the pattern. It seemed to focus, then shimmered out of sight. I thumped my head in frustration, going back over what Simon had said.

It still could work. What, one little hitch and the whole thing goes up in smoke?

Then it hit me, the image like a sledgehammer, impossible to miss. It exploded in my head with such force that I bit my tongue, the sting seeming to clarify the thoughts even more. The lost boys must have noticed something in me change as all three crowded in.

"What?" asked Simon. "You know what to do? How to get rid of the rats?"

"No," I replied through a smile. "I know how to get us out."

"What?" he repeated, his own face opening up into a grin. "Another way? Tell us for God's sake or I'm gonna throw you over the bloody edge."

"Going up in smoke," I said, picturing a trail of burning vapor rising up through the fractured rock, curling free from a vent on the surface. "We can get out through the incinerator."

FOR WHAT SEEMED LIKE FOREVER, nobody said a word. Two pairs of silver eyes and another of watery blue blinked at me as if I'd grown a four-foot beard in the last second.

"You think the chimney goes to the surface?" said Simon after a while.

"I know it does," I replied, remembering the day I'd been taken to Furnace, the view from the bus window of the Black Fort, shrouded in smoke that seemed to rise from the ground behind it. "It has to. Where else are they gonna put it without choking everyone to death?"

"Yeah, it makes sense," added Ozzie, his voice accelerating with excitement. "I'll bet you anything they placed the incinerator beneath another section of the gorge, saves drilling down through solid rock. And it would have to go to the surface. This place must have been inspected before it was opened, and an incinerator of any kind would need proper ventilation."

"You reckon this place was inspected?" asked Pete, an eyebrow cocked.

"Of course," the younger kid went on. "Every new prison would be inspected to make sure it was up to scratch. Obviously nobody's ever been back since to check, but they wouldn't have blocked off the incinerator chimney. What would be the point?"

"It's not like any of the inmates would ever find it," said Pete.

"Not alive, anyway," Ozzie added. "And even if they did, who would think to climb it?"

"They'd have to be crazy," I said.

"The only problem is getting to it," sighed Simon, standing up and loosening the tube tied around his waist. It coiled to the floor with a slap. "We gotta go through the infirmary."

I knew we'd have to go back into the prison, but I hadn't consciously acknowledged it until Simon had spoken. *No*, something in my head shouted. *You can't return. You're out now. Just stay out. You're not free, but you're not their prisoner either. You can survive out here. If you go back now, then you face the wheezers, the blacksuits, the warden.*

And whoever had been on the other end of the phone.

But I had to return. I was being forced back because of what I'd done to Zee. That's why we hadn't been able to make it up the steeple. That's why the rats were up there. Because I wasn't allowed to leave without him. I know I was delirious, my mind so exhausted that it couldn't think straight, but right then it made a perfect kind of sense. And it was that crazy logic that gave me the strength to stand up, because I knew what I had to do.

"So what are we waiting for?" I asked, resting a hand on the wall until my head stopped spinning, then squeezing back through the gap. "Let's make like a tree and leaf."

"Make like an atom and split," said Ozzie behind me.

"Make like diarrhea and run," came Pete's muffled voice, making us groan. Simon was the last one in, and we were halfway back to the cave before he suddenly chirped up.

"I've got one: let's make like a hockey player and get the puck outta here."

We were still laughing as we skidded down the slope that led back to the main cavern. I don't know why, I mean we were dead on our feet, and chances were that we would be dead on our backs within the hour, murdered by the blacksuits or the rats or worse. Maybe that *was* why. Maybe we were trying to laugh as much as we could before we met our dismal end. Because you never know which laugh is going to be your last.

It faded as we reached the low ceiling, replaced by the panicked cry of a distant siren. We dropped down onto our knees to scan the cavern ahead. At first I thought it was empty, and I was about to crawl under a rock when Simon grabbed my arm.

"You insane?" he whispered, using his other hand to point toward what I'd thought was a layer of darker rock against the fleshy red. Squinting into the merciless halogen beam, I saw a line of blacksuits standing motionlessly by the vault door, each holding a shotgun in one hand and a leashed dog in the other.

As we watched, three more strode from inside the compound, and behind them, looking nervous, was the warden. He barked something inaudible at the guards and gestured wildly to the various passageways that led from the giant room. Then he turned, his eyes sweeping the shadows. For a moment I thought he'd seen us because I felt cold fingers in my head, the floor and walls peeling away. Then the sensation passed. The warden shoved one of the blacksuits, and this time when he screamed I could hear him all too well.

"Find him!"

My empty cell had been discovered. And now there was an army standing in our way.

"Won't be long before they track us," said Simon. "Dogs'll pick up your scent from your cell."

"So what do we do?" I asked. "Hide out until it blows over?"

"You know as well as I do this ain't never gonna blow over. That's twice now you've vanished, and this time right under the warden's nose. They'll tear this place apart to find you."

"So what do we do?" I repeated. He looked at me, flashing a crescent of broken teeth beneath his starry eyes.

"We give 'em something to keep 'em busy."

I thought I knew where this was going.

"If there's a breach, then they'll be distracted. It will give us time to get in."

"But the rats aren't here," I said. "And we haven't got time to wait for them to get hungry. We need to go now."

His grin widened.

"That's why we need some bait."

BAIT

WE PLAYED PAPER, SCISSORS, ROCK for it. All of us, although there was no way Pete was going to be running from the rats with those stick-insect legs of his. Simon lost to him anyway, Pete's tiny hand covering about a third of his giant fist as paper beat rock. Ozzie got victory over me exactly the same way, and although he feigned disappointment, saying how he never got to be the hero, the relief coming off him was so potent I could almost see it.

"Gonna whup yo' ass, boy," said Simon, warming up his muscles like we were about to start a boxing match.

"You're mine," I replied, flexing my aching fingers. "On one. Three, two, one."

We flicked a hand out at each other and I squinted into the gloom to see Simon's fingers forked like scissors. They were snapping away at my paper like a piranha devouring a horse. He might as well have used them to open up my neck, because what I was about to do was suicide.

"Crap," I muttered.

"Yeah," the kid replied. "That sucks. You want me to do it?"

"Well—"

"Well, tough; rules is rules."

"Thanks a million." We almost started laughing, but it was stifled by the proximity of the warden and his blacksuits. Instead we ducked in toward each other, our whispered plans filling the pocket of rock like the hiss of a distant river.

"You only have to get them as far as here," said Simon. "Lead them down the slope and they'll sniff the blacksuits in the cavern. As soon as they're in, it will be chaos. It should give us enough time."

There was that word again, *should*.

"We'll hide over there," he went on, pointing the light at a cluster of broken rocks at the bottom of the slope. "We'll be ready to pull you in as soon as you appear. With any luck the rats won't see us and will plow right through into the cavern."

"And if they do see us?" I asked.

"Then we're screwed," he replied matter-of-factly. "Everybody set on what they have to do?"

"What do you mean, 'everybody'?" I said, a tremor belying my attempt at humor. "You three have just got to stay low and keep quiet."

"Okay," he corrected, handing me the flashlight. "Are *you* set on what you have to do?"

I didn't answer, just strapped the light to my waist, looked back up the slope, and tried to swallow.

"Good luck," said Simon. "Remember, lead them back through here. We'll be waiting for you."

Then they were gone, drowned in darkness as they scrabbled behind the cairn of stones. I started to climb, my heart juddering like an old engine about to stall. I was terrified already, the fear a bright white light that sat behind my eyes. I thought of the creature I'd seen in the steeple—the monkey? the ape? the kid?—the way it had torn into the blacksuit's arm like someone eating a hot dog.

My imagination swung into overdrive and I saw the rats pinning me down, felt their teeth pierce my skin, smelled their rancid breath, and realized it was *my* blood that dripped from their deformed muzzles.

What the hell was I doing?

I forced myself to concentrate on the path ahead, navigating the cluster of narrow passageways at the top of the slope. I wondered if I should be leaving a trail of something to help find my way back, then realized I'd be blistering down here at such an unholy pace I wouldn't have time to see the markings anyway. If I made it this far, that was.

I passed through the tiny cave where the lost boys had been sleeping, taking the tunnel out the back and the narrow passage that split off from that. I wasn't even sure if this was the right way—the couple of times I'd been here Simon had led, and I hadn't been paying all that much attention. Suddenly the tunnel seemed smaller. I noticed twists and turns that weren't there before. I was lost.

Then it angled down, the walls closing in, and I recognized that familiar stab of claustrophobia. The gorge was just along here. Maybe I should have made more of an effort to lose my way.

I pushed through the knuckle of tight rock and found myself in the endless swamp of liquid night—the abyss stretching out beyond the narrow shelf of rock and echoing to infinity above me. I looked up, picturing the rats gnawing away on the bones of the blacksuit. What should I do? Shout? Whistle? Scream?

"Hello?" I mumbled. No response. I tried again, louder this time. "Hello! Rats, are you up there?" It still wasn't loud enough. If the creatures hadn't heard Simon and me smashing our bone pins into the wall, then they wouldn't hear my pathetic cry. This time, when the words came, they were loud enough to carry. "I'm down here," I yelled, half shout and half scream. "Come and get me!"

I tensed my legs, ready to make a run for it. There was an insect click from the gap in the rock I'd just stepped through. I'd been counting on them coming at me down the wall. If they appeared behind me I was dead.

"Today's special: a skinny kid who's about to crap his pants," I bellowed, almost in tears. "Get it while it's hot."

Something shrieked in response, the sound dropping from above like a guillotine blade. Another noise, more shrill than the first but just as chilling. One more, a bass growl that seemed to make the very rock shake. In a couple of seconds the chasm was alive with a sickening chorus of grunts, screams, and wails that sounded heartbreakingly human. It reminded me of feeding time at the zoo, and I guess I wasn't far wrong.

Something sparked on above me, the twin specks of light distant but visible against the black canvas of the gorge. They blinked out, and when they lit up again there were two more beside them. Then four. Then too many to count. And when they all raced toward me down the steeple I thought for a moment that the sky was falling, the stars crashing to earth. It would have been beautiful if I didn't think it was the last thing I would ever see.

I ran, the rock scraping against my chest as I pushed myself through the gap, the flashlight swinging wildly, making the tunnel come to life. It was like being in one of those funhouse crazy walks where the floor and the walls are moving and you can barely stand up. Except on this ride if I so much as tripped I'd be skinned alive.

The screams on my tail were louder, the scrabble of their feet against rock so much quicker than my own clumsy steps. I couldn't believe they'd sped so easily down the same near-vertical slope that Simon and I had struggled so hard to climb.

I burst into the little cave, the savage cries like fingers trying to hook me back. Two giant leaps and I was out again, lungs burning as I charged down the passageway beyond. There was an instant of utter panic as I reached a junction, my brain too concerned with trying to make my legs work to remember which exit to take. I know I shouldn't have, but something made me glance over my shoulder.

It looked like a tidal wave of silver crashing and spitting toward me, gaining with impossible speed. My flashlight swung and the bodies attached to those eyes caught the light, the walls and floor alive with glistening red skin moving fast, too fast.

I threw myself at the middle passage, but before I reached it something thumped into me. It was like being hit by a train and I was on the floor before I knew what was happening, pinned down by a figure of knotted muscle.

I saw a needled jaw open in the fleshy mess of its face, lunging toward my neck. I squirmed, lashed out with my hands, twisted my body, and, more from luck than anything else, managed to raise my shoulder to block its attack. Its teeth sunk into the flesh of my upper arm and my skin turned to fire. But the pain seared through me like an electric charge, making my body buck.

The creature lost its balance, its lopsided body toppling to the side. It grabbed at me with gnarled hands but I kicked out, my heel connecting with its nose.

I didn't stop to see what damage I'd done. The other rats were almost on me, their howls rising to a crescendo as they watched me make my escape. As the darkness of the tunnel closed in, I realized I'd lost the flashlight, but there was no going back for it. I was almost there, maybe another ten or fifteen paces before the slope that dropped down to the cavern.

It was more like five. I felt my foot plunge off the edge, my stomach flipping as I fell. It wasn't a long drop, my descent broken by the uneven slope. Before I could even pull myself to my feet I felt hands on me, dragging me across the floor, panicked whispers in my ear.

"Quick! Get him in!"

It was too dark to see where I was going, but I didn't care. Blood was pouring down my arm, the wound like hot coals embedded under the skin. I stopped moving, three bodies pressed against mine as the screams resonated off the walls.

There was a thump as something landed close to us, the menacing growl of an injured animal from the other side of the pile of broken rocks. Then the bodies began to patter on the ground like hail, a storm of claws that thrashed less than a meter from where we cowered. Someone was holding my head, pulling me close, and I took some comfort from the fact that at least I wasn't going to die on my own.

There was a distant call, then a shot. Two more, followed by choked wails. I heard the scuffle of legs as the rats charged away from us, pictured them flooding under the low ceiling into the cavern, red in tooth and claw, eyes blazing as they stampeded toward the blacksuits.

The sound of shotgun fire was like a New Year's fireworks display. The figure holding me moved, getting to his feet and pulling me up with him.

"Good job," said Simon from the shadows. "I can't believe that worked. You okay?"

"I'm okay," I lied, tearing a strip from my overalls and attempting to tie it around the wound. The pain was spreading, making my entire arm throb. I could feel it in my neck too, and wondered if the rat had spread its disease to me, if the flesh on my face would start rotting, if I'd suddenly develop a taste for blood. Simon flinched when he saw what I was doing, then grabbed the makeshift bandage and tied it tight.

"You should go," said Ozzie, peering out from behind the cluster of stones and nodding an all clear. "The distraction won't last for long."

"You're not coming with us?" I said.

"No, I'm going to stay with Pete. Just make sure you come back for us."

"You can bet your life on it," I promised.

"That's exactly what I'm doing," he replied.

Simon was already moving, his eyes glinting as he jogged toward the low roof that separated us from the cavern. All the rats had made their way through, and by the sounds of it they were going to work on the blacksuits. The shotgun blasts were growing less frequent, replaced by wet cries and snapping bones. I wasn't sure I wanted to see what was happening through there, but I didn't have a choice.

We ducked down, peered under the rock. The halogen lights gave the scene the feel of a theater performance, and I was happy to believe the illusion. Everywhere I looked there was movement. Directly ahead a blacksuit was on the floor, gun lying uselessly out of reach as the rats piled on top of him. Past that, another of the guards was firing at one of the creatures, the flash of his weapon turning the rat into sushi. The line of suits near the door was holding, the giants using the butts of their guns and their massive fists to keep the approaching horde at bay. The dogs too were in their element, teeth locked around throats and limbs.

There was no way in hell I was running through there.

I turned to Simon but he motioned for me to be quiet, nodding out at the carnage. Sure enough the blacksuits were winning, their firepower too much for the rats to withstand. The creatures—those still alive and still with a sufficient number of limbs attached—were scuttling toward the outer walls of the cave, heading for the shadows and the passageways that led from it.

And the guards were following, reloading their guns as they ran, pumping shells into chambers and firing round after round at the fleeing figures. I could hear them shouting at one another, their deep voices full of what I thought was fear but which could just as easily have been excitement, or relish.

Seconds later, by some miracle, the cavern was clear—except for the unrecognizable shapes that squirmed and squealed in their beds of blood. The sound of gunfire echoed through the darkened tunnels, and it wouldn't be long before the suits returned, or the rats if they somehow managed to get the upper hand.

There were no goodbyes this time, no hugs and promises. Simon and I both glanced back to take a final look at Ozzie and Pete, but they had already gone. And with nothing else to keep us we dropped under the low ceiling, clambered to our feet, and started to run.

GOODBYES

IT SEEMED LIKE THE LONGEST DISTANCE I'd ever had to cross in my life. It only took us fifteen seconds to run the length of the cavern—if you can call my drunken, desperate limp a run—but it seemed like an eternity. Time ground to a halt as if inviting me to study the writhing shapes we passed, the shredded suits, creatures turned inside out, the pitiful cries of monsters who had once been like us.

A hulking shape loomed from a tunnel to my right, a blacksuit with a rat clamped to his shoulders like a backpack. Locked together in some horrific ballet of punches and bites, neither of them noticed us. I felt fingers on my ankle from another unrecognizable shape beneath me, but they were too weak to hold me back.

There was only one time I thought we'd had it, just as we reached the damaged vault door that led back into the compound. A blacksuit sat against the wall, his legs shredded, shotgun resting in his lap. He raised it as he saw us approach, his expression one of surprise. Simon was on him in a flash, a blow from his giant arm sending the guard slumping to the side.

Then we were in, bathed in crimson light and deafened by the siren that blasted from hidden speakers. There were two blacksuits in the passageway ahead, but they were running in the opposite direction. I noticed the warden between them, buffeted back to his quarters, and the trio vanished into his room without a backward glance.

We sped after them, reaching the junction where I'd heard the phone, but the air was clear now, no hint of whatever it was I'd felt before. Or maybe I was just too pumped up to notice it, my body nothing more than an engine as we crashed down the corridor that led to the infirmary. I thought there might be a guard outside the door, one final obstacle between us and the incinerator, but the way ahead was clear.

The plastic curtain slapped my face as we pushed through it, and I batted the slats away from my eyes to see the room ahead abandoned, no sign of the wheezers. Maybe they'd fled back to their quarters, scared into hiding by the siren, which swept around the room like a trapped wasp.

I realized I was still running and forced my legs to stop and rest. Simon jogged ahead, reaching the curtain at the other side of the room and peeking through it before turning to me.

"It's clear," he said as if he couldn't believe it.

"I've got to find him," I stuttered back. "I'm not going without him, not now."

I was expecting an argument but Simon nodded, moving toward the right-hand line of beds still concealed behind their screens.

"You look that side, I'll check over here."

I wrenched open the first screen, not caring about noise. It was still empty. So was the one after that. I paused outside Gary's compartment, unable to bring myself to look inside. I knew we'd have to leave him. Knew he deserved to be left. But if I saw him there, I didn't think I'd be able to go without him.

"Alex!" I spun, saw Simon half inside a cubicle waving at me. I sprinted over, avoiding the trolleys that littered the aisle, and dashed through the curtains. Behind them was Zee. He was strapped to the bed but there were no marks on his skin, no IV stand by his side. Just a small face looking up at us with eyes as wide as pickled eggs.

"No way," he said. "This has got to be a dream."

"You okay?" I asked as Simon ran back outside, returning seconds later with a scalpel. "They touch you?"

"No," Zee replied, his grin so wide it looked like it was going to stretch right off his face. "No, they stuck me with some of that black stuff, but it just knocked me out for a bit. Don't feel any different." He tried to ease his body to one side as Simon cut through the leather straps, the blade slicing them open as if they were butter. "I knew you'd come back for me," Zee said. "I knew you wouldn't leave me."

I felt my heart twist, guilt rising up from my guts like vomit. I tried to smile at him, then looked away.

"Have you seen Donovan?" I asked. "Is he still here?"

"I don't know," Zee replied, pulling his arms free from the severed straps and rubbing the ugly welts that had formed. "We can't see anything with these screens. I think so, though. I mean, I don't know why he wouldn't be."

"I'll be right back," I said, walking out into the aisle.

"You can't release him," said Simon as he continued to saw through Zee's restraints. "He's too far gone."

I hung my head, thinking about the last time I'd seen Donovan in solitary confinement, and what the hallucination had said to me.

You don't have to free me to save me.

"I know," I said, but I was the only one who heard it. I walked down the row, three cubicles, then peered past the screen. The metal sarcophagus was still there, angled against the wall, the IV stand in place now with four bags of nightmare black hooked up to it. The tubes ran the liquid death into the arms and neck of a creature that couldn't have been Donovan, but was.

He was monstrous, both in size and in appearance. All his limbs were now grotesquely deformed, the muscles like hunks of meat beneath greasy pastry. His neck was a mess of tendons as taut as steel cables, and perched on top was a shapeless face, all jaw and roughly hewn cheekbones decorated with half-healed scars. His silver eyes watched me enter with no sign of recognition. With no sign of anything human.

"Donovan," was the only word that slipped from my lips. His mouth split open, tombstone teeth flashing in the muted light. I thought about the first time I'd seen him smile, up in our cells on the day I'd arrived at Furnace. And all the times since, a beam of sunshine that more than once was the only thing that had stopped me throwing myself off the eighth level of the prison. There was none of that warmth now, no compassion. There was nothing there but the hateful sneer of a blacksuit. And it broke my heart.

Donovan lurched forward, the chains around his arms and legs and chest squealing as the metal struggled to constrain him. He growled, the noise like a machine lodged in his deformed throat.

"It's okay," I said, unable to hold back the tears anymore. "It's okay, D, I'm gonna get you out of here."

He fought against his chains again, his solid steel casket

rocking. The grin was still plastered on his face, his cold eyes promising me nothing but death if he managed to get out.

I knew what I had to do.

I crept past the screen into the next compartment, the bed empty and stripped except for the dirty pillow. I picked it up, held it to my chest as I blinked away the tears. Images kept flashing before me, the times I'd spent with Donovan up top in gen pop. The meal we'd had with Monty in the kitchen, the way he'd cried eating the steak. The look on his face when he realized escape wasn't just a dream. His excitement when we loaded the last of the gloves into the crevice in Room Two, when he'd asked me if we should just go, the night before the blood watch had come and taken him.

"I'm sorry, D," I said, the words nothing more than sobs. "I'm so sorry."

I walked back to Donovan, barely able to see where I was going through my blurred vision. He started struggling again when he saw me, the growl growing fiercer, breaking up at the end into what sounded like a grating laugh. It was the final straw. That thing before me wasn't Donovan, not anymore. Everything good about him had been stripped away.

I pictured him as I wanted to remember him, sitting beside me on my bunk and giggling, slapping my back as his tuneful laughter filled the cell, making my spirits soar.

You don't have to free me to save me.

"I know," I repeated, reaching up and pushing the pillow against his face. I was sobbing so hard I could barely hold it, his body rocking so wildly that some of the links in his chains stretched out of shape. But they held, and I pushed, howling now as I heard the muffled gasps. I pushed until I felt his body grow still, the tendons in his neck relaxing. I pushed until I felt the mouth beneath the pillow droop, one last dull groan fading into silence. And I kept pushing, because I couldn't bear to pull the pillow away to see what I'd done.

"You're free," I said. I closed my eyes, saw Donovan as he had been. One last smile, then he faded. "You're free. You're free." And I kept saying it even when I felt the hands on my shoulders pulling me away. I plunged my head into Zee's neck, feeling his sobs beneath my own. "You're free. You're free. You're free."

"We have to go," said Simon, and I let them both steer me out of the cubicle, the pillow still gripped in my hands.

I didn't look back.

THE INCINERATOR

WE DIDN'T RUN THIS TIME. Even though the sounds of the blacksuits could be heard over the endless drone of the siren. We walked across the infirmary, somehow knowing we had enough time, that we were going to make it.

Zee pried the pillow from my hands as we reached the plastic curtain, laying it tenderly on the stone. I know it sounds stupid but I didn't want to leave it. I couldn't tell you why.

"You did the right thing," Zee said quietly, wiping the tears from his eyes. "He wouldn't want us standing around weeping. Let's get out of here. For Donovan."

We pressed through the door, the plastic slats like cold fingers on my face. The corridor beyond was deserted, the surgical rooms on either side empty behind their electronic seals. Several more steps and we'd reached the incinerator. The air here was warm, and a jolt of panic ran through me as I pictured us walking in to find the furnace burning, our path out blocked by a wall of fire.

But when Simon eased down the handle and opened the door, the room beyond was lit only by the cold lights in the ceiling, the incinerator grilles wide open like a welcoming embrace. The bodies had gone, but there were others here now, five of them, watching us with what I could swear was envy. Simon closed the door behind us, cutting off a dog in mid-howl. The blacksuits were close, but they couldn't stop us. Not now.

"I hope you've got a good reason for being in here," said Zee, staring into the furnace. "I don't fancy getting cozy with the dead guys again."

"It's our way out," I said. "The incinerator, the chimney. It goes all the way up."

Zee frowned, then his face blossomed into a smile.

"You've done it again," he said. "That's brilliant. Have we got the gear, the climbing stuff?"

"Nope," answered Simon, taking a step toward the furnace. "We're gonna have to do this without help."

"Well what are we waiting for?" Zee moved to join him as the sound of shouting rose up behind us. Simon clambered into the oven, then Zee, and I followed, trying not to think about the source of the ashes that clumped around my feet, that danced in the air and collected in my mouth.

It took a while for us to build the courage to look up. For all we knew there could be a metal grate bolted into the ceiling. The chimney could be a foot wide. The walls could be as smooth as silk.

But when we did tilt our heads up, our choked sigh of relief echoed back at us from the metal sides of the incinerator. Above us, stretching into darkness, was a vertical tunnel of rough rock maybe a meter and a half in width.

And coming down it was the unmistakable scent of fresh air.

We let it fall on us, closing our eyes and imagining spring rain and sea breezes. Okay, it was a mile or so above us and we had no idea if we could actually reach it, but right now that breath of cool wind was all we needed. It was part of a world we thought we'd never see again, never feel, never breathe. It was a link to the surface, the chink in Furnace's armor. Bathing in that draft we were as good as free.

"We gonna stand around all day or get the hell out of here?" asked Simon, holding out his mammoth hand. I put my foot in it, grabbing his arm for balance as he hoisted me up to the ceiling of the incinerator. I eased myself into the chimney, running my hands across the rock until I found something I could cling onto.

"Got it," I said, my voice ringing up the walls as if trying to beat me to the top. I could feel the soot and smoke of dead things against my fingers. "Christ, this thing could do with a wash."

My shoulder was killing me where I'd been bitten, but I ignored the pain as best I could, lifting up a leg and bracing it against the wall. The chimney was narrow enough to wedge my body in, back and feet on opposite sides, allowing me to shuffle my way up without the need for handholds every few meters. I inched up painfully slowly, but with every passing hair's breadth I felt the tension peeling away, the stress and the panic dissolving into smoke and rising up alongside me.

We were doing it. We were getting out.

There was a scuffle beneath me as Zee got in, moaning under his breath about how uncomfortable it was. We pushed up a bit more before Simon's tinny "Mind if I join you?" resonated from the stone.

"Only if you don't peek up my skirt," laughed Zee.

It was tough going, but every time I felt my legs cramp I just spread them, bracing my arms on either side of the chimney and tilting my neck back to lock myself in place. With no light I couldn't tell how far we'd climbed, but it must have been fifteen meters or so. Only a few hundred left to go, I thought.

"I hope neither of you needs to take a whiz while we're in here," said Simon. "Not unless you let me overtake you first."

I tried not to laugh, knowing it would probably make me lose my grip, plummet back into the furnace. Instead I shifted my body around, climbing in the conventional way for a while in an attempt to use some different muscles. It was as I was scanning the wall for any hint of a grip, impossible in the smothering gloom, that I noticed something up ahead. It looked like a flash of silver, so small it barely registered in my vision. I blinked the sweat from my tear-ravaged eyes, tried to focus on it.

A silver penny, unblinking. It was a rat. It had to be. How the hell had it got in here? It didn't matter. Right now we were stuck in a narrow pipe with it, and there was no other way to go except down.

I was about to warn the others when something in my head clicked. For a second I didn't understand it, or maybe I just didn't believe it. But the more I stared at that pinpoint of silver the more difficult it was to deny it.

"Do you see that?" I said.

"What?" asked Zee. "I can't see anything, your butt's in the way."

"That," I said, gripping the wall tight so they could look up past me. "That dot."

"Dot?" mumbled Simon from farther down. "You going crazy?"

"No way," interrupted Zee. "Is that . . . ?"

"It can't be," added Simon.

"But it is," I said, imagining its warmth on my skin even though I knew it was impossible from this distance. "It's daylight."

We were so busy cheering that none of us noticed the change in the chimney, the thickening of the air. I coughed, thinking it was just the exertion of the climb. But then Simon spluttered too, Zee's whoops of delight becoming a rattle. I opened my mouth but no oxygen flowed in, only an acrid cloud that lined my windpipe. I coughed again, this time convinced I'd hacked up a lung.

"Oh no," said Simon. I didn't need to look down to know what he was talking about, but I did anyway. I could make out the silhouettes of the two boys beneath me, squirming against the wall as they tried to escape the growing flames.

The incinerator had been lit.

I tried to double my speed, tried to scramble up the rock to outrun the smoke. It was pointless. I didn't know whether the blacksuits had discovered our escape or whether it was just another of the cruel twists of fate that Furnace was so, so good at, but there was no way we could go on.

I heard Simon coughing again, too many times for him to have been able to draw a breath. Zee was wheezing like one of the gas masks, his fingers grasping at my legs for support. But I had none to give. With another racking splutter I felt my grip on the wall come loose. I tried to wedge my back against the rock but I was spasming too much, the smoke in my lungs, in my eyes.

There wasn't even enough air for me to curse the blacksuits, curse the warden, curse our crappy luck, curse God. The smoke was in my head now, a pungent cloud even darker and filthier than the chimney. I knew I was passing out, knew I couldn't hold on any longer.

I took one last look at the speck of daylight, keeping my eyes open even though they burned. Then I was falling, thumping into

Zee, our tangled limbs hitting Simon, all of us plummeting toward the fire below.

At least it will be quick, was the last thing I thought. *At least we'll be free*. And I wondered if Donovan would be there, wherever we were going.

But we weren't that lucky. It wasn't quick. We weren't free. I don't remember hitting the inferno, the pain too much for my body to register. I could hear the shouts, though, the cries of the blacksuits, the shudder of the furnace as it was shut down. I could feel their hands on me, dragging me out, slapping my skin where the flames had taken root.

And I could see the warden, his soulless eyes making me wish I had burned to death. My vision went before my hearing, and I could hear him laugh—wild, lunatic cackles of delight. When they faded, his voice was just as terrifying, penetrating the darkness inside my head.

"My my, look what the rats dragged in. Get them into surgery, prep the wheezers. We can still use them."

Then my hearing went too, my senses deserting me in the face of what was to come. I prayed for death, prayed to be taken away, prayed for somebody to free me the same way I had freed Donovan. But even as I felt myself being carried through the door I knew that death wouldn't come for me here, not now. It wouldn't dare.

Because the true horror of Furnace was about to begin.

ALEX HAS FAILED TWICE TO ESCAPE FROM FURNACE.
NOW HE'S BEING TAKEN TO THE LAB . . .

"UNIQUELY HORRIFYING." —REALMS OF FANTASY

DEATH SENTENCE

ESCAPE FROM FURNACE

A THRILLER BY THE AUTHOR OF *LOCKDOWN* AND *SOLITARY*

ALEXANDER GORDON SMITH

WHAT WILL THEY TURN ALEX INTO?
FIND OUT IN

DEATH SENTENCE:
ESCAPE FROM FURNACE 3

THE IV

WELCOME BACK, OLD FRIEND.

I thought I heard the tunnel walls laughing as I was carried through them—deep chuckles that could have been distant earthquakes. Somewhere inside I knew it must have been the echo of the blacksuits, but the injuries in my mind were just as bad as the ones on my skin and reality was a distant memory. I was living inside a nightmare now, a place where Furnace was a creature that howled with delight as we were pulled back into its belly, dragged to the infirmary.

Every atom of my being was in agony. God knows how badly I'd been burned when I'd hit the incinerator flames. I would have opened my eyes to see if I'd been barbecued, but they wouldn't obey. I would have lifted a hand to check that I still had my eyes, but I couldn't find the strength. I would have screamed, but there was barely enough air in my smoke-ravaged lungs to breathe.

So instead I tried to shut down my brain. Tried to forget that I'd ever been alive. Tried to flood my body with absence—a black tide that would douse the pain in my flesh. Maybe if I could do that then death would sneak in, snatch me up right from under their noses. It worked for the fraction of a second until I heard the voice.

"Oh no you don't, Alex," the warden hissed, snapping me back into my body. "Death can't have what belongs to me." The whisper grew louder, accompanied by wicked shrieks I knew all too well. "Get those wheezers to work. We haven't got long. And find me an IV, *now*!"

I was lowered onto something that should have been soft but which felt like acid against my burnt skin. I tried once more to leave my head. Maybe if I could just escape my skull for an instant then death would take me, carry me up through the rock toward that sliver of daylight I had glimpsed only minutes ago.

Then I felt the needle in my arm, and something cold rushed into my veins. I knew exactly what it was. I'd seen it before on Gary, on Donovan—a drip full of evil, not quite black, not quite silver, with specks of starlight floating in its dark weight. It was the warden's poison, the stuff that turned you into a monster.

I tried to fight it, to buck my body until the needle came out, but the pain was too great and I could feel the leather straps holding me tight against the infirmary bed. The panic grew like a living thing in my chest and I made one last mental effort to escape, to leave my flesh behind and vanish like smoke. But the liquid nightmare flowed into me like molten lead, filling my veins and arteries and weighing me down. And it's impossible to escape anything when the chains are inside you.

It was only a matter of seconds before it reached my brain. To my surprise it numbed the agony. I felt the same way I had years ago—a lifetime ago—when I'd broken my wrist and the doctors had given me morphine. It was like I was no longer connected to anything physical, like my mind was free.

I should have known better than to hope. For a blissful instant I felt nothing, then the floodgates opened and something far worse than physical pain burst into my head.

This time I managed to scream.

It was as if the warden had ridden into my mind on the wave of poison, because I could swear his voice came from inside my skull.

It's over, he said, the sound of him causing rotten images to sprout from the shadows in my head. I saw something that looked like flyblown meat, something else that could have been a dead dog, there for only a second before evaporating. The warden continued: *Everything you ever were, everything you are now, and everything you ever wanted to be, it's over.*

I wanted to argue, wanted to open my mouth and tell him he was wrong, but his words were like maggots burrowing into the flesh of my brain. They gorged and grew fat on his dry laughter, revealing visions so horrific that I couldn't bear to make sense of them.

There is nothing to be gained in fighting. What flows inside you now is far more powerful than that fallacy you call a soul. Let it take you, for without it you are nothing.

"I am something . . . I am Alex . . ." I tried to say, but even inside my own head his voice was stronger than mine.

You are nothing, you can be nothing. Surrender yourself and be done. You were never Alex Sawyer, because Alex Sawyer never existed.

"You're wrong. I'm . . ." I began, but my words were so weak I could barely hear them. He cut me off with another laugh, and this time when he spoke his voice was like fingers sliding into my brain.

Alex Sawyer never existed. You are one of us.

The fingers flexed, as if they were pulling something out of me, and with nothing more than a whimper I fell into the gaping emptiness that had once been my soul.

I WAS STANDING IN A MUDDY TRENCH, and for a moment I thought I was free. Then I glanced up at the sky and saw an endless void of darkness and knew that I was dreaming.

To my left and right were slick earth walls the color of blood, sheer and too high to climb. Not that I'd have wanted to—beyond I could make out dull explosions that shook the air and caused a fine rain of soil. I was about to take my eyes from the sides of the trench when I noticed a vague shape in the mud. I couldn't quite make out what it was until two slits appeared and a pair of eyes stared back at me.

By the time a mouth had opened up beneath those eyes and unleashed a groan of desperation I was already running. The ground gripped my feet the way it always does in dreams, slowing my escape. And when I looked down it was hands I saw pushing from the mud—cracked and broken fingers snatching at my legs. I kicked out at them, trying not to lose my balance, trying not to fall.

But there were simply too many, dozens of hands and faces emerging from the soil like the living dead. I felt the world spin, saw the ground rush up to meet me. There was no impact. Before I could land, the trench seemed to freeze—all except for a puddle of filth right beneath my face. The muddy water bulged up, then slowly parted to reveal a face beneath, caked in dirt but still familiar.

"What do you want?" I asked it, although my voice made no sound.

The mouth opened and moved as though it was speaking, but again I could hear nothing.

"Who are you?" I asked wordlessly, studying the eyes, the nose, trying to remember where I'd seen the face before. It didn't stop talking, but there may as well have been a sheet of soundproof glass between us. I focused on its lips, caked in mud but visible.

Don't . . . I made out, reading the way they moved.

forget . . . It could have been any of a million words but somehow I knew. Just like I knew what was coming next.

your name, the figure mimed. I opened my mouth to reply, but before I could do so the face morphed into an expression of pure terror, its eyes like diamonds set into the wet earth. It was only then that I recognized myself in the mud, the face a mirror image of my own. It—*I*—tried to say something else, but my mirror face was sucked back into the ground, mud filling its mouth and nose, flowing over its still-open eyes until nothing remained.

"Wait!" I yelled. "Wait!"

Then the rest of the trench once again found life, zombie hands grabbing my legs and clothes and head and pulling me down into the grave. My heart lurched, the sensation of being buried alive too terrifying for my sleeping mind. The trench exploded into dust, darkness flooding in like water and propelling me back to the surface. I rose from the dream like a drowning man, gasping for air and clutching at the night.

It didn't take long for me to remember that the real world was even more horrific than my nightmare.

But far worse was the fact that, for several seconds after waking, I couldn't remember who I was.

GOFISH

ALEXANDER GORDON SMITH

What did you want to be when you grew up?

As far back as I can remember, I've wanted to be a writer. I don't remember really ever wanting to be anything else when I was growing up (except the usual helicopter pilot/rock star/Green Beret combination). I used to be obsessed by stories, writing them and drawing pictures for them, then stapling them into actual little books that I would pretend were real. I vaguely remember taking one into a bookshop once, complete with a hand-drawn bar code, and telling the cashier that I wanted to buy it because I was the author! The first time I walked into a shop and saw my book there (an actual book, not a homemade one) was one of the best moments of my life, a real dream come true. The only other job I'd still like to do is be a truck driver, driving from coast to coast in the States. Sometimes I think I'll take a year off from writing and give it a go!

What's your first childhood memory?

My earliest memory is actually a dream I had when I was very young, maybe four. I'll never forget it because it was so traumatic. Me and my family (my mum, dad, and sister) were walking down a path next to a beach. There were palm trees growing on both sides, and as we walked past one, a cave-man dropped down next to us and grabbed my mum. He said, "It's time to change mummies." Then he ran off with her! I don't remember waking up. I don't remember much at all about my childhood, to be honest, but I remember being absolutely terrified in that dream!

What's your most embarrassing childhood memory?

Crikey, that's tough. . . . There are so many of them! There are the usual suspects: calling my teacher "mum" whilst crying in front of the whole class, falling in a puddle at playtime and having a massive wet patch on my ass, wearing my under-pants over my trousers one day because I thought it made me look like Superman (honestly!), being forced by my mum to wear sandals to secondary school, going up to my sister in the middle of a shop and wrestling her to the floor (as we often did) before realizing it wasn't my sister; the list is endless. Thanks for forcing me to relive those awkward moments! To be honest though, the memories that are most embarrassing, and most shameful, are when I was a teenager and I stole a load of books from my mum and sold them so I could have a bit of cash. Some of them were irre-placeable, and I felt so awful. The guilt that Alex in *Lockdown* feels for being a thief is partly my own guilt at doing some-thing so terrible. It is a horrible, horrible feeling.

What's your favorite childhood memory?

I think quite a few of my favorite childhood memories made it into *Lockdown* as well. When Alex gets sent to Furnace, when he spends his first few nights buried alive at the bottom of the world, he tries to remember the good times in his life, and I used my own memories to make it as poignant as possible. I've always loved Christmas, and although I don't remember many years specifically from when I was young, I do remember the breathless excitement of Christmas morning, lying awake waiting for your parents, then going downstairs and seeing the presents under the tree. Nothing beats it! And summer, too. I have hazy memories of beaches and football, picnics and sunshine. Nothing specific, just pure childhood bliss.

As a young person, who did you look up to most?

My parents were my heroes when I was a kid. They still are, to be honest! Even though they got divorced when I was really young, they gave us a wonderful childhood. There were loads of reasons why I looked up to them, but one of them was the fact that they were both creative; they both made up their own stories and told them to us at bedtime. I thought that was such an amazing thing, and it really did inspire me to tell stories of my own. I also looked up to writers. We never had an author visit at my school, but I remember seeing them on the television and their pictures on book jackets and being totally in awe. These guys wrote books, real books! To me, as a kid, writers were gods.

What was your worst subject in school?

I'd have to pick between math and physical education. I was pretty hopeless at both! At least with math though, I didn't have to run around the school field in the bitterly cold wind and rain feigning asthma attacks to get out of a cross-country race. As a teenager, I decided that I didn't need an education because I was going to be the next Stephen King—I was writing my first horror novel at the time. When it came to doing my A-Levels at age eighteen, I was so confident in my future as a best-selling millionaire writer that I didn't write a single word in one of my exams and fell asleep in another! Of course when my book was universally rejected (for being too gory, which isn't surprising really as it was about angels that ate people), I realized my mistake and had to retake my final year at school. Nightmare.

What was your best subject in school?

English, without a doubt. I loved it. When we weren't reading books, we were being encouraged to write our own stories, which was just amazing for me. English lessons felt like holidays in the school week and I would have sat in my English class all day if I could. I remember writing one of my first proper stories in middle school (aged around ten), called "The Valleys of Olaf Karnoff." It was a total rip-off of *The Lord of the Rings*, but I was so proud of it!

What was your first job?

My first ever job was working in McDonald's. And yes, it was awful! I was sixteen or seventeen and I was only there for three weeks, but that was enough. A ten-hour shift on the fries station left me with calloused hands and oil burns up my arms; it was like some medieval torture chamber! It wasn't all bad, though. For lunch, we were allowed to make up our own burgers, so I used to construct these elaborate towers made up of six quarter pounders and gallons of sauce. Yum! And once we had a firefight with the guns they use to squirt sauce on burgers, which was awesome! The best thing about working in McDonald's was that it really made me realize how much I wanted to be a writer, to do my own thing. The day they told me I was management material was the day I gave my notice and went home and really started working on my novel.

How did you get your first book published?

Getting published was an adventure in its own right! I've been writing since I was a kid, but other than the horror novel that ruined my A-Levels, I never sent anything off for publication. In the summer of 2005, my little brother Jamie (who was nine) and I decided that we were going to try and write a book together. We both loved reading and we wanted to see if we could write something really cool, a book that we'd both love to read. We came up with the idea of *The Inventors*—two young inventors who have to save the world from an evil genius—and set to work writing it. In the end though, we spent more time actually trying to build the inventions in the book than we did writing. We wanted to know exactly what it was like to be two inventors, so Jamie designed and built dozens of gadgets, machines, and traps and tested them on me (which was an interesting, if not entirely pleasant, experience—especially the rocket boots). Although we had plotted most of the novel and developed our characters and knew exactly what was going to happen, we only actually wrote about 13,000 words.

At the end of the holiday, Jamie spotted a competition being run by a national bookshop chain. All they wanted was the first three chapters and a synopsis, so we entered. After that, school began again and we kind of forgot about the novel. A few months later, I got a phone call telling me that our book had been shortlisted for the award. It was pretty much the best phone call I had ever received in my life, until they went on to say that they needed the full manuscript by the end of the next week. I told them that we had only written 13,000 words, and they answered that if we couldn't give them the manuscript, then we weren't eligible. "Can you do it?" they asked. I said no, thinking it was impossible. As soon as I put the phone down, though, I realized this was our chance to be published, this was our big break. If we didn't take it, or at least try to take it, we would regret it forever.

So we started writing, really writing. Like I said, we had the story in our heads, we knew what was going to happen, so it flowed beautifully. Seven days later, we had a total of

96,000 words and a finished book. The experience nearly killed me—11,000 words a day—but to be honest, the mad rush actually gave the book so much of its energy. I've written every book in the same white heat ever since. We got it to the post office about one minute before it closed the day of the deadline, then we kept our fingers crossed!

How did you celebrate publishing your first book?

Finding out that I was going to be published was just incredible. I'll never forget the phone call from Faber, my UK publisher. They'd been trying to get hold of Jamie and me for ages because of the competition we'd entered, but we'd already found out that we hadn't won. Part of the runner-up prize was that somebody from Faber would call us up and offer feedback on our book, which I didn't really want to hear because I was so disappointed! So after leaving several messages on my answering machine, Faber finally got hold of me and told me they wanted to publish *The Inventors*. I was so shocked that I dropped the phone, then banged my head on the desk picking it up. I was worried for a while I'd dreamed the whole thing while concussed! I ran straight round to tell mum the news, then went into town with her and my gran for a celebratory lunch (Jamie was at school, so he had to wait to hear the news). My gran actually got drunk and ended up swinging around a lamppost in the middle of the street! All in all, it was one of the best days of my life.

Do you plan your stories?

I never really plan out my books. Weirdly, it's because I don't have the patience for it. When I get an idea, I like to throw myself into it straightaway. I get gripped by that adventure and pulled along by it, and half of the fun of writing is seeing where you end up. If I plot too much—and I have tried it—it feels too much like writing by numbers. It loses something on the page, feels too formulaic. It's a cliché, I know, but letting your characters grow and develop by themselves is amazing; it's what writing is really about for me. That's why it's so important to get your characters spot on, to know them inside out. If you really understand them, then they will be free to evolve, to act according to their own needs and fears, and the story will practically write itself! I love that about writing— you can be halfway through a chapter and have an idea of where it's heading, then suddenly one of the characters will break away and do something completely unexpected, and you're wrenched off course down a completely new path. Admittedly, sometimes it doesn't go anywhere and you have to backtrack, but most of the time, it leads to something much better and more exciting than you had originally envisioned.

For books like the Furnace series, I really didn't want to sit down and work out how, or if, Alex would get out. I knew that if I had this planned out from the start, then his adventure, and his horror, wouldn't be as convincing as it should be. I really wanted to feel like I was in Furnace with Alex, as if I *was* Alex, and so when I started writing, I had no idea how, or if, he would make his break. Hopefully, his experience is much more realistic because of this. Having said that, I do have a very rough story arc in my head for all five books— and I mean *very* rough. To start a series of books with absolutely no idea of where they are going could be literary suicide!

Where do you write your books?

I always write on the laptop, and tend to move around the house during the day so I'm always in a sunny room. If it's really nice, I'll sit out in the garden and work. It's a hard life! I used to write in notebooks, but my handwriting is so bad that I wouldn't be able to decipher half the notes I'd made. I do have an office in town, but I tend to use it when I need to do other bits and pieces of work. It feels too official there to write books!

Which of your characters is most like you?

Definitely Alex. In many ways Alex *is* me—in the first draft, we even had exactly the same name. I feel very close to Alex for a number of reasons, not least that I went through a stage, when I was a teenager, of being a bit of a troublemaker—nothing as serious as him, but stealing things from my family, getting into fights, roaming the streets at night, drinking in biker bars. I vividly remember what it was like to rebel, to feel yourself becoming independent, the excitement but at the same time the fear, and the sadness of losing the child you had once been, all mixed up into a permanent lead ball in your stomach. When I started writing the book, Alex's voice was so similar to mine. In a way, I guess, he was a version of me that could have existed—that may exist—in another reality.

The other reason I feel so close to Alex is that shortly after I started writing *Lockdown*, I suffered a personal tragedy. It was a really dark time for me, and I almost stopped writing altogether. But *Lockdown* was one of the things that got me through the experience. I began to see Furnace—this horrific penitentiary built beneath the ground—as a symbol for this nightmare period I was going through in my life. Alex was trapped inside the prison, I was trapped somewhere without walls, but just as bad. I knew that if Alex didn't make it out of Furnace, or at least try, then I would never get over this tragedy. So Alex's fear and pain and desperation and hope are really my fear and pain and desperation and hope. That's what gives the book so much of its drive and its power.

Alex isn't an ordinary hero. Why did you make him a thief and a bully?

I didn't want Alex to be a conventional do-gooder hero. Right from the start, you know he's a criminal and a bully, albeit a reluctant bully. He's less interested in hurting people than in what he can get out of it, which is money. It didn't seem realistic to me that an innocent kid would be framed for murder, it had to be someone who had broken the law, who was heading for prison anyway. Alex certainly isn't a nice guy—and I'll bet there were plenty of kids at his school happy to see him locked up for life. But when you get inside his head, you do come to understand him, to learn more about why he acts the way he does. It's not like he's had a bad upbringing or a traumatic childhood, and he's certainly no Oliver Twist—stealing to stay alive. But he's a complex character, a real person, and there are many different sides to his personality. Ironically, by the end of the book, Alex has committed far worse crimes than those he was guilty of on the outside, but the reasons for committing those crimes are different. There won't be many readers who see Alex as a good guy when they start the book, but there won't be any who see him as a bad guy by the end.

Were you trying to make a comment on the prison system?

Not intentionally. The thought of being convicted of a crime you didn't commit, and spending your life in jail, is absolutely terrifying. When I was writing the book, I wasn't attempting to make any kind of political point or statement about the prison system in the UK or in the U.S. I wanted it to be a horror story, pure and simple. In fact, the biggest problem I thought readers would have with the book was believing that a teenager could be sentenced to life without possibility of parole. It was only after I'd finished *Lockdown* that I read an article about teenagers in the States who had suffered this exact fate—literally locked away for the rest of their lives. It is a tragic and distressing thought that, for some young people, there is no second chance (of course, you can say the same about their victims . . .). I'm not sure if any of these individuals were wrongly convicted, but if so, I can't imagine a worse nightmare.

I don't think the prison system is perfect, I don't think there is as much focus on rehabilitation as there needs to be. And whilst real prisons aren't full of monsters and mutant dogs, they do all seem to be based on an atmosphere of terror and violence. Surely the punishment in going to prison is losing your freedom, not being forced to live in a hell on Earth. But, like I say, I'm no expert on the matter and would never pretend to be. Part of what I wanted to show was that the label of "criminal" isn't so clean-cut as most people think. Alex is a criminal, and he's not a nice guy to start with, but he's not a killer. It's only when he gets to Furnace that he is forced to commit the crimes that he was accused of, and only then to stay alive. Alex changes so much during the course of the series, for better and for worse, and maybe that's the point—people can change, we need to help them change for the better before it's too late.

When you finish a book, who reads it first?
It's always my sister, my mum, and my girlfriend. I send them each chapter as it's written, and get angry e-mails from them if I don't send them over fast enough!

Did you do any research for *Lockdown*?
I didn't do too much—I always prefer to throw myself into a story, research just feels too much like work! However, my little brother Jamie did help me out with a few things. He suggested going to visit a prison, to get a sense of the atmo-

sphere and an idea of what it is like to be locked up. We tried visiting a real prison, but they wouldn't let us in! So instead, we went to a medieval dungeon in town (Norwich is a very old city and full of them). It was buried deep beneath the ground and the lights barely worked. I walked into an old cell to have a look around and Jamie locked me in! It was pitch black in there and terrifying—I kept expecting to feel ghostly hands on me, dragging me into the darkness. It was really useful though, as it gave me a real sense of what it was like for Alex the first night he is locked up in Furnace.

I got revenge on Jamie a few weeks later when I made a life-size Wheezer (I'm always making real-life versions of things in the book, I find it helps me describe them). I took it round to his house after he'd gone to bed one night and left it outside his room. When he got up for a wee in the middle of the night, he almost died!

The funniest thing that happened when researching Furnace involved guns. I hate guns, but I thought I owed it to myself as a writer to at least know what it was like to fire one. I have a friend who goes shooting for rabbits in the country-side and he invited me along one weekend. I didn't really want to shoot a rabbit, so he told me the best thing to aim at was a cowpat—a massive mound of cow dung. Now when you shoot a cowpat with a shotgun, it literally explodes; it's like watching a poo volcano! At one point on the trip, my friend and I found a particularly large cowpat and we both shot it at the same time, using both barrels. It rose up like a tidal wave, got caught by the wind, and landed on my friend's thirteen-year-old brother. The poor guy had to spend the rest of the day absolutely covered, head to toe, in cow manure! But learning how to fire a gun helped me make the book as realistic and as believable as possible.

Are you a morning person or a night owl?

I'm definitely not a morning person. . . . Although saying that, I do force myself to get up fairly early because I do my best writing in the morning. For some reason, I don't seem to be able to write after lunch, it just doesn't flow. Which is annoying really as I'd quite like to write into the night. Instead, I just end up spending most evenings watching films, reading books, or playing video games. Shame!

What's your idea of the best meal ever?

The best meal ever has to be a hot, steaming plate of macaroni cheese with bits of bacon in. It really is heaven! Every year for my birthday, Mum offers to cook anything I like, and every year it's the same. I really could live on macaroni cheese—breakfast, lunch, and dinner, three hundred and sixty-five days a year—if I thought it wouldn't kill me!

Which do you like better: cats or dogs?

I love cats *and* dogs. I have two enormous cats, Midge and Grub. They are brilliant company when I'm writing (except when they sleep on the laptop). But I would love to get a dog one day, a massive Saint Bernard called Donovan.

What do you value most in your friends?

Wow, tough question. I think the thing I value most in friendship is the ability to be totally and utterly relaxed with somebody. To feel like you don't have to make an effort to impress them or entertain them. My friends often just turn up at the door and stay all day, and we'll watch telly or play video games and chat and eat takeaway or BBQ and just have fun. I feel totally at ease with them, totally relaxed. We're equals, and we trust each other implicitly, and that's why we're friends.

What makes you laugh out loud?
Most things, I think! I have quite a loud laugh, a Brian Blessed laugh, and it doesn't take much to set it off. I've even had neighbors complain that I laugh too much! I would like to say that sophisticated humor and Shakespearean wit make me laugh out loud, but to be honest, there's nothing funnier than fart jokes and watching cats do stupid things on YouTube. Oh, and seeing people get hit in the crotch with footballs.

What's your favorite song?
There are too many to list, and it depends entirely on my mood. My playlist can include anything from "Sweet Child O' Mine" by Guns N' Roses to "Dance of the Knights" by Prokofiev. Oh, and "Don't Stop Believin'" by Journey, of course.

What are you most afraid of?
I'm a tiny bit afraid of everything, to be honest! But my worst fear is probably flying. I hate it. I try to avoid it as much as possible, but when I am forced to get on a plane, I have to be physically restrained from running up and down the aisle screaming, and I'm a nervous wreck for about a week afterwards. Even thinking about it now is making me feel queasy! But I guess an even bigger fear is waking up one morning and realizing I've forgotten how to write. I think all authors probably have nightmares about that.

What time of year do you like best?
I like all the seasons, each one has its charm. Summer has to be my favorite, because of lazy days on the beach. But my favorite day of the year is always Christmas.

What's your favorite TV show?
Again, there are too many to mention! I'm a huge fan of American drama—*The Wire, The Sopranos, Sons of Anarchy, The West Wing, Lost,* and, of course, the absolutely amazing *Battlestar Galactica.* You guys just make the best television in the world! Although saying that, nothing can ever beat *Doctor Who.*

If you were stranded on a desert island, who would you want for company?
Scarlett Johansson . . . Ow, I mean my girlfriend, of course!

If you could travel in time, where would you go?
The future! I'd want to see what happens to the human race in, say, a thousand years' time—whether we've made contact with aliens, whether we've developed faster-than-light travel and teleportation, what kind of new gadgets there are, and, most importantly, whether we've actually survived.

What's the best advice you have ever received about writing?
It's something that all authors advise, and the thing I always tell young writers when they ask: Enjoy yourselves. Pick an idea that you love, that excites you, make sure it's a story that you want to tell. You have to want to experience that adventure yourself, you have to want to live it—even with *Lockdown,* I wanted to be there with Alex, if only for the excitement of trying to find a way out. Don't do what so many writers do and pick an idea just because you think it will sell, or because you think it will fit the current fiction market. Your heart won't be in it, and a reader (and a publisher) will sense that. Be brave, go with the ideas that you find thrilling, let yourself be carried away. For me, that's the best part of writ-

ing—the fact that you get to have these adventures, that inside your head they're as real as your day-to-day life.

Also don't worry about making your first draft perfect. Let the story pull you along at its own speed, get the first draft finished, and there will be plenty of time to polish it.

And read! It's the best education a writer can have.

What do you want readers to remember about your books?

Like all authors, I'd like readers to remember they had an amazing time reading my books, that they were carried away by the story, that they were left breathless by the excitement, left giggling to themselves at the funny bits, and left peering under the bed at night by the horror. I want them to remember the characters like they were old friends, and remember the story like it was something they had actually been through, that they had experienced for real. I want them to remember that this was as much an adventure for them as it was for the hero of the book.

What would you do if you ever stopped writing?

I can't see myself ever stopping writing, but if I do, then there are a few other things I'd like to try. At the moment I'm in the process of producing a horror film with my sister, and that's definitely something I'd like to do more of, even though it's really hard work. I'd also love to develop video games one day. So long as I get the chance to be creative, and I don't get bored, then I'm happy. And of course, I'd still love to be a trucker!

What do you like best about yourself?

I guess it would be the fact that I love life. I still wake up in the morning and feel like I've got the whole world to explore, that I'm about to embark on a new adventure. I'm an optimist and an idealist. Life just makes me happy. It's a great feeling!

What is your worst habit?
Being an optimist and an idealist makes me a rubbish realist, so I'm always getting into trouble for not paying enough attention to the boring stuff like accounts and bills and taxes. Yawn! I also pick my nose. But I'm a flicker, not an eater, so it's not too bad.

What do you consider to be your greatest accomplishment?
It has to be getting published for the first time, walking into a bookshop, and seeing my first novel on the shelves. It was the most amazing thing ever, the culmination of all my childhood dreams, and the grin was on my face for months afterwards. In fact, I'm still grinning about it now! I was so proud to have published a book, and that sense of accomplishment, the knowledge that my books will always be out there, long after I've gone, is still astonishing. It just gets better with each new book!

What do you wish you could do better?
Everything!

What would your readers be most surprised to learn about you?
I write thousands of words a week on the computer, but I can only type with two fingers, three counting my thumb!

For more from Alexander Gordon Smith, please visit us.macmillan.com/lockdown.

Six chilling tales

AVAILABLE FROM SQUARE FISH

The Adoration of Jenna Fox
Mary E. Pearson
ISBN: 978-0-312-59441-1
$8.99 US / $11.50 Can

*What happened to Jenna Fox?
And who is she, really?*

The Compound
S. A. Bodeen
ISBN: 978-0-312-57860-2
$8.99 US / $11.50 Can

*Eli's father built the Compound to
keep his family safe. But are they
safe—or sorry?*

Dead Connection
Charlie Price
ISBN: 978-0-312-37966-7
$7.99 US / $10.25 Can

*Can Murray's ability to talk
to dead people help him find
a missing cheerleader?*

Holdup
Terri Fields
ISBN: 978-0-312-56130-7
$8.99 US / $11.50 Can

*The most dangerous thing at Burger
Heaven should be greasy food,
not a maniac with a gun.*

The Love Curse of the Rumbaughs
Jack Gantos
ISBN: 978-0-312-38052-6
$7.99 US / $8.99 Can

*Ivy has two great loves, her mother
and taxidermy.*

Zombie Blondes
Brian James
ISBN: 978-0-312-57375-1
$8.99 US / $11.50 Can

*All of the girls in Hannah's
new school are blonde and
popular—and dead.*

SQUARE FISH
WWW.SQUAREFISHBOOKS.COM
AVAILABLE WHEREVER BOOKS ARE SOLD